D0196205

CROW WINTER

CROW WINTER

A NOVEL

KAREN McBRIDE

HARPERAVENUE

Crow Winter
Text and illustration copyright © 2019 by Karen McBride
All rights reserved.

Published by Harper Avenue, an imprint of HarperCollins Publishers Ltd

First edition

HarperCollins books may be purchased for educational, business or
sales promotional use through our Special Markets Department.

HarperCollins Publishers Ltd
Bay Adelaide Centre, East Tower
22 Adelaide Street West, 41st Floor
Toronto, Ontario, Canada
M5H 4E3

www.harpercollins.ca

Library and Archives Canada Cataloguing in Publication
information is available upon request

ISBN 978-1-4434-5967-9

Printed and bound in the United States of America
LSC/H 9 8 7 6 5 4 3 2 1

For Dad and all those under the blue skies of Timiskaming

If you talk to animals they will talk with you
and you will know each other.

If you do not talk to them you will not know them,
and what you do not know you will fear.

What one fears one destroys.

—Chief Dan George, *My Heart Soars*

CROW WINTER

1

HOMECOMING

I always thought it would be Raven.

The one who finally decided it was time to teach me. Raven seemed like the right fit. In all the big stories, he's the leading man. A beautiful bird with glossy black feathers. He's strong and graceful. Got a sharp wit and clever tongue. I heard that he found the First People on the beaches of the West Coast. That he stole the sun one day just for the fun of it. Tough, self-assured, a good sense of humour. All the things a real Spirit Guide should be.

As I drive, I press the lever down to wash the windshield and watch as the pale blue liquid shoots onto the glass. I hold it down longer than I should, watching as the wipers move back and forth. Most of the bugs come off in the first pass, but a particularly juicy one stays put. No matter. I know this road well. The early-August corn is high in the fields on either side of me. I roll the windows down to let the fresh country air into the car. A flurry of birds rushes into the sky from one of the fields as I pass. I track their silhouettes for as long as I can, then return to scanning the highway stretched out in front of me.

Raven was always the one the elders and other storytellers told us about. Tales of how he stole Crow's potlatch. How he made that proud bird sing and sing and sing until his voice was nothing but a croak, all while Raven gorged himself on food. How he'd created the world and then messed it up. A trickster and a transformer. A herald of change, sometimes by accident and

3

sometimes on purpose. A writer who only ever uses ink, who thinks that using pencil means admitting to mistakes.

And yet I know why it couldn't ever have been Raven. He doesn't belong to us. The Indians of Spirit Bear Point don't tell stories about *Kakagi*. Sure, I can smirk knowingly when I hear people talk about him here and there, but he's not mine. Me and Raven—we're different beasts. Hell, me and Raven aren't even the same kind of Indian. We aren't even neighbours. Something like three thousand kilometres separates us. No, it could never have been Raven.

Then Wisakedjak maybe? "Whisky jack," as my pale-skin brothers and sisters call him. Funny how saying it like that makes people understand. As if it's unheard of that the White Man might know a few words of a Native language, leastways enough to understand what we're saying. But no. Easier to throw in alcohol. Another Indian always hounded by booze.

He's a trickster too. One of many in a long line. A brother or cousin to Raven and Coyote. Wisakedjak is closer to home, a neighbour who lives in the next town over. He's a nice guy, a friend to the People. But he's not a friend of mine. He lives farther south and farther west. So, it wasn't Wisakedjak either. That's his Cree name, and I am not Cree.

Anishnaabeg call him something else.

Nanabush.

Yes. Now that I've said it, thought it, felt it, I know that it's right. It's a name that has a certain weight on the tongue. A taste. Like lit sage in a windowless room. Or aluminum foil on an old filling.

All the stories about Nanabush read like the memoirs of an ancient troublemaker. Someone with the power to do great things but who doesn't want to put in the work. The old, good tales they tell around a fire say he was here when the world was young. That he was a child of the People and of the gods—if you can call them gods. Not our word, but I don't know what else to think. He had power, but so did everyone. Power that is unnoticed becomes stale. So Nanabush did what he wanted. Served himself and his interests. I think of him as a creature of endless summer. Someone who says, "I have time, so I'll do it later." Later, later, later, until it's too late.

Then again, I remember hearing how G'tchi Manitou sent him here to teach the People. His first task: naming all of the plants and animals. That must have been difficult. I have a hard enough time choosing a name for pets. I can't imagine having to figure out that a silverfish should be called a silverfish. But he did it. That Nanabush. He named everything from the eagle in the sky to the fish in the sea.

I never understood how he could be a brilliant shapeshifter one moment and then the next he's tumbling naked down a hillside. Makes me wonder how he stacks up against all the stories about him. Smart guy, dumb choices?

Is that why he came to me? So I could piece his story back together? He's looking for a chance to rewrite his history.

I'm getting ahead of myself. After all, that crow only shows up when I'm sleeping. Could be a dream. Or a hallucination. Thinking about it only raises more questions. Who is Nanabush and why would I pick that figment of my imagination to fixate on?

Honestly, we're strangers. I'm making all of this up to try to reconcile the mess that is my life. No job. Dead dad. Why not enlist some made-up shapeshifter to try to teach me a few lessons in the old ways?

Could that be it? Nanabush, the Spirit Guide.

Well, if that's the case, then I should introduce myself.

Hello, Nanabush. My name is Hazel Ellis. Can't wait to get to know you.
That's a lie, but I think it anyway.

I keep driving, across the bridge that hangs above a river of clear, fresh water, through the Québécois town of Ste-Marie des Oblats, until I cross into Rez country. The houses get smaller and the lawns are less tidy, filled with toys, bicycles abandoned haphazardly as the kids raced in for dinner. Some of the yards are even littered with garbage. That's what happens when you miss pickup day. One good breeze and the lawn doubles as a trash pile. A pack of Rez dogs crosses in front of my car and I have to slow down. They're led by a boxer-mix with one white ear who pauses to look at me while his packmates hurry to the other side of the road.

As I drive past the motley pack, a weathered wooden sign in the shape of a medicine wheel comes into view, telling me: "*Minwa pijawok!* Welcome to Spirit Bear Point First Nation."

2

THE BLUE SKIES

The sky is always clearer here. Rows of birch, aspen, and pine stretch until their limbs touch the clouds. When the wind weaves through the trees, it's as if waves are crashing onto the shore of a sea. People here take it for granted because they haven't left this place. But I know what I'm talking about. I've been there. These leaves sound like the ocean.

The Trans-Canada cuts right through the reserve, which means there's always traffic. The only gas station runs out of gas so often that it's more of a corner store. Sometimes we have to boil our water before we drink it, but that's only if pipes burst. Spirit Bear Point is far from perfect. But I don't care. It's home.

A line of cars and two transports hauling logs pass too quickly along the highway that's a stone's throw from my front door. The speed limit here is fifty kilometres per hour. Which feels like a crawl from the ninety kilometres per hour of the Trans-Canada. But seriously? It's always made me crazy how fast people speed through the Rez. Just because you don't have to make any real turns to get back on the open road doesn't mean you can speed through and hit whatever stray dog or kid is running around.

The first transport's horn bellows like a steam engine as two little kids with scraped knees walking by jump up and down excitedly on the roadside. They pump their arms repeatedly to sign to the second trucker to pull his horn, but they're left disappointed.

I watch as they throw obscene gestures at the back end of the transport before picking up their bikes and pushing them across the road toward the trailer park.

"Any more boxes left in that old Toyota?"

Mom is standing in the entryway. She's leaning against the door frame with her arms crossed, watching me. Her face creases into a small smile. My mother, Nora Ellis, is who people envision when they think of Native women. Perfect brown skin, white even teeth; fine lines at the edges of her eyes that are the only sign of her age. Her jaw is angled, and she has cheekbones that most people get by using makeup and a paint-by-numbers guide. Her dark hair pulled half back from her face means she's been in the kitchen baking beans or bannock or maybe even both.

I shake my head. "Nah, this is the last one."

"Bring it inside. You've got a lot of unpacking to do. I don't want these boxes and bags in the front room forever, you know."

I readjust the box in my arms, nudge the back door of my navy blue Toyota shut, and start for the front steps. The gravel crunches under my feet, distracting me. A crow croaks loudly on the power line above my head, startling me so much that I nearly drop the box. I turn to look and that black bird, with its shiny feathers and dark eyes, is staring right back at me. A flicker of recognition brushes my skin with goosebumps.

"Nanabush."

And just like that, my mother has my attention. I look at her incredulously. "What?"

She nods to the bird on the wire. "He used to change into a crow. At least that's what my mother told me. You ask Terrance Sutherland, though, and he'll tell you it was a rabbit. That Nanabush was *always* a rabbit. But I don't believe it. I think a crow's better, don't you?"

I keep my eyes on her a moment longer before looking up at the black bird again. It's still staring down at us. Tilting its little head back and forth, ruffling its feathers as it readjusts on the line when the wind picks up and shakes the wire. The crow lets out a few more caws before I look away, although I can still feel its gaze. I wonder if I've got something shiny on, but then I remember that's a magpie thing. Or is that crows too?

All I can think about are crows. What are they symbols of? I remember all those highly caffeinated 8:30 a.m. English literature lectures. Crows are ominous. They spell doom for the person who hears them. They're mysterious and sometimes magical. Signifying intelligence, destiny. What's the nursery rhyme again?

One for sorrow,
two for mirth,
three for a wedding,
and four for a birth.
five for silver,
six for gold,
and seven for a secret never to be told.

Sorrow it is. Fitting.

They remember faces, too. I can hear my dad's voice in my head, echoing like a cheesy soap flashback. *Crows are smarter than we give them credit for. They're memory and truth and creation.*

Funny how you always remember something you're trying to forget. Can't think of him now. I just got home. There'll be time for those memories later. I push him from my head, but he won't go.

They're manipulative, though. Don't ever forget who the most famous crow of them all was. Shapeshifter.

Trickster.

"Hazel?"

Mom's talking to me again. I turn to look at her, smile. "Did you say something?"

"I said that you came home at a good time. Weather's still nice. Come on," she says.

The door shuts with a thud, setting off a soft tinkle from the magnetic República Dominicana chime that's stuck up near the top. I kick off my shoes and turn into the living room. I step over the large pile of boxes and bags, dropping the one with miscellaneous items onto the couch. The warm scent of my mother's famous baked beans invites me into the kitchen, where she's standing at the counter, the sleeves of her plaid button-down rolled up to her elbows. She's wearing a T-shirt that says, "Tax Exempt."

"Supper should be ready in maybe fifteen minutes. I'm just waiting on the bannock to get nice and golden. You want some lemonade?"

"Geez, is this a powwow feast or something?"

"Tsk, no. It's just Minute Maid. I love you, kid, but lemons were not on sale this week."

Mom lifts the lid off the crockpot, scrunching her nose, and quickly replaces the cover. I watch her and the simple, easy way she moves about the kitchen. She barely has to look when she reaches up into the cupboards. Everything in here has stayed the same since my older brother was a baby. Sure, the cupboards have been repainted and the tile on the floor has been replaced, but it's still the same kitchen. It's got the same memories locked inside the yellowing cabinets and the mock-granite countertops.

Being here is comforting and makes me feel safe. It's a relief. Coming home is my way to pause while I try to figure out the next part of my life. I don't know if that means learning how to move on, but for now I'm happy to be here. City life has a way of devouring a person, and a year ago, right after everything went to shit, I gladly welcomed the distraction. School was my way of forgetting and ignoring all of the hurt that had built up inside of me. But once I had finished, crossed the stage, held my degree? It all rushed back into my life. I spent all of July shut up in my apartment, shifting between anger and disbelief until I couldn't stand it anymore.

"You glad to be home?" Mom asks, brushing loose strands of hair from her eyes as she continues to adjust the flavour of the beans.

I plunk myself onto one of the stools at the island and lean forward onto my elbows. "Yeah, it's a nice change. I'm excited to sleep tonight without someone stomping around in the apartment above me."

"Mm-hmm," she says. "It's a good place to recharge those old batteries, eh?" She moves over to the stove and flicks on the oven light, then bends down to peer through the tempered glass at the bannock. She clicks her tongue, muttering about it taking forever.

"Yeah," I answer. "I mean, it's not like I have anything lined up for myself here, but I guess that'll be a worry for another day. I should just shut up and enjoy the wide-openness of not having to work."

She straightens up as she looks at me. "Weird not to be going back to school?"

I nod. "But like, it's not like I had a whole bunch of friends there or anything. Most of the people I hung out with were Gus's friends. I'm not *missing* anyone. Just, I dunno, the freedom and the structure."

"Bit contradictory there, kid," she says with a smile. Mom comes over and pulls me into a side hug. "Ah, you'll be fine, just you wait. You'll settle in and before you know it you'll be happy that this is your new normal again."

"Uh-huh. Hope you're right."

She kisses the top of my head and walks back over to the counter to check on the crockpot once more. The rich, woody scent of maple syrup and liquid smoke fills the room as Mom spoons the beans into two mismatched floral-patterned bowls. I watch the way her shoulders shift as she breathes in. She pauses momentarily, the wooden spoon hovering over the crockpot. She clears her throat. "I'm gonna need your help picking out a monument."

"What?" I say, caught off guard. "Are you serious?"

Mom's moved from the counter to stand at the island across from where I'm sitting. "Yeah, I don't know if I'll pick the right thing. I mean, your father was always so particular about good materials. I think if I go alone, I'll muck it up."

"Jesus, Mom, can't you at least let me unpack a little before we start with this?"

"I'm sorry, Hazel, but you being home to help with his last wishes and all has got me thinking about it." She places her hands on the countertop of the island and grips a little. She's doing her best to keep her emotions tucked away, but they're creeping up on her. "I can't stand the thought of him lying in that place without any sign that says he's there. There's grass there now, you know? It's not just some big patch of dirt anymore, but plain old stupid grass. The same kind that dogs piss on."

I reach out and put my hand overtop hers and she stops talking. "*Kaye Mâmâ*, it's okay. Let's just eat, all right?"

She nods and I stand up to move to the table.

Outside, the crow is cawing.

✖ ✖ ✖

My bedroom, like much of this house, has remained unchanged since the day I left for university. The walls are a golden yellow that glows when the morning light pours through the windows, and the duvet is covered in daisies. The window looks out onto the front lawn and the pair of skinny evergreens planted there. I can also see the highway from here, which made it a great place to watch the school bus zoom by on those days back in high school when I hit the snooze button one too many times.

I'm taking a break from hanging up clothes to dig through the biggest of my sealed boxes. It's mostly books. Getting it up the five stairs of our split-level house proved to be very difficult. Mom even cursed a few times, twice calling the books stowed away inside the box *wabi-jishkish.* A fair judgment, considering most of them are the remains of my hard-earned, very White, very male-centric English degree.

I settle the books into their new home on the worn bookshelf in the corner. It's made of light wood—birch or something—and has been left natural. The only stains on it are the five letters of my name written in the untidy scrawl that six-year-old me thought was wildly artistic. I used black wax pencil. Mom was so mad when she found me etching my mark into the beautifully crafted bookcase. I remember her shouting that it had been built by my grandfather back before he was *ogima,* so it was a big deal that I had ruined such an important family heirloom. But she never tried to remove it. Maybe it eventually became a sweet memory of a younger me. Or maybe she knew trying to wash it away would only smudge it more.

At this rate, I'll never finish unpacking. I'm terrible at finishing anything. A trait I blame wholeheartedly on my father. I would need two extra hands to count how many projects around this house have been started and left: three different versions of the same bench, two doors that are only half stained, one door frame that's got a decorative piece that falls out seemingly at random, the tile in the kitchen that doesn't quite reach the edges of the walls, not to mention the deck that drops off without stairs or a railing. All those things started. Left to stay unfinished.

I can feel the tightly bound pieces of myself threaten to tumble and fall apart. A year and a half out from his death and I'm still struggling to be normal. Most days, I try to keep my grief inside myself. Look fine, feel awful. But being here has me too close to it, to everything from before. So instead I swallow to push it away. Down, down, down, until it isn't there.

Moving without thinking, I unpack as much of my stuff as I possibly can. Books. Clothes. Movies. Some art to make the walls a little less sunny. I spend the majority of my time putting up a corkboard that displays the past four years of my life. Years in pictures showing only the highlights. Makes it seem like I was only ever happy.

I pin up a picture of me and my older brother, Gus. It's from my second year of university, at a pub that we'd always go to with friends. It was warm and inviting. Even had a fireplace and comfortable chairs. Most importantly, the drinks were cheap and there was a jukebox. Every night at a certain time—probably closer to midnight than to last call—this woman would come in selling flowers, a Polaroid camera hanging from her neck. The regulars rarely got suckered into buying anything from her, but on this night, we made an exception. It was Gus's twenty-eighth birthday and we were out celebrating. Gus wasn't a big partier, so we had gone to dinner and then for drinks at our favourite place. Someone tried to convince him to go bowling, but Gus adamantly refused. Mostly because he didn't want to take the bus to get there.

We did almost everything together during those years I was in Ottawa. People used to tell us how lucky we were that we got along as well as we did. We'd get a lot of, "Oh, I could never live with my siblings." For us, it was fine. We've lived together pretty much our whole lives, so it was nothing new. You can yell at your brother about eating your favourite cereal in a way that you just can't with a regular roommate. Plus, we have the same sense of humour and Gus always does the dishes. He's kind of a neat freak.

That night, after too many pints, he wanted his birthday documented in a way that couldn't be erased by a thumb tap. He motioned the lady over, stuck his big old arm around my shoulders, and pulled me closer. I was laughing so hard because he had made some joke—I don't remember it now—and the camera caught that perfect moment of the two of us. Real happiness on both our faces.

Gus doesn't smile so big anymore.

He's still in Ottawa. He works for the Council of Algonquin Indians now. Does work to right wrongs against our People. *Toiling.* That's what he calls it. He always talks about his job that way. It's the type of work that makes you feel like you aren't making progress even though you come home with your mind and heart aching. He says it's like working in a mine. You get stuff done, but the air down there is still killing you slowly. Until recently, he worked as part of the Truth and Reconciliation Commission. Helping those of us still suffering from second-wave cultural genocide to find peace. Which is a fancy way of saying he helped people apply for the money that was owed to them by the Canadian government.

Thinking of my brother makes me happy. He's one of the lucky ones. One of the kids who made it off the reserve. He didn't always hang with the best crowds, but that never made him lose sight of the freedom of leaving the Rez. Like so many of the kids who studied in the country's capital, Gus majored in political science and minored in social justice. He keeps talking about going back to get his MBA. I don't think he'll go.

There's a small knock on the door frame and I turn to see Mom. Her hair's down now and is falling over her shoulders like a silvery-black waterfall. She's got Pocahontas hair.

"Unpacking going well?" she asks.

"Mostly." I shrug. "I didn't realize how much I own. There's stuff here that I completely forgot I had."

"Need a break yet? There's lots of berries out by the quarry this time of year. Would be nice to have some." Mom walks into the room and sits down on the bed facing the wall where I've put up the corkboard. She leans back on her hands and smiles. "When's that from?"

Without even needing to turn around, I know she's pointing at the picture of me and Gus. "Gus's birthday. His twenty-eighth."

She whistles lowly through her teeth. "Nice that you and Angus got to be in the same city after leaving home. I've always been happy that you two got along."

"Not always. There was that time that I wanted to hang out with him and his friends and they told me to go with them into the bush behind the house and they just left me there."

"He was young. Brothers do that."

"I was young too! Like, six maybe?"

"Oh, you were fine. It's always good to get lost in the woods at least once when you're little. Brings out the Indian in the kid."

"Don't think it worked for me because I've still got the worst sense of direction. I feel like the least-Indian Indian ever. Oh my god, I say that and you are *literally* braiding your hair right now."

She tosses the finished braid over her shoulder. "Hey, when you go out to the quarry, take a look at that old road, will you?"

"Why? You wanna open it up again?"

Mom shakes her head. "No, but your dad was interested in its possibilities, so maybe you should be too?"

I press my lips together into a hard line. "Dad liked to start and not finish things all the time. Maybe the quarry should stay that way?"

She shrugs off the question and turns her attention away from me. I watch her for a while longer, trying to find answers to her suggestion in her features. What possibilities can come from an overgrown hole in the ground?

Mom brings her gaze back to me after staring at the rest of the pictures on the corkboard. I can tell she's looking at the ones of me and my father because she's got water in her eyes. They're great pictures—one of us at Disney World, another one of the two of us in matching motorcycle jackets.

I had no idea she'd be in this bad shape. Granted, she's not falling apart into a weepy mess at every mention of Dad, but the fact that there are tears at all is enough. Mom has always been the strong one. Always happy. And now, well, she's not. She wears this grin on her face, but the smile never reaches her eyes. I know because I can't see the lines at the corners of them. When she really smiles, the wrinkles make her look like she's grinning bigger than she is. She's had them forever, the crow's feet. Most people think that wrinkles are bad, that they show your age, but not Mom. She has worn those crow's feet with pride since the day she noticed them.

"They're gifts from Nanabush," she'd say. "I remember my mom—your *gôkom*—used to say that the Great Shapeshifter liked to visit us in our dreams. He shows up so much that eventually we get these little lines on our eyes from where he's walked. And the dust in the corners of them, by your nose? That's bits of the Spirit World. Stuff that he brings over with him when he visits."

She tears her eyes away from the pictures and finally notices me staring at her. She blinks once or twice and tilts her head. "Jesus, you look like your dad when you do that."

I try to say something, but nothing comes out. I end up looking away.

Mom continues, "He had this way of looking at someone, didn't matter who, and he could see them. Not like just seeing a person like looking at their clothes or what dumb haircut they have—trust me, he did that too—but he could *see* a person. When that man looked at you with those big old grey eyes, he saw through you."

"But my eyes are brown." What a stupid thing to say.

She smiles but winces too. "Yeah, you got my eyes. Sorry about that one, kid." She moves to stand, brushing her hands on the front of her jeans as she stretches. She comes over to me, places her hands on my shoulders and looks at me. "Nah. My colour. But those are still his eyes."

The knot in my throat quickly moves into my eyes and makes them water, so Mom puts her arms around me. I don't want to cry, so I make strangled noises until I've got myself under control and she lets me go. She pats my cheek before turning to leave the room. For a long while I stare at the spot where she had been standing. When I convince myself to move again, I reach up to wipe away tears that aren't there.

I got sick of crying months ago.

Sick and tired.
That's what he was too.
Now I'm just tired.

☒ ☒ ☒

Mom's earlier suggestion to pick berries turned out to be the distraction I needed. Classic Mom. Therapy that also includes benefits for her. Being home is tougher than I thought it would be. I can see traces of my father everywhere. I expect him to walk in the door any moment. I keep thinking I'll see his truck pull into the driveway. I'll hear him whistling to himself as he walks up the steps to our house. It's starting to eat away at me, building up until I feel the anxiety threatening to make me panic or lose my breath.

Outside, the fear almost disappears. The trees that surround me are thrumming with the summer buzz of cicadas. Everything is so close in this forest, it's as if I'm inside a living, breathing creature. The air snuggles in like an embrace. Mom used to say that there was magic in this place. Every tree, every leaf, every little flower bud, and every birdsong carries a story and piece of our people. She used to read the bark of the birches back here and tell me my future. Nothing she said ever came true.

I follow a well-worn trail through the forest behind our house. I've walked this path so many times I could probably do it in my sleep. I move between the trees slowly but easily. This trek has always calmed me. The best berries grow past the first throng of trees. If I keep walking through the growth of wooden giants, I'll come out into a huge clearing. I can't tell if it's perfectly round, but from the middle of it, it feels eerily so. It looks like it was clear-cut, that some human had a hand in creating this place, but that's not the case. People have tried finding evidence of a lumber company in this location and found nothing. As far as we Natives can be sure, the clearing has been here as long as we have, perhaps longer. I can only assume there are stories and myths linked to it, long forgotten. Dad used to say it was faeries, which he heard from his Irish great-grandmother. Mom insisted that faeries only make circles of mushrooms, not clearings in forests. Plus, she hated the idea of someone else's stories from across the ocean finding roots here.

Whatever the reason for it, this clearing in the middle of the bush is beautiful. It's probably sacred, but now I'm the only one who sees it. Mom doesn't come back here. Something about the air feeling funny. I don't mind. If it does feel strange, it's only for a moment. All it takes is one light breeze to brush along the grass and the glade will settle.

I take a moment to glance up at the sky. When we were kids, I used to think I could see the curve of the world up there. I'd stare at the way the sky seemed to blend into a blue arc and I'd feel like I was at the centre of something—that there was a reason I was here. I still experience a small flutter of excitement, but now I know that's left over from my youth, my self-involved sense of importance. And yet, here I am smiling. I take one deep breath in, the smell of cedar filling my lungs, and slowly let it out, feeling the wind pick up and breathe with me.

A bird croaks from somewhere in the trees, the sound echoing and carrying along the air for a moment before disappearing among the other calls and whistles. My footsteps are light as I move through the grass toward the edge of the glade, the earth a carpet beneath me. The second I make it past the pines, the air closes in tightly. Whatever haze of bliss had been over me before is gone and I feel a weight in my chest. My shoulders slump back down and I accept the familiar discomfort as I weave in and out of the trees. The first patch of raspberries is nearby. They grow all along the northern edge of the forest and continue to follow the sloping dirt road that leads down to the quarry.

I smell the rock and water of the old open-pit mine before I see it. This place is familiar in a way that goes beyond my own memory. The land has been in my dad's family for generations, even before someone came along and started digging into it. I read something once that said Indigenous People are tied to the land through memory that exists in the absence of sensory experience. It's in our blood. I'm not sure if that's true for everyone, but I know that this place is a part of me and has been for years beyond my own counting.

I'm standing on the cusp of the far side of the quarry. I tend to keep a good distance from the edge because just beyond it is a drop of about a hundred feet to the water. When I was little, my best friend, Mia, and I would come out here and dare each other to get close enough to hang our legs over. She always got closer than I did, what with my fear of heights, but neither of us ever made it to the edge. Plus, the fact that we were told to stay totally clear of the place was enough thrill for a goody two-shoes like me. It scared me back then and it still scares me. It's been over a hundred years since the pit was operational, and even then, it wasn't a very successful mine. For years, rumours and stories flew around the community like little birds fluttering from ear to ear. They said that the mine had to close because people kept dying or there were accidents that couldn't be explained. Elders like Old Tommy Knight said his ancestors cursed the place. The White Man took and took and took without ever giving thanks. No tobacco was offered, so Mother Earth decided to call in her debts and snatch back what she was owed.

I've always thought that story was too dark. Mother Earth as a vengeful spirit doesn't seem right. Those were just stories made up by parents to keep their kids away. The quarry closed so long ago, the reasons faded with it. The land around it is fertile, but nothing's ever been done with it. The property has been in my dad's name forever, so if anyone was to do something about it, it would have been him.

I'm glad it's a dead investment. I get this place all to myself. The old road that leads here is overgrown—too difficult for even the most seasoned bush explorers. The rocky terrain around the quarry makes it dangerous, even without the drop into the terrifyingly clear water below. The years haven't been kind to the weathered and winding road that was used to haul the caches of silver. Now, one wrong step could mean an ugly fall.

I step out of the woods and amble toward the growth of raspberry bushes that has made its home between the forest and the quarry's edge. The wind picks up, creating rippling patterns along the water. It's colder than it should be at this time of year. I tuck my arm in close to my body, clutching the empty margarine container tightly, as I gather the deep-red berries, each one making a soft plunking noise as it hits the plastic. It's quite some time before I pick enough to even cover the bottom of the container. After a while, I settle into a rhythm, relaxing enough to sing quietly. It's an old hand drum song that my mom used to sing to me. Even alone, I'm self-conscious about what I sound like, so I sing slowly and softly, and only use my full voice at the end of the song. As soon as the last word slips past my lips, a trio of black-winged birds explodes from the tree closest to me. I jump and almost drop my berries. Their calls echo across the expanse of the quarry in perfect time. I watch the birds until they're specks on the horizon.

I make it back to the house as the sun slips beyond the edge of the western sky. Mom's out on the back porch, sitting at the table. Her chair is pushed out from it and her feet are resting on another one beside her. She's got the phone pinched between her ear and shoulder as she picks at her nails. I catch bits of her conversation as I get closer to the house. She hasn't spotted me yet.

"I don't know what Abe was thinking." She pauses and listens while the other person on the line talks. "Mm-hmm, yeah. Had plans for it, that's for sure. Guess it's something the kids are gonna have to talk about since he left it to them."

What is this about? Dad left us a bunch of land, that I know, but this is something specific.

"Well, if it wasn't for that damn deal, maybe we'd have more wiggle room." She glances at me as I walk up the steps to the deck. "I'll talk to you later. Hazel just got back. Okay, I will. Bye." Mom ends the call and places the phone down on the table. "Good berry adventure?"

I nod and move to sit at the head of the table, placing the container down in front of me. "Who was that?"

"Your auntie. She says hello, by the way."

"What were you talking about?"

She gives me a noncommittal shrug. "Your dad's will."

"Oh," I say, looking away. "You want my help or something?"

She shakes her head. "No, no. I've got it under control for now."

"'Kay, if you're sure."

When I look back at Mom, she's staring at me curiously. My stomach pitches and I can feel my eyes go wide.

"What? You're looking at me so weird right now and it's kinda freaking me out."

"Oh," she says, blinking for a moment. "Sorry, kid. It's just . . ."

She plucks something from my shoulder. Mom twirls the gleaming black feather between her thumb and forefinger.

I can only blink at her.

Her smile comes back, bigger this time. "A gift from Nanabush. Guess he's got your back, huh?"

3

ÀNDEG

I exhale and my breath fogs into the night air. There are stars hanging in the expanse above me, blinking down at my collapsed body. My hands seem to sink into the ground, making it difficult to push myself up. I blink once, twice. My eyes are open, but I can't see beyond the tall, naked trees silhouetted by starlight. Fear starts deep in my gut, threatening to take over. I swallow it and send it away. Something whispers to me in the dark.

—*Hazel.*

Calm spreads through me and I rise, slowly and carefully. I listen, trying to hear the voice who seems to know me. Curiosity presses me to move forward in the dark. My footsteps dissolve in the space around me, the ground eating them up before they can make a sound. Erasing me like I'm not here.

But where *is* here?

—*It is where you need to be.*

"Who's there?" I wait, my own voice echoing into the cold air, the hair on my arms pulling toward the sky, but there is no answer. I walk forward. This time, I can hear my steps. Or maybe that's the double-beat drumming of my heart?

—*Keep moving.*

I swallow, but my mouth has gone dry and it does little to ease my discomfort. I keep walking, even without a destination. The fear starts to creep back into my body, making me tremble. I feel the air get colder and soon the ground is covered in a crisp blanket of snow. I hear it crunch beneath my feet. I want to pull the shroud of darkness off me, so I bring my hands to my face. And that's when I realize I'm crying. Or I *have been* crying. Am I still?

Something flutters past me and I stop. My pulse pounds in my ears, so fast I can't count the beats. I'm getting dizzy. Like when they fan the drum at a powwow and another pickup starts and then another and another, so you just keep dancing and dancing, making your way around the arbour with no idea of when they might finally stop so you can rest your feet.

—*How do you expect to move on when you keep stopping like that?*

"Was that you?"

—*Was what me?*

"The wings. Just now."

—*Yes.*

There's a flutter of movement that I can almost see. Wings brush the side of my face, smooth and cool and impatient. Faster than before. I close my eyes, a small act to help me listen.

"What are you?"

—*Does it matter? I'm here. That should be enough.*

"It isn't," I say. "You're nothing but empty words right now. Show yourself."

Two grey eyes flicker like beacons in the darkness, and I know they're staring me. Looking me up and down, studying everything from the way I stand to the curve of my eyelashes. They stare and stare, and because they are the only light I can see, I stare right back. As my eyes start to adjust, I pick up the smooth outline of a black bird. I blink and it comes into focus. It's too big to be a raven, so that means it's far too big to be a crow. I've never seen a bird like this one before. But by the way it looks at me, I can tell it's seen me. It knows me.

I shudder. I feel vulnerable under this bird's gaze. It tilts its head this way and that as it surveys me, blinking a few times before ruffling its feathers and opening its beak to caw at me. It's so normal that it upsets me. I expected the voice I heard. How disappointing.

—*Can you see now?*

The bird's beak is shut, but it looks at me, expecting an answer.

This whole thing is starting to lose its mysticism, and my frustration is growing again. I want answers, not more questions and riddles. It's making me grind my teeth. "No. You're just lines in the dark."

—*As are you. Yet, here we both are, looking for a way out.*

"And you can give that to me?"

—*We could trade. Help me and I'll help you. Fair, don't you think?*

The look on this bird's face is familiar. Like a predator cornering its prey. His eyes glimmer warmly, but I do not trust him. He speaks as if I have already agreed to whatever bargain he offers. As I look him over, it dawns on me.

"Wait. I know you, I do. I thought I didn't, but it's making sense now. You're Nanabush."

—*"The Great Shapeshifter" sounds nicer, better, and more formal, since we're strangers.*

"That isn't true," I say. "You and I have met before. You know me."

—*I do, yes.*

"And since you're on a first-name basis with me, it's only fair that I use yours." I move my gaze from him and take in my surroundings as light from an aurora reaches me. Birch trees—I can smell the bark—are silhouetted in the dark. Nanabush is perched on the low hanging branches, looking down at me.

—*Fine, so be it.*

"This whole thing, it's lucid dreaming, isn't it? Where you're aware that you're dreaming? Let me change it. Where's all the magic?"

—You people claim you want to dream about magic when everything around you has been created out of the Great Magic of the Earth and the Sky. The air that all living things breathe gives the gift of life, but it can also take life away. Is that not magical?

"I wouldn't say death is magical. Might be for the person who wants it, but the rest of us left behind are stuck with pain and grief and anger that we can't unpack."

His laughter startles me.

—People take dying for granted.

"What's that supposed to mean? It's awful. I've seen it. Your body fails and shuts down until you're trapped inside of it." My voice shrinks and breaks. "Just a husk of someone who used to mean so much."

—You mean your father?

His words cut clean and clear through me. Nanabush looks at me again and my ears start to ring. It's quiet at first, but I can feel it pushing into the space behind my eyes. I try to press the pain from my head, but I can't.

"You don't know anything about that," I say.

He's still gazing at me and I hate it. Makes me feel naked. I lash out.

"Aren't you supposed to be a sage? Give me a vision quest or leave me alone." I wince as the ringing gets louder.

—You're not ready for that.

"That's rich. I mean, if I'm dreaming, then technically you're just a figment of my imagination." I cut myself off with a laugh. "I don't think *I'm* ready."

Silence settles between us uncomfortably until all I can hear and feel is the ringing. But the quiet, it fits us like a pair of too-big shoes, making me stumble back into conversation.

"I want to wake up now."

Nanabush laughs, a ragged croaking that echoes around us.

—*Then open your eyes.*

"They're already open. You're all I can see."

—*Do you see me? I don't think that you do. Look harder.* He spreads his feathers wide, his whole form growing until he's bigger than me. He looks down at me, his head twisting and twitching.

"I see you!" I snap, screaming at him. "Lines in the dark. All around me."

—*And that's what it's like. Being here? Like trying to draw lines in the dark.* His beak opens in laughter again. Nanabush flaps his wings, sending a rush of air that whips and pushes me to the ground.

"Stop it! *Stop it!* I want to wake up!"

I grip my hands to my head to stop the ringing. Why won't it stop? The world around me is swallowed up by Nanabush's growing shadow, punctuated by the clacking of his beak.

I cry out into the darkness. And I'm back in my bedroom. When my eyes finally open, the pain's gone, but the ringing persists. Slowly, the street lamp's glow comes to life on the walls of my bedroom. I run my hand over my eyes and back into my hair. There's sweat on my forehead. I tell myself to calm down, it wasn't real. Inhale deeply until I can breathe normally again. The clock beside my bed reads 3:04. The ringing isn't just in my ears. Now that I'm awake, I can hear it properly. It's the kettle.

Mom's awake too. Some irrational, still-dreaming part of me wonders if she had the same dream that I did. She's making tea. She does this whenever she can't sleep. She swears by the tea leaves, saying they help you fall asleep and stay asleep. For a moment I consider staying in bed, pulling the covers up so they're nearly over my head, leaving space for me to breathe, as I make deals with my brain to let me fall back into a dreamless sleep. But that's pointless because the more I tell myself to shut my eyes, the more I don't want to. I'm afraid that there'll be black wings and grey eyes waiting for me on the other side.

Pushing off the covers, I swing my legs around and stand up. I stumble but catch myself against the bedside table. My body starts to ache like I've just finished a half-marathon. I stretch to push the pain from my muscles before I tiptoe out into the hallway.

Downstairs, I hear Mom humming to herself. She stops when I appear in the door frame, but only for a moment. She reaches into the cupboard and pulls down an elaborately decorated box. She's chosen a blend from a bookstore in the next town over: Labrador tea. People around here say it can cure almost anything. I've even heard that it can help a woman induce labour, when her baby is being stubborn and refuses to leave her. That's what helped Mia when her little girl kept pushing back her due date. Or maybe it was a coincidence. Can't be sure now anyhow, seeing as the kid's been here for five years.

Wordlessly, Mom grabs a second mug from the cupboard before she brews tea for us both. She gives me a smile and takes both mugs in her hands. I watch as she walks over to the island and sits down, then move to join her. We sit in silence for the better part of ten minutes while we wait for our tea to cool. Steam rises from the mugs. Mine has a picture of Mickey Mouse on it. Mom's reads, "Bowler of the Month." The seconds tick by. Mom grabs her mug with both hands, brings it to her lips, and attempts to take a sip. It's still too hot. She scrunches her nose and shakes her head before putting the mug back down on the island.

She doesn't ask me why I'm up. I give her the same kindness. Neither of us drinks the tea.

4

WÎGWAS

In the morning, I take my time going down the stairs, running my fingers along the edge of the wall like I've done since I was a kid. The movement is old, part of who I am by now, but I still pay attention to the way the paint dimples. There's a beaded breast-plate that belonged to my dad hanging on the wall. It has these long pieces of thin leather with the smallest jingles I've ever seen hanging from them. When my fingers touch them, they chime together daintily.

Back when I was a kid, putting my hand on the wall was a way to keep myself from falling as I went down one stair two feet at a time, but now I guess it's just a habit. The movement feels good, comforting. I don't quite smile, but the sounds of the jingles reassure me. Remind me that home will always be home. Only now it's different. I pause a moment, then run my fingers along the jingles once more. I watch as they sway against the wall, knocking into each other, slowing down until they stop completely. Then I make my way into the kitchen.

"Morning, kid," says Mom. "Beans are hot in the crockpot if you want them for breakfast. Bought a loaf of Sadie Jocko's bread a couple of days ago. Should still be good if you want a slice."

She's at the counter, cutting vegetables and squinting at a recipe book that's propped open against the sugar and flour canisters.

"*Kaye Mâmâ*, wear your glasses." I pick them up from the counter and offer them to her.

"I don't need those damn things." She leans in closer to the book.

I click my tongue. "Yes, you do. It's your own fault you picked out that silly pair. Besides, it's just me and you here. What do you care what you look like? Wouldn't want you putting in two table-spoons of sugar instead of two tablespoons of salt."

"Oh my god, Hazel, it doesn't call for that much salt."

"That was just an example. Here. Take them and put them on your face, *gôkom.*"

She gasps, swatting at me with her hand. I know enough to hop back before she can make contact. A smile spreads across my face and I can feel a laugh bubble up from my stomach.

"*Animizie binòdjish!* Calling me an old woman. I got carded the other day at the LCBO, you know."

"Yeah, probably to make sure that you weren't some escapee from the seniors' home."

Another swat. She's smiling, though, so I know I'm in the clear.

"Starting to think I should've made Gus come home instead."

"Pfft. Gus has been calling you an old lady *way* longer than I have. You'd have it much worse if he was here."

"Your brother's an ass."

"Yup. Lucky for us he's a lovable one."

"It's that stupid grin of his."

"Mm-hmm."

"I miss that grin."

I stop smiling. So does she.

Mom finally takes her glasses from my outstretched hand and puts them on. She dusts her fingers off on her apron, then goes back to cutting the vegetables. Her eyes widen when she looks back at the recipe, and I know it's because she can actually read the words. I want to say, "I told you so," but the playful moment is gone. Shame, though. It felt nice.

I clear my throat and walk over to the fridge to have somewhere else to look. This silence is different than before. Last night, it was like we understood each other without talking. Now, it's like she's stepped on one of those land mines you see in movies, where someone triggers it but as long as they stay still it won't explode. Any movement, or even a droplet of sweat, will set it off. I don't know if those exist, but that's how it feels right now. Tension. A wrong move or word will release something bad into this room. Something destructive.

Memories.

Boom. There's us taking a road trip to Ottawa in the early 1990s. And over here, by the fridge, that's Gus and Dad on the day Gus bought his first four-wheeler. Oh, and there, next to the patio door, that's a picture from Christmas. Didn't know it would be our last Christmas together. We look happy, huddled close like that. Smiles aren't real, though. How could they be? Christmas around a hospital bed isn't Christmas, even if there's garland draped across the window blinds.

"Hazel?"

I don't turn to face her, instead keep my gaze focused on the inside of the fridge. "Yeah?"

"Think you could get me the carrots from the veggie drawer? I got everything else but those. What the hell kind of tomato-veggie soup is this going to be without the carrots."

"See? This is why you needed your glasses."

"Oh hush, *animizie binòdjish*."

"Look, if I can't call you an old lady, you can't call me that. And don't think I don't know you mean it *meanly*." I hand her the bag of carrots.

She gives me a small smile. No crow's feet, though.

I pull the orange juice out of the fridge and grab a glass from the cupboard, then get distracted by the thought of that home-made bread she mentioned. I slice off two pieces and put them into the toaster. When I'm done, I notice my glass has juice in it.

"Thanks."

"No problem."

"It's not full, though."

"You never drink a full glass. I'm just saving you the trouble of wasting food. Doesn't grow on trees, you know."

"Dunno, last I checked, oranges grew on trees."

"*This* is why I can call you *animizie* all I want. Take your damn juice and get out of my kitchen already."

"Okay, okay! Stop trying to hit me. Don't make me call Child Services on you."

"Tsk, oh my god."

"Can you at least let me know when my toast is ready?"

"Yeah, yeah. Now gwan outta here, you!"

I grab my juice and head off into the living room. I flick the television on and flop onto the couch. I absently scroll through the channels until I find something for background noise. It doesn't take me long to zone out. I'm staring in the direction of the TV, but I'm not seeing it. My head is somewhere else entirely.

Lines in the dark.

I've dreamt of birds before, but nothing like what happened last night. Nanabush felt so real, so present, more than a dream. How could it be? I was asleep, so it had to have been a dream. There should be nothing more to consider. Normally, I can reconcile the real and the unreal. Dreams are supposed to be difficult to understand. Impossible things happen in them all the time. There's a moment, right after I wake up, when the truth and fiction are blurred, and I panic. That uneasy feeling hasn't left me. Like I can't convince myself that what I saw was made up, illogical, irrational.

In my head, it's still real.

I'd sound completely batshit crazy if I tried to explain this to anyone. I wouldn't even know where to start. I cover my eyes with my hand and lean back against the couch.

The more I think about the dream, the quicker it fades away. It's all fragments. Like an echo on the other side of a canyon where the words are muddled until they aren't words anymore, just sounds. Bird calls in a forest. Sentences in a language I can't understand. Thinking about Nanabush sitting in that dark wood is making my head throb.

I slump on the couch, slowly sliding against it until I'm lying down. The sound coming from the TV starts to soften. I let myself drift off. Can I get back to the dream? Scary or not, I know that I need to return to it. I want to find it all again—the birchbark and the bird in the branches. I don't want the echo; I want the voice who spoke the words.

I smell sweetgrass and fire. Did Mom light a candle?

There's wind, strong and fierce. It's coming from the Western doorway, the door closest to the Spirit World, so it brings voices with it. Whispers and whistles. I hear them around me, quiet and loud, like they're inside of my head and right beside me at the same time. I start walking, the snow crunching beneath me, my feet in moccasins made of moosehide and white rabbit fur. The beading looks like it was done by my grandmother. I recognize her style. Around me there are wigwams—huts made of bent branches and pelts. Each of them cloaked in darkness. At the head of the camp stands a beautiful giant teepee. Firelight makes the animal hide stretched over the poles glow. Moonlight makes the snow glisten and sparkle. The wind picks up as I walk. I hum an honour song.

Smoke rises from the great teepee, now in front of me, its light peeking through the edges of the doorway. As I move closer, I hear the sounds of people speaking inside. Their voices are biting with anger but hushed, like they are telling secrets. Each voice is old but lilted with the melody of youth. Turning my ear to the teepee hide, I listen until I can understand. How many are inside the tent? I pause, close my eyes so that I can count. Seven voices. I move around the great hut and pause at the doorway. I do not go in.

—*I will go. I am needed now. I am the carrier of Thought, a healer of wounds and minds.* The first voice, creaking and whispering, is the wind that lives between giant, ancient birch trees as they rock back and forth.

The second voice is like the heat of a wood fire that is burning in a pit dug into the earth. —*No, Tabasenimidiwin. You are too quick-footed. You will end the grief before it has had time to be felt. You cannot go. It must be me, Sagi'idiwin. I am the carrier of Spirit.*

—*You are wrong for this as well, Sagi'idiwin. It should be me, Manadji'idiwin, the carrier of Honour.* The third voice is an oak: proud, bent, but unbroken.

—*Honour will do no good at a time like this. It is honour that opens old wounds. I will bring our noshis the healing that is needed. Send the carrier of Belief. Send me, Tebwewin.* The fourth voice speaks with the determination of a stream upon a boulder, careful and calm in the knowledge that it will win with patience.

—*Tebwewin is only one-half of true Belief. I will go to our noshis. Gweyâkwâdiziwin is the carrier of Faith.* This fifth voice speaks like water upon a mountain. The rain of a landslide.

With the sixth voice comes the softness of cool air, scented by wildflowers and honey. Sticky and bright. —*Faith is not needed now. Faith will only hold back our noshis. I will go. I am the carrier of Light.*

And last is a voice like thunder in the heat of a summer evening. Warm and ominous. Foreboding. Gentle. —*It is too soon for you to go, Kaye Nibwâkawin. You will give the teaching without healing. If any of us shall go, it must be me, Sôginijiwin. I am the carrier of Heart.*

All of the voices speak at once in a language I can understand but not hear. It is too much for me, so I step back from the doorway. As the wind picks up again from the West, I turn my head to follow its breeze. There, away from the circle of wigwams, stands another small home, covered in dark furs that ripple like waves on water in the night wind. Smoke rises from the opening at the top, but no light comes from the edges of the door. I feel drawn to it. I need to move closer.

The snow crunches and swallows each of my steps so loudly that I am sure the voices in the teepee will hear me, but their arguments have grown louder and they are only concerned with themselves. At the entrance of the small wigwam, nothing in my body tells me to stop, no voice cries out that what I am doing is wrong, so I reach forward and lift the pelt covering the doorway. I bend my head low as I duck into the dark interior. It looks as if a fire was going, but it's been dead for a while. Only embers glow, huddled inside of the charcoal of the pit. Smoke dances into the air. Here, I smell sage.

The wind carries the voices from the teepee to me, but I do not listen.

Across the remains of the fire is a long piece of bark. As I stare at it, it moves. This could be a trick of the smoke. Looking closer, I can tell that it's birchbark. The edges are curled but have hardened. Birchbark is quickest to catch fire but also best to keep out water.

I bend down to take the bark in my hands, to turn it over and see its underbelly. But when I reach for it, a flurry of dark wings pushes the bark aside. The wigwam comes alive with my startled scream and the frantic rustle of feathers. A whip of wind blows the door open, letting in the moonlight. I peek out from my fingers in time to watch the bird fly through the doorway and down the path I took to get to the village. Its feathers are like ink against the snow until it is swallowed up by the trees surrounding the clearing.

The wind carrying the voices to me dies.

I take a deep breath and step back out into the night. The crow's caws are all around me, but the bird with the grey eyes is gone.

The voices stop when they hear the crow's words echoing into the night. It is a while before I hear the oldest of them speak again.

—*We have argued too long. Someone has let the Trickster out of his prison. Now we can only watch as he stumbles over teachings that should have been ours to give.*

"Hazel?"

Mom is standing directly in front of me, the look on her face telling me that I've been doing something weird or something that warrants that raised eyebrow of disapproval. I quickly push myself up into a sitting position and pat down my hair.

"What? Why are you looking at me like that?"

"I've been telling you your toast is ready for about five minutes now."

"Have you? I couldn't even hear you."

"Well, when you're watching this mind-numbing ghost-hunting crap, it's easy to ignore your ever-so-loving mother when she shouts at you."

I want to laugh. She's being sweet and funny, but I can't seem to focus.

"The hell's in that orange juice? The look on your face right now, kid."

"I must just be tired. You know, didn't sleep great."

"Mm-hmm."

"Anyway, sorry. You said my toast popped?"

"Long time ago. So, when you're ready, there's two pieces of hard, cold bread waiting for you in the toaster."

She turns, heading back into the kitchen. Before she can leave me altogether, I stop her.

"Hey, Mom?"

"Yeah?"

"You didn't light any candles or anything?"

"No. Been cooking this whole time."

"And the soup? You didn't put sage in your soup, did you?"

She shakes her head. Her hand is on the door frame as she looks me over in that way that only moms and grade one teachers know how to do. "No. Sage is for ceremonies and cleansing. And turkey." Her voice starts to trail away as she disappears around the corner. "Now come get your damn toast before I throw some peanut butter on it and give it to the dog."

I nod and sigh quietly, but the smell of smoke is still in my hair.

5

CATCH UP

The chains hanging from the swing set rattle when Mia and I plunk ourselves into the seats. The school playground is practically ancient, made of unpainted wood and metal assembled long before safety standards were a concern. It should probably be updated, but the Rez doesn't have the money to spare for something like that. Instead, they bypass the problem by putting three teachers on recess duty when school's in session. Right now, Mia and I have the place all to ourselves.

Mia brushes the bangs from her face, tucking her long hair behind her ears. She's been ranting for the whole walk from my place to the school about her life on the Rez. Complaining is one of our favourite pastimes.

She grumbles, "And I mean, like, what's the point of trying to even apply for a house when I know it's going to go to someone whose last name is the same as someone on Council. They gotta do something about the way the supply and demand works. I can't even bring myself to be bothered to do it anymore. But, like, I'm gonna do it anyway. I would rather just bitch about it than have to face the reality of the situation, you know?"

"That's still a big thing here, eh?"

"Oh god, Hazel, you have no idea. I have been here forever and I still want to poke my goddamn eyes out every time I see those announcements in the *Newsletter*. Like, jab-jab. Done." Mia shakes her head. "It's the same thing. Biweekly disappointment.

Shit, if I wanted that kind of regular letdown, I'd have stayed with my ex."

I snort. "How's he doing anyway? You guys have a better arrangement?"

"Heh. He's all right and it's all right. I mean he's got custody once a month. I guess you could say he's doing the bare minimum. I should've seen that coming. He only ever did the bare minimum in school too." She shudders, making the chains on her swing shudder along with her. "Mistakes we make in high school, huh?"

"At least you got a great kid out of it."

Mia throws her head back and laughs in that ascending giggle of hers. "Bless you, Hazel, and the way you make light of any situation that shouldn't be made light of. Yeah, you're right, though. Emmy's the one good thing that piece of work gave me. Even if we were only teenagers when I had her."

"I don't know how you managed being a mom. No, no"—I draw a little star in the air with my finger—"*Manage*. You're still doing it and will for, like . . . ever, so that's super impressive."

"When you think about it, I was kinda on trend. It just made sense to go with it. I mean, how many other Rez girls were pregnant while you and I were in high school?"

I start counting in my head and then begin numbering them off on my fingers. "Started with Gracie. Then, like, months later, it was her best friend, Paula. And the next year, it was Natalie, Sam, Leanne."

"And me. Don't forget me."

"Right, then you. And Kayla and Mackenzie."

"Then a few of the White girls from the hick towns got in on the action too and there were at least three of them."

"Dammit, I need another hand to do this count on."

"Does that mean I was trendy? Or was I trying too hard to be included in that one? Was it tacky of me? Was I being tacky getting knocked up?" She's grinning at me when I look over at her, and we both burst out in laughter that echoes the length of the playground.

"Tough call, honestly, Mia. I like your kid the best, so I'm gonna go ahead and say you brought an element of class to the whole thing. I could be biased, though." I kick my legs out a bit to get my swing moving again.

"True, true. Can't rely on your judgment. Ugh, what's the point of your big old education then?"

"Oh, all judgment is biased in some way or another. Take my final thoughts and run with them. As in, you're the best."

"'Kay den. I like that. I *am* the best."

Satisfied with the height of my swing, I relax my legs and simply let the motion run its course as I start to slow. Mia's doing the same thing. Our swings don't ever align, but we're just fine without perfect symmetry.

"How's unpacking going? Not gonna lie, I'm a bit offended that you've been here a week and this is the first time we're hanging out, but I'm gonna let it slide." Mia grips the chains of her swing. I can feel her looking at me, waiting with anticipation for my answer. She offered the question with a joke, which means she's trying to keep things light so I can't hear the real question she's asking.

How are you?

But it's not the bouncing, boring, one-off question you ask someone you know when you run into them at the grocery store. It's the one with the stress on the *are*. How *are* you? How are you holding up? How are you dealing with the death of your father? How are you coping with the fact that you're going to have to live in the place where you grew up and where he had always been, knowing full well he's not going to be there? That he'll never be there ever again?

A loaded question that she hasn't asked.

"Well," I begin, looking down at my feet as they start to drag through the sand. "I haven't done as much as I should have. Like, I've got my books and the other important stuff. You know, pictures and memories and shit."

"Unpacking memories sounds intense."

I shrug. "It can be."

"You miss the city yet?" She kicks out her legs to get her swing to go higher. The breeze makes her long hair trail behind her like a black flag.

"No, not yet," I say. "Honestly, I needed a break from all of it. It's nice to be somewhere I can see the stars at night."

"Oh yeah, eh?" Mia drops her legs, so she slows down. "How's your mom?"

"She's good. She's always good. No. That's a total lie. She's good until she's not, but it's not like we talk about it that much anyway. On the surface she's good."

"Does that still count?"

My swing finally stops and I take a moment before looking at her. The moment is more for her than for me. I can gather myself quickly enough to avoid crying, but I can't guarantee that Mia knows how to keep her face from instantly expressing some form of pity. God, I hate the pity. The way people look at you like you're damaged. Or it's more like you've got something stuck in your teeth. People know they should probably tell you that there's this thing taking all of their attention away from listening to you, but they don't know how to say it without offending you.

"I don't know. At this point, all of us are just playing this whole grief thing by ear, so . . ."

Mia's cheeks flush with embarrassment and she looks away from me quickly. "Yeah, that makes sense, huh? I'm asking the worst questions, aren't I?"

"You're asking the expected questions. It's . . . it's normal." I give her a little smile to let her know that I didn't mean to make her feel awkward. "Hell, I'm glad you're asking questions. You know that Danielle full-on changes the subject when I so much as hint at talking about my dad? Or if I manage to sneak in an actual feeling in a text or something, she is always like, 'Awww. Yeah, that must be tough. Awww. Awww.' I fucking hate *awww*. If I could somehow punch her through the phone, I one-hundred-percent would. Don't *awww* me, you bitch."

Mia snorts and laughs. "Been holding that back for a while?"

I laugh too as I shake my head. "You have no idea. Do you remember at my dad's funeral how she was walking around from group to group, trying to make everyone comment on how much weight she lost? Who *does* that? Just because you're my cousin doesn't mean you can use this time to show off your latest fad diet results to all our relatives. How fucked up is that?"

"Super fucked up."

We let silence settle between us as we both sit nearly motionless on our swings. A breeze picks up, weaving through the branches of the trees along the edge of the playground fence. The sound of the leaves brushing together fills the air. Waves of heat from the late-summer sun radiate off the pavement lining the inner courtyard of the grounds. I watch them shimmer for a while until my vision blurs. A bird call makes me start.

"You all right there, Hazel?"

"Mm?"

"You just did the whole 'someone walked across my grave' body-shake thing."

"Oh, yeah. Kinda . . . I dunno."

Mia looks at me long and hard. When I glance at her again, she's got one eyebrow raised—she knows I'm not telling her everything.

"Okay, first of all, it isn't fair that that glare of yours is extra strong now because you're a mom. But, if I'm being forced to be honest," I say, pausing to take a deep breath, "I've been having these dreams lately."

"Welcome to the world of the livingly lucid, Hazel."

"Tsk. No, no, it's more than that."

"Ehhhnn, I'm just teasin' you. Go on, tell me all about this dream."

"It's not just one dream. There's been two now. They aren't the same. But they have this . . . this . . . this weird weight that stays with me. Like they're more than just dreams."

"Shit, you been vision-questing, you?"

"Mia, you aren't making this easy."

"Sorry, sorry. Go on. I'll be good, I promise."

"What happens in the dreams isn't important. Actually, maybe it is, but telling you all that is gonna take too much time, so I'm just gonna focus on the good part." I sigh. "The big deal is that I have this feeling. No, shit, that's not right either. I know. I *know* that it's him."

"Your dad?"

"No, I don't think so. I guess it *could* be my dad, but I haven't dreamt of him since the week after the funeral."

"Oh, okay, sorry. Go on."

But I pause. I look down at the ground in front of me again and I chew on my lip. I get goosebumps even though the sun's high in the sky.

"I've been seeing Nanabush." The hair on the back of my neck stands on end as if feathers have brushed my skin, and I instantly reach up and whip my head around, expecting to see the fluttering wings of a black bird as it flies away. I rub my neck as I slowly turn back to look at Mia. She blinks a few times before responding.

"Oh, that's the big reveal?"

I give her a glare as I swiftly bring my hand back to rest in my lap. "I guess that's it. But, no, Mia, it's a big deal. I know it has to be because of how the dreams feel. It's like they aren't even dreams at all. They just happen to happen when I'm sleeping. But it's like an experience or something. Maybe it *is* a vision quest, but, shit, I didn't think we did that. Algonquins, I mean. It's a dream that I know is a dream, but it's more like real life than a dream, even though it *is* a dream."

"Sounds like a movie or something. Like *Inception* but with birds."

I laugh. "I know, right?"

"Might be a good movie. Write that shit down."

"My luck they'll get some White girl to play me. Probably Jennifer Lawrence."

"At least she's funny."

"She'd probably win an Oscar for it, I bet."

"Get Meryl Streep to play your mom. She'll probably win an Oscar too."

"White people always win when they tell our stories, eh?"

Mia giggles and moves to get up off her swing. She stretches and then turns to look at me. "Nobody tells our stories. When's the last time you saw an Indian on the screen who wasn't riding a horse somewhere in the American desert or gripping a bottle of 50 or something?"

We start to make our way out of the playground and back to the main road. As we walk, the dust from the dirt road billows like muddy clouds around our feet, leaving imprints of the day on our clothes and on our hands.

"But what's the big deal with Nanabush, then?" Mia asks, squinting to keep the sun from her eyes as she looks at me.

"What do you mean?"

"The way you're talking about your dreams is like they're trying to tell you something. Did you think of googling it?"

I nod. "I did, but it's all general stuff. You know, crows mean death and shit like that. Besides, the dream dictionary I've got at home is ridiculously Freudian. Like everything is about sex in some awkward way or another. And I just don't get that feeling from this dream."

"Don't feel like snaggin' yourself a Nish demigod?"

I shake my head and quickly cross my arms to hug myself. "Nope. Not this one. He feels too . . . familial. Like I know him."

"You sure he's not your dad in disguise?"

I shake my head. "No. Can't explain how I know, but there's this feeling in my gut or whatever that tells me it's not him."

"Maybe he's your cuzziiiin, ehhhnn?"

This gets a smile and a laugh from me. "Ever sick! But no, he's always a bird in my dreams. I haven't seen him as a person yet."

"Aww, you mean you don't know if he's one of them Disney Indians? Like Kocoum?"

I shake my head. "Doubt it."

"Is that it for the dream then?" Mia glances at her watch and then off in the direction of her parents' place. She's one of the only people I know who wears a watch. "My ma's good with my kid, but she's not so good with patience. If I show up later than I planned, I won't hear the end of it from her."

"Yeah," I say. "That's pretty much it."

"Maybe just wait and see what happens next?" She pauses,

looks down at the ground, and sighs as she kicks a few stones around with the edge of her shoe. Her voice deepens with the serious expression on her face. "Hazel, you've been through a lot. I mean, it can't be easy being back here without your dad."

I wince, but she keeps talking.

"Maybe this weird Nanabush dreaming is your brain trying to work that out. When'd these dreams start?"

"My first night back and then again the next day."

"But not before then?"

My voice is small when I answer her. "No. Not before then."

"See? That makes total sense. Maybe that's all it is. Just your head trying to come to terms with what's been going on in your life."

"Yeah, I guess that . . ." I clear my throat and look at her for a second before nodding.

"If this keeps up, then maybe we go and find ourselves an elder and we have a nice little chat? Sound like a plan?"

Mia reaches out and places both of her hands on my shoulders as she turns me to face her properly. She can tell that the moment is weird, that we're not the type of friends who reach out and touch each other, but she's committed to the gesture at this point, so she tightens her grip on me. "This moving home shit is hard. Even harder for you. If you need me, just text or call or, Christ, send up some smoke signals, okay? I have to get going now but get at me later and we'll keep talking. Nanabush and all."

I bring my hands up and lightly tap hers. "Okay, sounds good. You better get home. Don't want to give your mom a reason to scold you."

"Ugh, seriously. In my twenties and she still wants to try and ground me." Mia flashes me a grin as she steps back. "See you later."

I wave and watch her walk up the road for a bit before I turn and head for home. I know she meant well with the way she decided that my dreams are just dreams, but there's something off about it. What about the voices? I should have told her about the voices. There were seven of them. Seven's an important number to us. They all had names and spoke like they were living and breathing and outside of me. I know I couldn't have made them up. I don't have that big of an imagination, do I?

If I'm imagining a Native demigod, then maybe?

I wipe my face to get rid of the dusty sweat that's formed there but also to try to get a hold of myself. The things I'm thinking seem to be moving in circles. That can't be a bad thing, though. Natives, we have all kinds of circles. Hoop dancers tell whole stories with circles. Then there's our round dance, where we link hands and move around the powwow arena in a circle. But the way I'm thinking isn't like those things. It's more like a dreamcatcher.

Now that I've thought it, the dreamcatcher makes sense. Sometimes the circle is perfect and sometimes it's not—depends on the branch. And what about the web? It's like a judgment net for dreams. The good dreams can slip through the holes in the web while the nightmares get stuck and are turned to dust when the morning sunlight hits them.

What about Nanabush?

He makes it through the web and he stays with me, days after he's left. I don't think he's a dream that can just disappear. I think he wants to be seen.

The gravel crunches under my feet as I start the long walk up my driveway. The sound is louder than it should be. Everything is louder and brighter than it should be. Instinctively, I glance up to see a black bird sitting on the telephone wire like it's been waiting for me. It looks at me and I look right back at it. I don't stop walking and I don't tear my eyes away. The bird tilts its head, asking a question.

So I answer, "I see you, Nanabush."

The crow lets out a loud croak, ruffling its feathers before spreading its wings and launching itself into the air. It flies right down to me, so close that I can feel the air from the wingbeats as it hovers in front of me. I stop walking, willing myself to keep from blinking. I'm afraid that if I blink, Nanabush will vanish.

—*Am I still a line in the dark?*

"I thought nightmares burned up in the light of day?"

—*Who said I was a nightmare?*

"You haven't proved otherwise."

—*Nightmares can't find you in the daytime. Didn't your parents tell you that?*

"This isn't real."

—*No? Doesn't this feel real to you?*

Keeping my eyes on Nanabush, I bring my hand up and tentatively reach my fingertips out toward the crow in front of me. It doesn't recoil or fly off. It beats its wings, waiting. My fingers prickle in anticipation of the smooth, silky touch of the black feathers as they glisten in the sunlight.

Contact.

And then nothing.

I watch with my mouth hanging open as the bird dissolves in front of me. The breeze picks up and takes the last few feathers of what could have been something real with it. I don't want to blink.

"Should I be worried about you there, kid?"

I look over at the front steps where my mom is standing, watching me.

"I—didn't you see that?"

She shakes her head. "See what? Come on and get in the truck. I need help getting groceries today. Your auntie wants me to help her make chili for that hockey fundraiser thing your cousin's a part of, so let's go."

My fingers brush through the air before dropping down to my side. "Yeah, okay. Let's go. You should probably drive, though."

"As if that was even an option." She gives me a grin as she walks down the steps. Mom pauses before moving over to the silver '99 Ford Ranger. "Hi-yah, this is grim."

"What?" I ask, glancing again over my shoulder to the place where Nanabush was only moments before.

She shrugs and looks up. "The sky. The way the clouds keep hanging out by the horizon. I think we might get a crow winter this year."

I look at her curiously.

"That's what it's called when it snows too soon for it to be called winter," she says, walking over to the truck. "Like, the second week in October or maybe even earlier."

"Huh," I say, moving to join her. "I've never heard that saying before."

"We haven't had one for a long time. Last one was probably about twelve years ago, so you were too young to care. It's real annoying because everything dies before it's supposed to." She clicks her tongue disapprovingly. "Let's hope it doesn't happen."

She gets in the truck and I open the passenger-side door to get in next to her. Mom expertly backs the Ranger out of the driveway and onto the highway. As she shifts gears, I take one last look up at the telephone wire.

A crow looks back.

6

HEADSTONE

"The corn's high, eh?"

"Yeah, it is."

Then silence. Each time Mom and I try to start up a conversation this happens. I guess there's too much on our minds today. It's hard to act like everything is fine when you're going tombstone shopping.

It's such a weird thing to do and I have no other way to phrase it. After all, that's the perfect description. We have to go to a yard full of granite and other elegant polished stones to pick out the right one to stick in the ground on top of my dead dad's head. It's like picking out a new outfit for a special occasion. Or maybe it's more like buying a car. You need to choose something that you'll be happy with for a long time—an investment piece. Something with good mileage and fog lights.

Traffic has been steady the whole drive. Mostly, we've had to slow down because of the long lines of RVs that pack the highway in both directions. The last full week of summer vacation has always meant traffic. Families want to sneak in that final bit of fun before sending their kids back to school. We've avoided the morning rush of regular between-town commuters by leaving just before noon. It's relatively smooth sailing, save for the odd Sûreté du Québec patrol car.

We're going to the next French town over from Ste-Marie des Oblats. The funeral home that took care of my dad's arrangements is there. They've got an understanding with the guy who sells monuments. Some dark package deal: "Let us handle your death and you get fifteen percent off your tombstone!" A discount's a discount, though. So we drive the thirty minutes to Ville St-Michel.

The countryside between the two towns is scenic. The road follows the Àmibi River after it curves behind the Band Office and meets the Kitchissippi. Farmland stretches in long, narrow lots that reach toward the water's edge. Fields of corn and wheat colour the landscape in stalks of green and yellow. Here and there, rows of expertly placed evergreen trees separate the lots, hiding the neighbouring crops from each other. There aren't many barns. The land here is too fertile to waste on livestock.

Mom takes in an audible breath when we see the town sign. I look over at her. She's sitting stock-straight in her seat, her grip tightening on the steering wheel until the veins on the back of her hands stick out. She keeps her gaze focused on the road in front of her. I wonder what's going on in her head. Is she filled with the same fearful anticipation as me?

When we talk about Dad, it's indirectly and never for long. Usually, we offer a few jokes to each other. Poke fun at the fact that he's not here instead of acknowledging the painful truth of his absence. Knowing we have to spend the next twenty minutes or so talking openly about his death is going to be hard. Mom and I don't know how to have that conversation. Thankfully, there'll be at least one other person to help with that when we get to the monument place, even if it is a salesman.

The gentle ticking of the turn signal puts me on edge. I look out the window at the business as we pull into the gravel parking lot. The building looks unassuming, like any other store with glass doors and a brick facade. There's a sign above the entrance that reads, "Monuments Lepage." Outside, there's a collection of blank granite monuments. This must be a sample of what they have in stock.

Mom turns off the truck and undoes her seat belt but doesn't move. I unbuckle myself. Careful to not disturb the quiet, I hold onto the belt as it slowly slides back into place. We sit like that for the better part of three minutes until Mom exhales harshly and turns to me.

"Let's go in and get it over with, okay?"

I nod curtly as tension begins to pull at my body. "Yup."

When I step out of the air conditioning of the truck, the hot, humid air hits me like a damp towel. I instantly feel sticky. Out here, I'm glad that I wore a T-shirt and shorts, but once we step inside, I know I'm going to feel differently. This seems like something you should dress up for. Like when you decide to go to the expensive mall, the one with all the designer stores that each have their own security guard policing the entrance. You want to look like you can afford to be there, even if that's a lie.

Mom and I both reach for the door. I pull back and she tugs it open, motioning for me to go ahead. I give her another nod, then stuff my hands into my pockets as I timidly walk into the building.

Inside, it's deathly cold, pun intended. I pull my shoulders up toward my ears as we approach the reception desk. A man wearing a long, white work coat stands at the cash register, fiddling with a granite cup, trying to make the rectangular business cards fit into a too-small and shallow bowl. When I take a better look around, I notice that almost everything is made of granite. I suppose when you're good at something, you shouldn't be modest.

The man looks up, nearly scattering the cards everywhere. He places them down on the countertop and wipes his hands on his jacket. When he moves around the counter to where Mom and I are standing, I notice he's wearing heavy steel-toe boots covered in dirt. He must be the one who works with the stone. He flashes us a surprisingly broad smile that neither of us can properly return and says, *"Bonjour."*

"Hi, I'm Nora. I called earlier about a monument?" She says the last bit like a question, her voice lilting up at the end.

"Ah, *oui.* I remember you from the phone call." His English is heavily accented, and he pauses, waving a hand about when he struggles to find the right word. *"Mon nom c'est Stéphane."*

Mom shakes his hand when he holds it out to her. "Nice to meet you, Stéphane."

Stéphane clasps his hands together and exhales. *"Bon,* let's get started. We can go and look in the yard to see the samples."

He motions for us to follow him out a side door. I wince when the sunlight reflecting off a piece of red granite hits me in the eyes. The yard is small but packed with rows of rocks in various shapes, sizes, and colours. Some are finished with such intense polish that they seem to give off their own light. The stones are mostly in shades of white, black, and grey, but there are a few blue and red ones that stand out. I can't decide if uniqueness is what you go for when you choose a headstone. Death might be the one time we're better off fitting in.

"You can see we have lots of stones for you to pick from," says Stéphane as he leads us through the rows. "Do you think you want something classic or . . . ?"

"Classic?" asks Mom. "Are you kidding? Does that mean there are other stone categories to choose from?"

"Oui, there is *contemporain, moderne*—all kinds of things." Stéphane gestures with his hands, pointing out which stones fall under each category.

"Uh-huh," she replies.

She glances over at me as Stéphane goes on about the different kinds of speckles found in each of the granite blocks and how that changes the price. The look she gives me is hard to read. Like she's fed up with this whole ordeal. I guess I understand. Dad's been dead a year and a half and we're still dealing with the arrangements.

She huffs and suggests, "Something black, how 'bout?"

Stéphane looks back at us and nods before clapping his hands again. Must be a nervous tic. He points toward the farthest row. "*Bon choix, madame.* We have a lot of nice black stones. This one here is black galaxy."

He points to a deep-black headstone flecked with thousands of tiny white and yellow dots that are meant to look like stars against the night sky. The stone is polished to a glossy and unblemished finish.

"What do you think, Hazel?" Mom asks.

I look it over, wonder what it'll look like with my father's name carved into it. "I don't know. You know I'm not good at making decisions."

Mom takes a deep breath as she thinks it over. "It's a pretty rock. Grey would be too boring and red just seems gaudy. Let's go with this one."

Stéphane's eyebrows go up, grazing the bits of hair hanging over his forehead. "Are you sure? I don't think I've ever had someone pick so fast."

"Yeah," says Mom. "I'm sure. This isn't something I want to spend all day doing. Abraham's been without a monument for so long, I don't think he would like it if I made him wait too much longer."

Stéphane blinks, still taken aback by Mom's quick decision-making. He nods and pulls a piece of paper and pencil from his coat pocket to write down the model number and colour. He sticks the pencil behind his ear and then shuffles past us. Mom and I file back into the building behind him. She doesn't look at me much when we walk back inside. Her expression is still hard, stoic. She wants this day to be over.

Stéphane clears his throat when he notices the silence beginning to stretch out too long. "Do you have some idea what you would like on the monument? I can provide you with a picture of what it will look like."

I don't say anything, but Mom nods and walks over to the counter as Stéphane moves behind it to grab paper. He shuffles back around it and places the paper down so that Mom and I can see properly as he begins sketching. He asks Mom if she wants to go with a flat or upright monument and then they keep talking, but I've stopped listening. I stare at the pencil as it drags and skips across the page. The lines are shaky, disconnected, and blurry from the softness of the graphite. The tombstone takes shape. Strong and stiff sides with a gentle curved top. As he sketches the details, the pencil scratches and tugs against the graph paper. My dad used to use this type of paper to design his own woodworking projects. Sketches were littered throughout the house, like doilies or tablecloths, some with coffee rings and others covered in sawdust and turpentine.

"I don't know. What do you think we should put on it?"

"Hm?" I yank my gaze up to find Mom and Stéphane looking at me. "Oh. I don't know. Is there a book of images to choose from or can we pick anything?"

Stéphane shrugs and scratches the back of his neck. "You can pick anything that you want. The machine can do whatever you want."

Mom and I exchange the same uninspired glance. I offer a shrug and she clicks her tongue.

"Did he have any hobbies?" asks Stéphane. "Sometimes people pick things like a book or a fish—if they like fishing."

Mom laughs. "Hobbies? Talking. That was one of his favourites. You got any pictures that'll show that?"

"Uh, maybe. I could check."

"No, no," says Mom, waving her hand to stop him. "I was kidding."

"Oh."

I look over the drawing he's created, let my eyes trace along the clear and straight lettering of my father's name as it touches the edges of the tiny blue squares of graph paper.

"What about a hammer?" I say, not taking my eyes off the sketch. "Woodworking was his hobby. He loved doing it. Even if he didn't finish too many of his projects."

Mom follows my gaze down to the drawing as she considers my suggestion. Her lips curl up into a small smile and she nods, pointing to the top of the headstone. "Right there, above his name. A fancy little hammer will look perfect."

Stéphane agrees and quickly tugs the drawing back over to himself to sketch in the final addition. He slides the paper over to us and we both agree that the stone is perfect. The dates that mark my dad's sixty-one years of life stare up at me. A bunch of numbers and letters carved into a piece of rock. Enough rain and wind and eventually they'll fade. Could memories do the same? Am I going to forget his voice? The way he laughed and how he would grin in that self-satisfied way every time he made a particularly bad pun. Forgetting is almost as frightening as losing. Frustrated, I sigh and turn away from the counter, tugging my hair down over my ears to hide the anger I know has brightened them.

"*Bon*, I'm happy that you like the stone," says Stéphane. He scribbles what looks like an order number onto the paper before moving over to the register. "There is just the bill that we have to settle."

"Mom," I say, gently tapping her arm, "I'm gonna wait outside by the truck."

Concern flashes across her face when she catches the glassiness in my gaze, but she nods and hands me the keys. "Here. In case you want to hop inside and get the AC flowing. I'll be there soon, kid."

I take the keys from her outstretched hand and head for the door. The wall of humid, sticky heat nearly takes my breath away as I try to get myself under control. Ours is the only vehicle in the lot. Stéphane must live nearby. What's working with death like? Do you become desensitized to it to the point where even the thought of your own death seems normal? Or maybe he simply compartmentalizes? Death at work, life at home. Leave the names and the dates with the stones. These are the questions I want answers to. Never mind the bullshit stuff he's been bothering us with: "Do you like black stone or red stone?" I walk over to the truck and move to lean against it. The metal burns when my skin hits it and I jump back, cursing.

"Be glad that I didn't buy a black one. That would've hurt something fierce." Mom crosses the parking lot to join me at the truck.

"That was fast," I say, tossing the keys back to her.

"Yeah, well, they take credit." She unlocks the truck and tugs the door open. Mom leans forward to turn the key in the ignition, adjusting the vents so the cold air blasts out the stifling interior heat. She waits a minute before getting in.

I join her in the truck. She's got her hands on the steering wheel, but she makes no move to drive us out of the lot. The only sound comes from the rush of the air conditioning. The beads on the end of the dreamcatcher hanging from the rearview mirror knock together quietly. But in here they might as well be church bells.

"Mom?"

She isn't crying, but there's pain on her face all the same. Her knuckles tighten on the wheel until all the blood is gone from them. She presses her lips together in a hard line as she exhales.

"It's the stupidest fucking thing," she says slowly.

I tense when she swears. Mom never really curses in front of me. Nothing worse than an occasional "Oh, shit!" ever comes out of her mouth. I'm about to ask her what she means, but she continues on her own.

"I had to use my credit card. It was so damn expensive that I had to use my *credit card*. Means I'm gonna have to pay it off *plus* interest. Can you believe that? Paying interest on a dead man's head." She pauses to take a ragged and choked breath in. She's fighting back tears, I can tell by the way she keeps trying to clear her throat. Mom frowns and drops her head to the steering wheel. "It's never going to end, is it? We're always going to be missing him, haunted by him. If anyone ever tells you ghosts aren't real, they're wrong. They don't wear white sheets and jump out at you in the middle of the night, but they haunt you all the same."

Speechless. The one sob she lets out is muffled by the whir of the air conditioning. I don't know how to answer. Should I even bother? Is this one of those times when I'd only be talking to fill the silence? I don't know how to make this better.

"Mom?" I sound small, like a child seeing their parent cry for the first time.

She moves her head slightly, acknowledging that she's heard me.

I was hoping that something would come to me if I just started talking, but that was a miserable assumption. Finally, I manage, "Do you want me to drive?"

Her shoulders and back heave as she draws in a long, deep breath. Slowly, she pushes herself up until she's sitting straight. Mom uses the heel of her hand to wipe her eyes before she looks at me. She smiles sadly and shakes her head. "No, I've got it under control."

"Yeah?"

"Yeah."

She sniffles once more before forcing herself to smile. It's something she does to try and remind herself to not let me see her break. One of those protect-your-kids-from-harm mom-traits that she can't quite shake. She puts the truck into drive. We pull out of the parking lot and turn onto the highway to head for home.

I stare out the window as the passing fields blur into an endless wall of green. I should tell a joke or something, fix the mood, but I can't. Because Mom's right—every day I think I should feel lighter, that the grief should start to disappear. It doesn't. It only waits. It starts to weigh on me and I sink farther into my seat. I want a distraction. Anything to take away the sting of this awful day. But it's too late.

My mind is swimming with ghosts.

¤ ¤ ¤

It takes Mom a while to recover from the mess at the monument place. It's been a week since we placed the order for Dad's tombstone and she's still wearing too bright a smile. She's doing what she can to stay cheery, but when I catch a glimpse of her, she's chewing her lip or picking her nails instead of humming or singing. We used to be a musical family when Dad was alive. Mom and Dad would sing together. I did what I could to learn the basics on piano and even Gus put his books aside to attempt keeping a beat with the tambourine. He was terrible.

Music always connected us, even if we had been arguing. Gus got himself out of trouble for skipping school once by composing his own song about why he did it. Dad couldn't stay mad at him after that. After all, Gus had learned that technique from the master himself. Dad used that on us all the time. Like once, a few summers before his lungs started to ache, Dad convinced us all that it was a good idea to try to catch a glimpse of the Perseid meteor shower. Gus had been home for a rare weekend away from work. I was home working a student summer job at the Band Office, for the Chief and Council. Dad got it in his head that it was important we do a bit of stargazing as a family since it was probably how our ancestors navigated as they moved from camp to camp during the changing seasons. Not exactly true, but Dad got into one of his moods, so he couldn't be convinced otherwise. Gus tried to argue that he didn't want to spend his last night home and that he'd much rather join his friends, but it was too late. Dad had already planned the evening.

The night was perfect. Hardly any moon, stars stretched out across the expanse above our heads like pinpricks in a curtain, and the air finally cool enough to be pleasant on the skin. Dad brought us all out onto the back porch and proudly pointed up at the sky. We looked up expectantly, hoping to catch a glimpse of a star shower. But nothing. For like fifteen minutes. Gus got impatient and threatened to head back inside, hoping he could still catch his friends for at least one drink, but Dad said, "No. Let's wait."

"Nothing's happening," I said. "Can't we go back inside, Dad?"

"It's been almost half an hour. We aren't going to see anything," Gus said.

"Tsk, no. Only fifteen minutes. Geez, Angus, you can't wait," said Dad. "Didn't your mom teach you about being patient?"

"She did," I chimed in. "Still does every single time we run errands. 'I'll just be a minute!' means she's going to be *at least* twenty minutes."

"That's true," said Gus. "And 'It's only gonna take me a second' easily means a solid hour."

"Hey!" scolded Mom, giving Gus a little smack on the arm with the back of her hand in the way Anishnaabe mothers do. "I never made you wait a whole hour."

"I'm kinda getting cold," I complained.

"Hi-yah, you're all spoilsports," Dad said. "It's going to come and if I let yiz go back in, you'll be jealous that only I saw it."

"They happen every year," said Gus as he looked down at his glowing phone. He scrolled with his thumb. "Google says they peak second week of August. Meaning we missed the best time, so oh well, let's try again next year." With that, he pivoted on his heel, brushing off Dad's hands, and headed to the door. His thumbs moved rapidly on the keyboard of his phone as he kept his head down.

I looked between Mom and Dad to see what their thoughts on the matter were, but neither of them looked back at me. Mom squeezed Dad's shoulder.

Gus paused at the patio door to glance at me. "Haze, can you drive me down to Robby's place?"

"Yeah, sure." Now that we were actually leaving, I was hesitant to go. Even if I was over the outing, I hated disappointing my father.

Gus tapped his foot impatiently, so I hurried to where he stood with his hand on the door. He yanked it open. Then Dad's smooth baritone lilted over to us. He was singing something clearly off the top of his head to what sounded like the tune of David Bowie's "Starman."

"There's a Nish Man all alone outside wondering if his kids will ever join him by his side. Just a Nish Man looking at the sky hoping that the stars might show up so that he won't feel like he lied."

Gus and I exchanged a look and a sigh. Gus in particular rolled his eyes but smiled. He nodded in Dad's direction and walked back over to him. How could we resist that?

A smile started on my face as I sang back to Dad, *"They told him: Yes, them kids noticed . . ."*

Gus continued off-key, *". . . that he didn't blow it."*

"Them kids are animizie," Mom finished.

Dad turned to us and grinned. "Ah-ha, I knew yiz couldn't resist a good song."

Gus smirked. "Cheap shot. But we're here now. Show us your meteors."

Standing side by side, we looked back up at the sky. Our excitement renewed by Dad's serenade, we searched hopefully for some sign of the shower. Finally, Dad's hand shot up and he pointed at a tiny glowing orb trailing across the treetops.

"There! Look at it go!" He laughed proudly. "See? Your dad's not a bullshitter after all!"

He turned to us, his hands up and ready for a pair of high-fives from my brother and me. But my own hand was already over my mouth holding back laughter, and Gus had a smirk plastered on his face.

"That's a satellite."

"Aw, bullshit."

In the end it didn't matter. We stayed out together, ignoring the sky and enjoying each other's company. Mom made hot chocolate and Dad built a fire. Eventually, someone grabbed a guitar and we sang together until late into the night. That's the way it was with us. Music brought us all together. Not so much anymore. Hard to continue a song when your lead singer cuts out partway through.

Now there isn't even an instrument in the house. Mom sold our old piano because the upkeep was too much to deal with while Dad was sick. Dad was the one who played guitar, so it was either pass it on or let it gather dust and slip slowly out of tune. Mom gave it to one of my cousins. Gus was so upset with her for that. He couldn't believe she'd just give something that precious away to someone who wasn't either of us. Mom shot back that Gus didn't know how to play and never cared much for the damn thing anyway. They didn't talk for a month.

Things between them are better now. I think Gus realized that he was taking out his anger on Mom, and he ended up backing off. Neither of them apologized, but they moved forward anyway.

My phone chimes, grabbing my attention and pulling me back into the present. Seems I like to spend more and more time in my memories these days. Must have something to do with being back home. I unlock the screen and read a message from Mom: "On my way home. Hope you didn't forget to take the stuff to the dump."

Shit.

I launch myself off the couch and rush to the door, snapping up the keys to Mom's pickup on the way. She put the garbage bags in the box before she left and I've let them sit there in the hot summer sun for the last hour. Gross. Not looking forward to throwing those out. We missed garbage day this week, so now it's my job to take them up to the dump. The one thing I've been tasked with doing and of course I've left it to the last minute. Classic Hazel.

The dump is located in the bush behind the far end of the reserve. It's pretty deep in the trees, about a kilometre beyond where the paved road ends. If you didn't know there was a heap of garbage stewing in the clearing at the end of the drive, you'd think you stumbled into untouched wilderness. The familiar sound of loose stones hitting the inside of the wheels as they bounce off the tires punctuates the constant rumble of the gravel. The drive is pleasant despite the fact that I keep hitting potholes that send my head dangerously close to the roof of the truck. It's a beautiful day. Hot, sunny, with the right amount of wind, so I've got the windows rolled down—which seemed like a good decision when I set out but isn't great now that I'm nearing the actual heap.

There's no other way to describe the smell of garbage. It's awful. The epitome of rot. I'd roll the windows up but that would only lock it in with me. This way I have a bit of air flow, even if it's nasty, hot garbage air.

There's a fork in the road with a sign that reads, "No dumping unless Spirit Bear Point member!" I wonder how they police that? It's not like they have someone sitting up here full-time. I signal right even though there's nothing but a dust cloud behind me. The clearing where we toss our trash is striking. Surrounded by lush trees and a wealth of wildflowers, the gaping trench in the ground is the last thing you notice about this place. The tree line frames a range of hills far in the distance that glow a vibrant green from where the sunlight hits the leaves and needles of the birches and pines. This place screams of life. And then there's the garbage.

The pile itself is farther down in the hole so that it isn't visible until you get closer. There are a few larger pieces that didn't quite make it in the hole: an old front-load washing machine with its door hanging on one hinge and what looks like the tub from a dryer sit on the cusp of the trench. That last piece is a waste. Someone could have used it as a firepit. What a shame.

I leave the truck running as I hop out to toss the trash. The black bags are hot to the touch and make a squelching sound when I lift them off the truck bed. I try to make the deposit as quickly as possible, rushing over to the edge of the trench while punctuating each step with a sincere and horrified "Ew." Not wanting to extend my visit much longer, I chuck the bags and hurry back to the truck, rubbing my hands on the front of my shorts.

The drive back is much more pleasant considering I'm going in the opposite direction of the smell. I take my time on the road, making sure to avoid potholes where I can. I don't remember it being this bumpy in the past. The road's never been paved, so it's always been a bit treacherous. Sort of enter-at-your-own-risk. Especially in the spring once the snow has melted. The whole thing turns into a swamp. If you don't have a vehicle with four-wheel drive, you're better off staying away.

Dad and I got stuck here once. It was so bad we had to leave the truck and walk home. I must've been six or so, because I had brought a picture book with me. We came up here to toss the trash after another missed garbage day and to do a bit of exploring. When we decided to go back home, the truck got lodged in the mud. Dad tried and tried to get us unstuck, but everything he did just dug those back wheels in deeper. I remember him trying his hardest not to curse. I think he said *sugar* a lot.

We started our walk back home. It shouldn't have taken us

as long as it did, but I slowed us down. Wildflowers are tempting to a little girl. The best part of the whole adventure was when we stopped and sat on this huge rock. Dad read the book to me. It was one of my favourites, about a little chick who learns what it takes to be a rooster. We sat together for a long time, and even though I'm sure Dad was worried about his truck, he never tried to rush me. He read that book, did all the voices, and sent us both into a fit of giggles. One of those perfect days that stay with you forever.

The dump sure is full of trash and treasures.

In a rush of shadows and dark wings, something black bursts out of the trees in front of me and I'm instantly pulled from my memories. I hit the brakes hard, jolting myself forward far enough that the seat belt tightens across my body. My hands are gripped solidly at ten and two on the wheel and my pulse pounds throughout my entire body. What the hell was that? From the passenger side window, I see a huge black bird in one of the trees along the road. He must be the culprit. The bird adjusts its feathers, unphased by what's happened. It fixes me with a stare, twists its head, and caws. That look is so familiar. It has to be him.

"Nanabush?"

Then my phone chirps and lights up, pulling my attention away from the crow. My foot's still on the break, so I take a second to check the message. Another one from Mom: "Monument place just called. Tombstone will be installed next week. Guess they're fast because business was dead this season. Ha. You almost home?"

I reply that I'm on my way, but I don't acknowledge the other stuff. Before driving off I need to take one more look at the crow. I want to meet his eyes and stare him down like he did me. But when I look back, he's gone. Maybe he moved to a different branch? I tilt my head back and crane my neck to check the other trees. Nothing. I even try sitting as quietly as I can to listen for its voice, but there's nothing. Only summer wind and silence.

Then one more ding: "Forgot to get butter. Can you get some in town? Thanks."

I sigh and resign myself to my next errand. Nanabush will have to wait. I ease my foot off the brake and let the truck roll into motion. The near-quiet gets to be too much, so I flick on the radio. Instantly, I smile. Any thoughts of crows and tombstones dissolve in a guitar riff and a collection of familiar *oohs* and *aahs*.

"Starman" is playing and now everything feels okay.

¤ ¤ ¤

The reserve exists outside the boundaries of regular time. Everything is too slow, too fast, too nothing. Every day ebbs by like there are forty hours instead of twenty-four. But then suddenly it's Friday and I've let another week go by. As I lie here in my room, time is grinding to a halt. I am wasting my life cooped up inside this house, and it's starting to take its toll. I'm supposed to be relaxing, using my excess free time to catch up on reading, maybe even sort through some of my childhood things, but I keep thinking about going back to Ottawa. I loved the city, the freedom of it. Maybe Gus would let me crash on his couch for a couple weeks while I try to find my own place. We lived together while I was at school, so it wouldn't be that hard to get along. If I'd had my way after I graduated, I would be there still. I'd hoped to get a job working at the Indigenous student services while I tried to figure out if I wanted to do a master's, but that didn't exactly pan out. Almost every job in Ottawa, including those at the university, demands you speak both official languages—which I definitely do not. Still, I miss it. Especially the coffee.

If I'm being honest with myself, I didn't leave much behind. I lived with Gus from first year onwards, so I never made friends the way most of the people in my program did. I had acquaintances I spoke to in class, but living off-campus right away did a number on my social network. Most of my friends were Gus's friends. Plus, I left each summer to come back home and work. Every Rez kid in post-secondary gets a guaranteed job that pays well, so why wouldn't I come back? I made a lot of good money working here. Didn't get much experience that would translate into the "real world," though. There's only so much you can learn when you're working as an artisan whipping out dreamcatcher after dreamcatcher every day. Guess I learned stuff that one summer when I was a secretary. Mostly how to fear phone calls from Council members.

Despite my dramatic longing for the city, I *do* love this place. The quiet, the trees, the water. All of it is beautiful. After all, I came home to find a way to remember how to be myself again. But man, is it hard. Too much space to fill. Too many reminders of grief. I haven't even seen Nanabush since that day on the dump road. If that was even him. Could've been a regular bird. Who knows? Maybe that mess at the monument place scared him off? Can't say I blame him for keeping his distance.

Nonetheless, I've been on edge since seeing the crow in person, with my waking eyes. I've spent the past two weeks trying to convince myself that what I saw couldn't have been real. All of this has to be some by-product of death. Grief must be manifesting itself as hallucinations. That has to be it. Or I'm going crazy. Or maybe there's more magic left in this world than people realize.

Grief. I'm going to go with grief.

I look over at the clock. It's nearly five.

Hauling myself off my bed, I shuffle into the hall and then down the stairs toward the kitchen. It's my turn to make dinner tonight, so I should figure something out before Mom saunters in and takes over. As I pull open the fridge, I hear her come in the door, humming tunelessly to herself. She calls out to me.

"I have good news for you!"

"Are you sure?"

She comes around the corner, tosses the mail onto the counter and clicks her tongue at me. "Whatchu mean, you? Of course I'm sure."

"It's just that the last time you said that to me, you were trying to set me up with that Hunter guy."

"That was good news too. He's cute. Plus, he has a real good job at the mine up north." She comes over to where I'm standing and reaches past me to grab a can of pop, which she cracks open quickly and sips from. "I think he's still single, you know."

"*Kaye Mâmâ!* It'll be tomorrow by the time you finally tell me what you came in here so excited about."

"Ah, all right, all right. No patience, you?" Mom smiles as she leans against the counter. "I ran into Joni at the post office and we started chatting. She asked about you and I said that you're starting to get cabin fever and I'm thinking that you're already planning your escape back to the big city."

"I might have left a suitcase packed on purpose, yeah."

"Oh my god, you have been here for almost a month. The kids are all back in school now. Get unpacked!"

"I'm working on it."

"Work harder."

We exchange a pair of playful glares. I point my lips at her. "What else did she say?"

"That she might have a job for you. Nothing long-term, just temporary. But it'll be nice for you to get out of the house." Her eyes crinkle as her lips part into a grin and her eyebrows shoot up toward her forehead. "Whatcha think?"

"I think I need more details."

"I knew you would say that. I told her you'd go into the Band Office tomorrow to find out everything you need to know." Mom places her pop down on the counter and walks into the hall to the pantry.

"That's it? You took a job for me without any information?"

Mom answers me from inside the pantry, so her voice is slightly muffled. "As if Joni would give you something you wouldn't like." She comes back around the corner with potatoes and an onion in her hand. "Just go in and find out more. It'll give you something to do, at least."

"True. Guess I can't argue with that."

She starts chopping up the potatoes, putting them into a pot. "Quit looking for excuses to argue, you."

"That mean you don't want me to point out that it's my turn to make dinner?"

"Yes, that's what I mean. Besides, I want to roast up some potatoes just how I like them and you don't know how to do that."

"You think I don't know how to roast potatoes?"

"Not like how I like them, I said."

"What special way do you like them that I can't possibly figure out?"

"Enough with the arguing. Git outta here and watch TV or something while I cook. You're too *animizie* in the kitchen. Gwan!" She shoos me out of her space with a wave of her hand.

I leave her be and make my way into the sitting room at the front of the house. The room glows from the sunlight beaming in through the bay window. There are plants everywhere in here. Proof of Mom's inherent talent with them. A trait that did not pass to me. One look from me and leaves wilt. I walk toward the window and stand in front of it, looking out at the highway at the end of our drive.

There's hardly any traffic right now, so my gaze wanders across the highway to the line of tall, trimmed cedar trees that hide the trailer park. From what I can see between the trees, the trailer closest to the road is empty. It has been for years, so the yard behind it is unkempt and wild, the long grass yellowed from days in the sun. Along the side of its faded white panelling, someone's painted the angry profile of an Indian with two feathers in his hair. The paint is old and has started to run and chip around the eyes from rain and wind. It's a wonder the Band hasn't boarded up the trailer's windows and doors yet. I doubt anyone is ever going to want to move into it now.

A truck with ridiculously huge wheels and a lifted frame speeds by, momentarily eclipsing my view of the park. I exhale and reach up to comb my fingers through my hair. A job is good. It's what I want. Something to keep me busy and distract me from my growing sadness and stagnation. I make the decision to take whatever Joni has to offer me.

Anything is better than waiting on a crow.

7

CEDAR BY
THE RIVERSIDE

Despite recent renovations, the atrium of the Band Office smells the same way it always has. It's like a mix of stale Maxwell House coffee, cigarette smoke from the chain-smokers who ignore the "Do not smoke within 5 metres of entryway" sign, lemon-scented wood polish, and the ever-present aroma of the cedar logs used to make the colossal building. I take a moment to glance up at the cathedral ceiling. Sunlight shines down through vaulted sky-lights to the ornately woven rug at the centre of the rotunda, traces of fading elegance of past funding. The Band Office was built in the early 1960s when the Canadian government was handing out grants left and right in the wake of Expo 67. The red cedar is another marker of just how much was spent to build it, since that wood had to be shipped in. The whole interior is decorated with as much Native art as possible. A few pieces are by local artists, but the rest is the run-of-the-mill, could-be-found-in-a-casino type of stuff.

I'm sitting on one of the carved wooden benches in the atrium, listening to the hum of soft music and the tapping of keys. The waiting area is positioned directly under the skylights, so that you feel important even if you have to wait forever to see somebody. The secretary working at the front desk is in her early twenties, like me. She went to the French high school in town, but we've chatted here and there over the years. This semi-ambiguous relationship means I can sit and wait for my meeting in a comfortable introverted silence, staring at my phone.

I flick my thumb along the glass screen and scroll through Instagram. Not much is new. That's a lie. There're all kinds of new posts, but it's pretty much the same as it was yesterday and the day before. Mia's posted a picture of her daughter playing on the merry-go-round at the park in town. Emmy's wearing the plaid shirt I got her. I spread my fingers on the screen and zoom in. The grin on her pretty little face lights the picture, making it lifelike instead of just a collection of pixels. As I zoom closer, the image dulls and blurs. But something in the corner of the frame makes my eyes go wide.

A crow, bigger than any real bird I've seen, is staring directly at the camera. It could be a coincidence. Maybe it's just a raven? They're bigger than crows.

But no. The bird is staring at me and I know that it's a crow. It's *my* crow. Exhaling becomes difficult. I taste chalk. I try to clear my throat. I make a strained choking sound instead, causing the secretary to glance away from her computer. I try to smile at her, but my attempt is made pathetic by the way I grit my teeth. I look away quickly. Doing my best to appear composed, I sit up straight and toss my hair confidently over one shoulder. Thankfully, she starts typing again and I pull myself together. I look back down at the picture. It returned to its normal size the second I moved my hand away from the phone, but I can still see the bird staring at me from beyond the glass. What does it want? I move my hand to zoom in once more, but the sound of raised voices coming closer startles me away.

"That goddamn Council doesn't know the first thing about business! They're idiots to think that a place like this can survive on Indian Affairs funding. Who do they think built every house on this reserve? Didn't come from the Liberals or the Conservatives or even the goddamn NDP!"

The man losing his shit is Heath Whittaker. He's the owner of the only construction company here. He's not wrong, his company *did* build about eighty percent of the buildings on the Rez, but he could lower his voice a little. Heath is going red in the face, making the white of his walrus moustache look even more brilliant.

"Now, Heath," comes the slow, even drawl of Vice-Chief Reggie Lee—the man who took over after my dad died. "You know that's not why we're saying no."

I know why they're saying no. Builder or not, Heath is a man obsessed with money. It's hardly a secret that he's one of the richest people on the Rez. He'll sell his culture out the second there's enough zeroes following a number. Everything's got a price tag for CEO Whittaker. CEO. People around here like to say that stands for "cheats everyone out." Again, they're not wrong.

"Then what the fuck is your ass-backward excuse this time? Some elder come and bless that fucking quarry back when the HBC still traded skins?" Heath shakes his head so aggressively that he almost knocks off his John Deere hat. For a second, I think he's thrown me a glance, but he ploughs forward with his rant. "The only way a reserve can survive nowadays is to build and develop. There ain't even any goddamn apartment buildings around here! No wonder there's a housing shortage. Every time someone tries to improve the place they get turned away because of some goddamn sacred ground."

Reggie starts to say something else, but Heath is already saying goodbye with his middle finger and storming out the front door. It's a shame the doors shut automatically and slowly behind him. Technology has put a damper on dramatic entrances and exits.

The atrium of the Band Office is suddenly silent following the departure of Heath's booming voice. The low country twang

of the radio comes out of the speakers in the ceiling and punctuates the sudden quiet. The secretary asks Reggie if he'd like her
to cancel his 1:00 meeting, but he shakes his head and smiles at
her before heading back into his office. I watch him go, keeping
my eyes on his back and the eagle embroidered on the buckskin
vest hanging off his shoulders. Reggie disappears around the corner. The secretary's eyes meet mine, but we quickly look away to
avoid holding any anxious gaze.

The mention of the quarry has me on edge. It's no secret
that it exists and that nothing's been done with it since the mine
closed. Not for lack of trying, though. People, businesses and
independents alike, had approached Dad in the past to try to get
him to work out a deal, but he always turned them down. I was
too young to know the reasons behind his refusal to sell. He'd
tell me that it wasn't the right time. That he was waiting for the
proper moment. I need to ask Mom about it.

"Is dat little Hazel Ellis?"

I slide my phone into my back pocket as I gather my face into
a proper smile. "Hi, Joni. It's me, all right."

Joan "Joni" Kitchisabek is the current head of the Lands and
Memberships department at Spirit Bear Point First Nation. She's
also the woman who used to babysit me and Gus when we were
little. I used to call her Auntie Joni because I was convinced she
was related to me. Turns out it was just a term of endearment
that attached itself to her when she began looking after us Ellis
kids. On the Rez, lots of kids have aunties who aren't actually
their aunties.

She gently taps my shoulder before pulling me into one of
her trademark warm bear hugs. "Tsk, you know you can still call
me Auntie! Goodness, you've ever grown up, you."

I let myself relax into her arms, feeling like I'm six years old.

"I know, I know. Just wanted to be a bit professional since I'm here on business and all."

Joni leans back from the hug, keeping her hands on my shoulders. There's a gentle sadness in her eyes as she looks at me. A look I've grown accustomed to. But she smiles in spite of herself. "Ah, to hell with business. You'll always be my little Hazelnut. Come on in, den. Lemme show you my office and den we can sit down and have a real chat."

She keeps her arm around my shoulders, leading me through the hallways of the Band Office, only letting go once we've stepped through the doorway of her own office. Shutting the door behind me, Joni walks around her desk and sits across from me. I can't help noticing how out of place she looks. Joni was always a considerate person who was better suited to caring for others rather than dealing with government and land politics. I wonder how she's handling it all. But here she is, sitting behind a huge wooden desk in front of a window with a view of the open field and grassy hills that lead down to the beach of the Àmibi River. Her office looks out onto the place where the people of Spirit Bear Point launch their canoes. It's a perfect spot, where the clear water runs smoothly overtop soft sand. Across the river, the land rises up toward a forest of pine trees.

"So," says Joni, resting her elbows on the desk and folding her hands together beneath her chin. "You liking being home again?"

"Eh, it's okay. Kinda weird, but I'm getting used to it now that it's been a few weeks. Biggest drawback is definitely how little there is to do in comparison to being in the city. How you all get by with waiting weeks to see new movies is a wonder to me," I say, doing my best to keep things light.

"We have more patience. I guess dat's why so many of us talk so slow."

"That must've skipped me. I'm terrible at waiting."

"You just need to practise. The more you wait, the better you get at it."

"Sounds like fun. Also sounds like it'll take a long time."

"You always did have your dad's sense of humour."

"Awkward, self-deprecating, and ill-timed?"

Another laugh. "No, no. Sharp. Your dad was always real sharp with the humour."

I shrug. This is better than the regular dad-conversation I've been forced to deal with, so I'm glad of the change. "Runs in the family."

"I'll bet." Joni leans back in her chair, her eyes and voice a bit distant as she repeats herself. "I'll bet."

I nervously run my palms along the tops of my jeans before I muster up the courage to get the conversation on track. I don't want to give her the chance to pity me with condolences. "My mom said you might have a job I could help with?"

"Hm? Oh, right! Yes, I told Nora dat I could use a smart little brain like yours on the job." Joni digs around in the drawers of her desk for a moment, muttering something under her breath about her absent-mindedness, then pulls out a few sheets of paper. "Right now, the Chief and Council have me working what feels like day and night on some membership tings. So I don't have time to get any of these files in order."

I take the papers from her outstretched hand. It's a list with what looks like names and numbers of files. "Wow. Okay. This is three, four . . . *five* pages long."

Joni sucks in air through her teeth as she grins sheepishly. "And each of dem names is a box filled with files."

Gingerly, I place the list back on her desk and take a breath in as I weigh the thought of the endless, mindless work Joni's asking me to do against the endless, mindless nothing I'd be doing at home. "Okay, yes. I'm in."

"Yeah? Good, good. I'm glad. I can't say dat you'll love the job, but it'll be something to do. Get your mind off being home and all dat."

Nice sidestep on the dead-dad stuff, Joni.

"Is there something you want me to sign?"

Joni shakes her head and waves her hand slightly in my direction. "Nah, not yet. I'll have to get Grace in finance to make you a real contract, and she's out of town till next Wednesday. But I want you to start Monday. For now, how about we shake on it?"

She's holding her hand out in front of her, pointing it at me. It hangs in the air while I stare at it longer than I should. The moment starts to get awkward and I can feel my face get hot from sympathetic embarrassment. Before she says anything else, I take her hand, giving it a small but definitive shake.

"Might not be in writing, but it's as good a yes as any. Don't you worry, little Hazelnut, you come in Monday, anyway, and we can go over all the other stuff den." Joni comes around the desk again and pulls me into another big hug. She still smells the same—cinnamon and vegetable oil.

I lean back from her hug, stepping away slightly. My gaze leaves hers and fixes on a point outside the window where the clouds are tracing lines across the sky. Joni moves back around the desk.

"Is there anything else you wanna ask me before you head out?" she asks as she lowers herself back into the faded leather chair.

"Um, yeah. There is something. Do you know what Heath Whittaker wants to do with my dad's quarry?"

When Joni looks at me with surprise, the lines on her face wrinkle. "The quarry? Oh, I don't know. I know he's been on about making a new housing development back dat way, but he can't get the right permits for the land."

"Yeah, I heard that much."

She purses her lips together before sticking them out as she thinks. "Other than dat, I don't know, me."

"So he can't get the permits because the land belongs to my brother and me now?"

Joni makes another uncertain face and shrugs. "Maybe? I don't know. Your ma might know more. Dat's not my area of expertise."

I bite back the chance to point out that she works in *Lands* and *Memberships*, opting to simply nod. "Okay, thanks anyway. And thanks for the job opportunity. Can't tell you how much this means to me."

"Don't mention it. Tell your ma I said hello when you see her."

"I will, Auntie Joni." The nickname puts a smile on her face.

With a wave, I turn and leave her office. The halls are practically empty as most people are hard at work in their own little worlds of education, management, health, or operations and maintenance. Chief and Council are at the opposite end of the building. That way, they don't interfere with the other departments and vice versa. Though that's hardly ever been close to the truth. I'm tempted to take the long way around and walk by Reggie's office. My meeting with Joni was short, so there's a chance that he's still riled up from his confrontation with Heath. I toss the idea around in my head a bit before heading down a different hall.

The wood on this side of the building is slightly lighter than the rest. The Chief and Council offices, located in the Migizî Wing, were built as an addition in 1987. It was Heath's company that did the work. It's matched to the original building in almost every single way, including the grandness of the ceilings, except for the wood. They tried to stain the eastern white cedar to match its red counterpart, but it only got so far before it risked looking tacky. It's still a beautiful and stunning piece of craftsmanship. But it's like a jigsaw puzzle—you can see where the pieces fit together.

The artwork on this side of the Band Office is pointedly Native, even more so than the stuff in the atrium. There are paintings and drawings of sad-looking Indians on the walls, an old and worn headdress that contributes to the whole problem of pan-Indianness, and what looks like an etched buffalo skull. I know for a fact that there were never buffalo here. We didn't hunt them and we didn't wear war bonnets. Sometimes the idea of reclaiming our culture erases the finer details, the things that make us Algonquin or Haida or Blackfoot, in the end. It's like a reprint of a famous artwork. The image is there, but the brush-strokes are gone.

I can see Reggie Lee's office at the end of the hall. It's one of my favourite places in the building. I spent more than a few evenings after school in the chair directly in front of its huge wooden desk, tracing the lines of the carved animals along each of the legs. As the sun goes down, the room lights up all pink and golden, filling the white cedar walls with pine-shaped shadows. When he was vice-chief, Dad used to bring me to work with him on nights when Mom couldn't pick me up or find a babysitter. It's been more than a year since an Ellis was last in that office. Nerves settle on my skin like porcupine quills and my palms sweat. I feel anxious, like I'm breaking some unwritten or unspoken law by walking through this half of the building unaccompanied and without the protection of my father's name. The door to the office is mostly closed. But as I get closer, I can hear Reggie's voice. He's talking and no one is answering. He must be on the phone.

". . . in here again, going on and on about that damn quarry. Yeah. Mm-hmm. There ain't nothing I can tell him about the situation without risking the whole deal Abe had in the first place."

I stop immediately. He's talking about my dad. What the hell does he mean by a deal? This sounds too familiar. Mom's said things that dropped hints here and there, but is this the same thing?

"Mm-hmm. Yeah. All right. I'll try that the next time he comes by. But what about Gagnon? Yeah, I know he wants to move forward, but there's nothing we can do yet without the transfer. No. No, there wasn't ever anything signed. That's the problem. That's what he left us all with, Brian."

Brian? He must be talking to the chief. Brian Howard has been chief of Spirit Bear Point for the past two terms. He used to work with Dad. On his kindest days, Dad used to joke that Brian was an idiot in a smart man's clothes. Not the nicest thing to say about him, but also not wrong. Brian's a guy who needs things explained to him seven times before he can understand. Dad was almost certain he only got voted in as chief because he knew how to dress. Looking cool in regalia doesn't mean you'll understand the first thing about politics.

Reggie keeps talking. "It's out of our hands right now. We gotta just wait. What's that? Oh, yeah. Yeah, I guess I could try that. See if they know anything and if they'd want to sign on his behalf. Okay. I'll get back to you. Yeah, you enjoy your conference. Oh, and hey, you're staying at the Best Western, ahn? The kitchen there makes these real good little buns. Can you bring me back a couple? Huh? Just put it in your suitcase in a napkin or something. It don't have to look pretty. 'Kay den. You have a good day."

The receiver hits the base awkwardly when he hangs up. I

hear him moving about, and if he's got the room set up similarly to the way my dad had it for years, I know I've got about six seconds before he comes around that corner and out into the hall. I waste no time in hurrying down the corridor back to the atrium. The secretary doesn't even look up when I walk past and out of the building altogether.

It's insufferably hot inside my car, thanks to the direct sunlight shining in it for the past hour, but I don't turn on the engine. Instead, I pull out my phone and stare down at the contact entry with my brother's name at the top. I need to talk to him. I need to tell him what I heard. I want to know why these people are talking about Dad. Why are they talking about the quarry? And why the hell don't I know about it?

Would Mom know the answers? Could I ask her without opening old wounds?

I start to break out in a sweat again.

I don't call Gus.

¤ ¤ ¤

My keys hit the front hall table in a heap when I toss them. I walk into the house, moving down the hall until I round the corner into the kitchen. I don't see Mom right away, but I hear her humming to herself. She's on the back porch, watering the tiny forest she has growing out there.

"I'm home. Just going to change. I want to go for a run before supper."

"Okay, kid," she answers.

After I've changed, I return to the kitchen. The counter is covered with a fine layer of flour. Mom's baking something. It must be bread. I look over at the stovetop, where a row of pans is

KAREN McBRIDE

covered with a damp tea towel. Mom likes to keep the bread on the stove while the oven heats up because she says it helps it rise quickly. It's nearly time for them to bake because there's a set of tiny rolling hills beneath the checked red fabric.

I move to stand in the doorway that leads out onto the porch. "Plants look good, Mom."

She looks up briefly and smiles. "*Meegwetch*. Been working hard on them all summer. 'Bout time that work paid off. How'd it go with Auntie Joni?"

I fiddle with the waistband on my running tights and nod. "Good, good. She's doing well. I still find it weird that she's in charge of all that stuff. What made her want to go into Lands and Memberships?"

"Oh, you know Joni. She likes helping people. Making sure people get what's owed to them seems right up her alley."

"Seems like more paperwork than she can handle."

"Which is why you've got a job now."

"Touché."

Mom finishes watering her plants and sets the can down on the table. She delicately tugs at the nearest chair so she can sit. She leans her back against the striped cushion and then motions for me to sit too. I shake my head.

"Gonna run soon, remember? If I sit there's a chance I won't get back up."

"Suit yourself." She places her hands on the armrests and settles farther into the chair. "What's on your mind, kiddo? You look like there's something on its way to bubble over inside of you. Spit it out."

She talks a lot about Dad being the one who could see right through a person, but she's pretty damn talented herself. "I heard some stuff at the Band Office today."

She scoffs. "What else is new? Who's on the chopping block now?"

"Us."

Mom's eyebrows shoot up around her hairline. She sits up straighter and nods to tell me to go on.

"Not by name. But I heard people talking about Dad. About the quarry." I don't know why, but I'm nervous. Saying this to her, I feel like I should hang my shoulders and avoid her eyes. Despite my dad being vice-chief for nearly sixteen years—a world record for anyone in Rez politics, I'm sure—our family name has remained, somewhat notoriously, far from the mouths of even the biggest gossips. No, saying the Ellis name in vain didn't come with a curse or because we had power. We were the good guys. Always have been.

Mom pushes the hair from her face with both hands before letting them fall back into her lap. There are lines along her forehead that I haven't noticed before. I keep my eyes on her. The sunlight reflecting off the glass table hits her in the face, making her look down, her eyes narrow. "What did they say? Who was talking?"

"Heath Whittaker and Reggie Lee."

"That damn Heath has been after the quarry forever."

"He's not getting it, though. I heard Reggie say something to that."

"Oh?"

I take a deep breath before answering. I let the air fill my lungs completely, holding it at the top of my inhale, then carefully, shakily, I let it go. "He said Dad made a deal. Said something about Abe leaving them with an unsigned problem."

Genuine confusion pulls Mom's eyebrows together. "And just what does that mean?"

"I thought you'd know. Sounded an awful lot like something you said before. Didn't you and Dad talk about this before he . . . ?" I still can't bring myself to say it.

"Land, yes. That was always the plan or deal we had. Your dad and I figured out what would go to you and Gus and what would go to me. Did you hear anything else when you were at the Band Office? What else did Reggie say?" She's looking at me like I have something she wants.

I can't explain why, but I don't want to tell her what I know. Maybe it's the way she skipped over the deal bit, but part of me wants to keep it all for myself. Hoard it so it stays with me. I want to bury the knowledge six feet under with him. My honesty wins out, though, and I say, "He said a name. Gagnon. Does that sound familiar at all?"

"Gagnon?" She pushes her lips out and they tremble slightly. "It sounds familiar. But, honestly, half the people in town are named Gagnon."

This is hard to believe. Mom and Dad shared everything with each other. How could she not know? Is she pretending to be confused? To not know anything? It doesn't make sense. They shared *everything*. They were perfect.

"Are you okay? Did you hear something else that upset you?"

I try to swallow back the emotion in my throat, but it's too much for me. "Why don't you know what I'm talking about, Mom? Why didn't Dad tell you?"

She looks hurt and it shows in the curve of her mouth. "I don't . . . I don't know. There were some things your dad and I didn't talk about. We had secrets. Every couple does."

The world goes blurry and I squeeze my eyes shut to push away the tears. "No. You didn't! You two didn't have secrets. Dad always said that."

This time, the hurt comes from a different place. She gives me a look I know well. It's one I've been getting since the wake, the funeral. Sympathy. Pity. "Sweetie, your dad had secrets."

"Not from me! Not from you!"

Softly, she replies, "From all of us."

I can't listen to this. I don't want to hear it. I have to go. I can't look at her. Mom calls to me, urges me to come back, but I'm already down the steps and sprinting along the driveway toward the road. I don't look back.

I just run.

8

MEMORIES AND WEEDS

I open this beak that I am forced to call my mouth and let out a series of caws. I listen as they echo across the tops of the trees. Other birds answer me, croaking from their places in the distance. They say things about the food they have found and the dangers nearby. Boring, typical conversations. I long for more than shouting about the taste of frogs and worms.

The last time I was on this side of the Medicine Wheel, the sweetgrass grew tall and the wigwams were built strong with pelts and hides. Now the grass is cut low to the ground, burnt in the spring to help it grow faster, only to be cut again. The wigwams are made of wood and rock and plastic and they crumble and flood—too hot in the summer and too cold in the winter. At least they're still building their own houses, but without the know-how of their ancestors, what's the point? Broken people build broken homes.

Spirit Bear Point sits on a piece of land surrounded by the Àmibi River. Follow that twisting line of water for long enough and it'll lead right to the highway of the people. In Kakone gîzis, during the harvest moon, the trees go from green to fire red and orange, and the air smells like warm earth and the sweetness of decay. Every morning, fog hangs like a shroud in the air, making it almost possible to forget the hundreds of pale faces settled not two kilometres southwest from the reserve. It's beautiful. Tagwagin is the perfect season for Spirit Bear Point. Now, however, it's still summer, or what remains of it. The leaves are thick and healthy. Even the dandelions and fireweed along the roadside are green and blossoming. The pine forests that border every neighbourhood in the thirty square kilometres of unsurrendered land chirp and call with life.

Doesn't sound like much when it's written down like that. Thirty square kilometres. As the crow flies it's only five kilometres from the farthest possible points. Which means that I can make it across the whole of what's left of this poor robbed territory in just a few minutes. It's beautiful and it's depressing. It's docked and limitless all at once.

And yet I want to be a part of it. I want to come back to this plane. Feel the warmth of the soil under my feet. Use fingers to touch skin and not plumage. More than anything, I want to be able to walk into my own home and shut the door. Push everything from the other side away. Before that happens, I need to convince the Seven that I'm worthy of mortal life. Ridiculous. Humans don't have to prove anything to anyone, and they are born and die every single second. But from me, the Seven, sitting high on the hill in their gargantuan teepee, demand so much more. Talking with big voices of stone and wood and honey and thunder. I am forced to earn my place. In the meantime, I'm stuck. I need to find a helper. The one who let me out. The one who can cross to the Spirit World and come back again.

Hazel.

I thought I would never meet another one like me in all of creation—in this world and the one watched over by those stuffy Seven Grandfathers. She's got something in her, a power, that makes her like me. Only, where I'm brilliantly clever and witty, she's got unyielding honesty and devotion. Less fun, but I can deal with that.

Hazel intrigues me. I haven't met another who could walk the boundaries between doorways as easily as me in so long. It's refreshing. This must be what parents feel like. Proud and only the tiniest bit jealous of what she's accomplished. I've been trying to get out of the Spirit World for years, and Hazel simply walks in and holds open the door for me. But maybe I'm assuming too much. I don't think she understands how important she could be. Someone need only show her the way. And that someone, thanks to her, is me.

She just doesn't realize her luck.

Although . . .

She's broken too. Like the rest of her People. I'll have to put her back together first. Not my strong suit. I hear, though, that if you strike enough blows with a hammer, you're bound to hit a nail. Hammers are curious things. At what point does a tool become a weapon?

A few beats of my wings and I'm flying over the brick walls she calls home. Built by her father and a few other carpenters, the house is a solid patchwork of rock and wood and leaf. The yard is filled with gentle hills covered in bright green grass. Or at least it would be if it wasn't completely blanketed in dandelions. Those bright yellow lions' heads do have a way of growing back no matter how many times you cut them down. Memories and weeds.

I swoop in closer, perching on the telephone wire connected to the house; it rocks slightly in a breeze that sends the aspens quaking like waves on the lake. I lose my balance a little, making a small noise that sends the nearby crows into a frenzy of caws and croaks. They're so irritating now that they've forgotten how to speak. Their groups used to be called "murders" because they were smart and cunning, but now I think that title is better suited to the urge you get when they won't shut up. Ignoring them, I turn my attention back to the brick house. The windows are open. Someone must be home. I can't tell which of the women it is from this distance. I have to get closer. It's a risk.

I move round the house and sit on the banister of the back porch, gazing into the kitchen. Ah, it's the mother, Nora, who's home. If it weren't for the long plait of black hair, I might have first guessed it was Hazel. They're strikingly similar despite the age gap. The same high cheekbones, the same self-conscious confidence about their walk, the same freckles around the eyes—oh, but the eyes are where they differ. Nora's dark, nearly black, eyes are gentle and comforting. Like the first warm hug after stepping in from the cold. But Hazel has her father's eyes. The kind that know more from one glance than years of study.

Like mine.

Ah, but the reason I look wise is because of years and years of trickery and fun on my part. Wisdom can be earned if you live long enough.

Nora would normally be humming to herself as she moves back and forth in the kitchen. But right now her face is hard, unreadable. Her eyes look distant, but they aren't red. Nora doesn't cry. Not anymore. I watch her move easily from the counter to the stove. She's baking something. She'll say it's because she loves doing it, but she does it because it keeps her mind from remembering. A task to keep herself busy while she does her best to forget the man who would come into the room grinning because he smelled cookies. Her husband, Abe. It's too bad she doesn't have anyone to spoil with those treats. After all, Hazel and her brother, Gus, aren't in the right place to offer their mother grandchildren. Broken people build broken homes.

After Nora sets a fresh batch of bread on the counter to cool, I resign myself to the fact that Hazel's not here. If not here, then where? If my comrades, those fools in feathers, would remember where to find their words, I could ask them, but no. Of course not. I always have to solve things on my own. This would be much easier if I could just remember my Anishnaabe shape. The second I made it through the veil from the Spirit World, I tried to remember how to walk on two legs, without wings, but something was wrong. I couldn't do it. Over and over, I wished for my moccasins, and every time I could not lose my feathers. Had things changed so much since I had been here last that there was nothing left for me? Nothing offered. Nothing laid out for my taking. There's power in prayer for gods. Can a god without worshippers still be called a god?

If it were that simple, I'm sure I could gather enough believers to help me reclaim my legs. But no. This whole problem reeks of the Seven. They've taken what little power I'd been given and locked it away where I can't get to it.

So, I've flown through this land ever since.

Gôkom used to say that too much time as a bird is bad for the mind.

You end up leaving a bit of yourself behind until there's almost nothing left and you're more bird than person. But Gôkom is gone and I'm still here, aren't I?

My first thought is to check the schoolyard. But I know that would be a waste of time. She would never go there alone. Instead, I follow the lines of the gravel roads, leading myself on a short tour of the reserve. Past the log walls of the Band Office and beyond the newly redesigned police station, the road changes to proper asphalt. It leads into what everyone calls "town" but what I'd call "land lost to the colonizers." Just past the sign spray-painted with the words "REZ LIFE," I find her.

Along a path lined with pine trees, into a glade that is sombre and beautiful, I see Hazel. She's almost completely still. If it wasn't for the jarring trembling of her shoulders, I could have mistaken her for one of the many statues standing watch over their silent charges. I ride the wind current over to where she's standing, but I don't land where she can see me. My eyes settle on her as she stares at the ground. Her dark hair is pulled away from her face, making it easy for me to see the tears on her cheeks. Until recently, there was nothing marking the place where she stands as anything special. There had been no stones or wooden crosses to offer any tribute. Just the weeds and the memory of a place remind her of where he lies. Now, she stares down at a monument of rock with his name carved into it.

I watch her for some time. Sadness looks lovely on her.

I open my beak and let out a caw that catches her attention. She looks up from the grass-covered ground and stares right at me. I'd smirk if I could. The knowing look in her gaze tells me that she finally sees me, acknowledges that I'm here in her world. Satisfaction sits in my belly like fresh moose meat—wild and rich. I've been trying to get her attention for what feels like weeks, and now that I have it, I'm that much closer to getting what I want. To fixing her. Who knows how long that could take, though? I can't be sure. Time is wasted by humans. It's a shame they've forgotten who I am and what I can do. I found them fire. I fought off the long night, so they could have sun. Hundreds of years of help and history and this is the thanks I get?

9

OGÂS

"What are you doing here, watching me like that?"

The ice in my voice is only a small taste of what I'm feeling. The last thing I need is this bird. He keeps showing up when he's not wanted. Should I tell him that? No. I'll hold back. The way he's looking at me, his little head twisting to and fro, those strange grey eyes blinking as they watch me closely, makes me uncomfortable and vulnerable. I'm chilled.

"This is ridiculous," I say, roughly brushing away the tear that's made its way onto my cheek. "I'm sick of thinking I'm hallucinating."

—*Then stop thinking like that. Can't you see that I'm real? As real as that square of grass at your feet. As real as the headstone guarding it.*

Anger rises from my stomach, flushing my face until even my ears feel hot. "What do you want, Nanabush?"

—*I've been looking for you. You weren't at home. Nora looked upset. What did you say to her?*

More anger bubbles up until it's in my throat. "What's it matter to you?"

Nanabush laughs. His cawing echoes across the open expanse of the cemetery. As if in answer, the wind picks up. He tilts his head sideways slightly, twitching in a way that almost convinces me that he's nothing but a bird. Except that the awareness in his eyes makes that impossible.

—Is it so far-fetched that I might actually care about you?

"Yes."

Another laugh. He rustles and readjusts his wings.

—I guess none of the old stories ever mentioned my caring and compassionate nature. They would be right, of course. I've always been a "me first" man.

"Stories used to say you weren't a man. Can't say they're wrong about that either, seeing as you're still a crow."

—Yes, I'd like to do something about that. While being a crow has its perks, I'm ready to get my real legs back.

"Then go ahead. Change. You're supposed to be this great shapeshifter. Prove to me that you're real by doing it right now. Give me a reason to want to believe in you."

The crow clacks his beak. He hesitates. The branch he's on wobbles in the wind and he adjusts his wings again to keep his balance. I watch him as he pointedly avoids my gaze, cawing a few times before preening. A few of his feathers fall from him, drifting slowly to the ground. Determined not to break my focus on the bird, I keep my eyes on him. They start to dry out and the urge to look away tugs at every part of me, but I don't stop staring. I don't give him a chance to fly off, to disappear somewhere between the rows of monuments.

After a moment, I snort derisively. "I knew you couldn't do it. You're nothing but an old crow."

Nanabush croaks at me, the colour of his eyes flickering from grey to black in anger.

—I am not just one of those mindless carrion eaters! I am Nanabush. I have been since the Earth was young. I was there when Glooskap and Malsum fought. I was there when the Thunderbirds came down from their mountains to bless the skies with rain. I was there when the first Winter came. I brought you fire. I ended the Long Night. Without me, you

Anishnaabe would have died long before the pale ones came across the water to colonize and slaughter each and every last one of you.

With every word he speaks, the sky darkens as Nanabush's shadow grows larger. I can feel some primal part of me screaming that I need to either fall to my knees or run. I shouldn't be able to commune with someone like him. But I can't move. The wind picks up again and tosses the few pieces of loose hair around my face until each touch feels like lashes from a whip. For the first time, I see the echo of the old powers of Nanabush. As if I know that he's not what he was. I understand him. Something connects us and I see him for the tired, unworshipped, forgotten soul that he is.

The sky brightens again, but the clouds don't clear. Nanabush's feathers are unkempt, out of place. Silver streaks the sleek black of his plumes. How old is he?

I breathe in deeply and say, "*Gashkenindam, àndeg.* I see you."

Nanabush doesn't say anything. He watches me. His head twitches from one side to the next in short, rapid movements. Then he shifts his wings and I can see him visibly relax, his feathers flattening against his body so that they no longer stand on end. He gleams in the dull, grey, cloud-covered light of late afternoon.

—*Meegwetch, little one.*

Something else should be said, but neither of us knows just what. Our conversations seem to come in waves. We talk at each other, we argue, we stand in silence, and we start again.

"Where does this leave us?" I ask, absently wringing my hands.

—*I'm here to help you. I thought that much was clear.*

"I don't know. You've been acting like a ghost with all your lurking and phantom comings and goings. Help wasn't first on my brain."

KAREN McBRIDE

A smirk plays in his eyes. The idea that he's created fear in me clearly excites him. An old god stuck in his old ways. If he could smile with that beak of his he'd be doing so now. Smugly.

"Help me with what?"

—*Don't you remember that night in the village? The voices in the great teepee with the fire that ever burns? They were talking about you. They want to fix you.*

The confusion in my voice is almost embarrassing. "And who's *they?*"

He spreads his wings open wide like arms in an exasperated shrug.

—They. *The big Seven.* The *Seven. The Grandfathers.*

"The teachings? I always thought they were just ways to live. Like 'Eat your vegetables.' That kind of thing."

Nanabush lets out a series of grinding croaks and caws that sound like a mix of ancient crow and Anishnaabemowin. I don't speak the language like I should; I don't understand it. But I understand him, clear as day. Cursing carries the same tone in every language.

—*You all stopped listening. They may only be remembered as Grandfather Teachings now, but they have always been more than that. Those missionaries taught that that god of theirs had angels. Well, G'tchi Manitou has the Seven.*

"If they're all real, then why the hell are they helping one Algonquin girl with a dead dad when they could be doing something about all of this? The poverty. The water we can't drink. The drugs and alcohol. What about all of those missing and murdered women? By comparison, I'm doing fine. I'm well off. Why waste time on me?"

Nanabush's shoulders droop and he winces. Like every word I've said is hitting him like a hail of arrows. But he's quick

116

to readjust. To fluff his brilliant plumage. Nanabush spreads his wings and moves closer to me, fluttering down from his perch on the oak to rest on the top of my father's monument. Up close, he's intimidating. Underneath his eyes, his flesh is red war paint. His tail feathers come together in a sharp point, the edges of each intricately barbed and flecked with silver. Each of his talons are abyssal black, as if they've been freshly polished, razor-edged to cut through skin, bone, and tendon. But his legs are scarred and marked. He's missing plumes along his chest and back. I can see the exhaustion behind his eyes.

The whole time I've been looking at him, he's been staring right back. No. That's not quite right. Observing. Like two animals in the wild, meeting where our territories overlap. The air between us, around us, hums. Nanabush shifts, stretching his feet.

—*The things you say. None of them are about you.*

This catches me off-guard and my face falls, lips parting slightly as my mouth tries to find the right words. Quickly, I pull myself together and find the heat of my anger again.

"And what's that supposed to mean? Of course they're about me. All of those things are our problems. If you spent any time living like an Indian person in the world they left us with, then you'd understand."

He shakes his head.

—*They're bigger than you. Things you can't fix on your own. Things I can't fix on my own. I'm here to fix you. And that's what I plan on doing. Do you think that if I had any idea why the Seven did what they did that I'd still be here? That I'd still be stuck like this?*

"What do you mean?"

Nanabush pauses before readjusting his feathers. The movement looks a little like a shrug. He means it to be casual, dismissive, but the tense way he clicks his beak says otherwise.

I take a step closer, forcing myself into his space the same way he's been pushing himself into mine. I want to see him flinch. I want to see more of the weakness he let me glimpse earlier. But he straightens up, folding his shoulders so that his wings sit comfortably and elegantly along his back.

I press, "What do you mean by that? Stuck like what, Nanabush?"

—*Stuck only talking to you. Someone like me is made to be admired, worshipped. If I had my way, I'd be chief of this reserve already.*

I take a moment to mull that over.

—*What? You think that sounds far-fetched?*

"The worshipping part sounds right. You'd love that. It's the chief thing that I'm not buying."

—*Why?*

"You have to understand politics for that job. And honestly? You've been out of the loop for a few thousand years."

—*Hundred. Few* hundred. *I haven't been gone that long.*

"Okay."

—*Hazel, quit wasting my time. Don't you want to know why I hunted you down today? Why I made a point of flying all the way here to this depressing place?*

"To continue your constant harassment of my used-to-be-normal life?"

If he could properly roll his eyes, I think he just might have.

He chirps back at me.

—*"Sweetie, your dad had secrets."*

It's remarkable, the way he can hurt me. And how he knows so much about my life as it happens. He must live in my shadow to be so close and still so hidden. I turn away from him, hiding the pain in my eyes. Hearing the words again, even in his voice, makes the fear real. It bubbles in the pit of my stomach and slowly up into my throat and mouth until I can taste it. I feel my hands shaking, my heart trembling.

My voice is sarcastic when I say, "What do you think you know about it?"

—*I know how much that one little sentence is eating you up inside. How badly you want to know the truth.*

"So?" I say.

—*Let me help you.*

I fight every urge to turn and walk away. Nanabush takes my silence as consent. He isn't wrong.

—*That's better. See? We can get along fine. You just need to not talk so much. I know, I know. I'm sorry. You don't have to make that nasty, scrunched-up face at me every time I try to make a joke about you. You need to relax if we're ever going to make this partnership work.*

"I'm not convinced that I want to get along with you."

—*This. This is what I'm talking about. Everything is so dark and depressing with you. It's a wonder your people can still handle being around you.*

"You're an asshole, you know that? All the stories about you left that out. I'll be sure to add it in when I pass this all on."

—*You will talk about me?*

"I don't know. Maybe. Once I figure out a way to tell this story without me sounding completely crazy."

Nanabush clacks his beak and makes a noise that sounds like laughter.

—*Make sure that you* tell *the story instead of writing it down. From what I've seen, people tend to take the written word too seriously. Truth and lies and stories have a hard time working together.*

It's clear that Nanabush is pleased. Something about him brightens as he straightens up. He's eager now. Eager to talk with me. I'm not sure if I'm sold on it yet. But this is better than going

KAREN McBRIDE

home. Better than talking to a headstone that won't answer back. I shift my weight and lean into my hip. Whatever sweat I had worked up on my run here has now completely cooled.

—*We had better give you a good story to tell then, eh, nishîmej?*

"How did you know about what my mom said to me? And what's it matter to you? Is this all part of the grieving process?" When I get worked up like this, I can't control how quickly I talk. Poor Nanabush. It's a firing squad of questions and he isn't wearing any armour.

—*I know because you were there . . . because we have this . . .*

He falters. The feathers of his brow come together.

—*I think we're connected. Sewn together like a fishing net. We're knotted together in so many places, I can't tell where they begin and where they end. I only know that we need to move together—one motion, one swoop—if we want to succeed.*

"Succeed at what?"

—*I don't . . .* He sighs. —*Tell me about the quarry.*

"Dad's quarry? What's there to tell? It's a quarry. I don't know what it was used for. I mean, I know it was mining, but that was something like a hundred years ago. It's all water and rock now."

—*How did it close?*

"People died or something."

—*And why would it bother you now?*

"Because I heard something. At the Band Office. There were people talking. Saying things that . . . that mean that . . ."

—*They said your father's name.*

No. Not answering that.

The old crow's eyes slowly turn milky. He stays that way for a long time, leaving me standing alone in the cemetery. I move closer to my father's headstone. The grass shifts and bends with each step I take, but Nanabush is motionless, perched on the

120

monument, watching me with his cloudy white eyes. A heavy feeling of dread settles in my bones. My hands shake as I reach, fingers outstretched, to touch the silken blackness of his wings. That same anticipation I felt the day he spoke to me outside my home—the day I could feel myself starting to go crazy—moves along my arms. There's something different about it this time. Maybe it's the startling closeness of the bird in front of me, or that acknowledging him has opened me up to feeling his power. The air around him, between us, thrums with energy. As I inch closer to him, my vision starts to blur and brighten.

My breath catches as I feel like I'm stumbling through grass and water, grasping for anything to ground me, something to help me find my feet. Voices, voices. So many voices. I can't see. Too bright. Like sunlight on glass. Bouncing, burning in my eyes.

Faded images come back to me. It's like looking at an old photograph that's been left out to age in the sun. I blink, squeezing my eyes shut to let the water back in. I smell cedar, sweetgrass. Everything around me is familiar, distant. It takes me a moment, but I recognize where I am. The Band Office, the hall directly in front of the office of the vice-chief. Only, the art, the books, the dents in the walls, they're all so new. This can't be the building I was in just a few hours before now. This is something else.

People are speaking. Clearer than earlier, but still far off, like I'm hearing them across time. Everything around me looks drained of colour. Not because it is old, but because it has already happened. Soft, blurred focus. These are memories. But whom do they belong to?

"Hazel?"

That voice I would know anywhere. My stomach drops. Emotion floods my eyes and my throat. I want to answer, but I can't. The sight of something—someone—stops me.

She's not quite up to my waist. Her dark hair is long, halfway down her back. She's wearing a corduroy dress. There's a small rip along the seam where the shoulder meets the sleeve, but it's been mended. The dress used to belong to her older cousin. It's her favourite.

"It's me," I whisper.

Hazel runs right through me. She's grinning. She pushes open the door to the office and I follow her, completely transfixed. She keeps running until she's around the desk and scooped up into his arms. I stop in the doorway.

Dad lifts little Hazel high into the air before pulling her close to him, kissing her cheek. Even though the colours are faint, Abe's grey eyes are alight with life and love. The way he looks at her tears at my heart. Jealousy of my past self leaves a taste of chalk in my mouth. It hurts knowing that they only have a handful of years left together. But here, they're carefree. There is only this moment and the next. Neither thinks of the one that will be the last. I'm more removed than ever, being so close to the past. To something I can never have again. I feel cold in my bones.

—*We're too far back.*

Nanabush's voice doesn't surprise me. I look his way. He makes a stifled croaking noise, blinks, and twitches his head to the right.

"It's been so long since I've seen Dad with his hair braided. It makes him look young. He's so happy. *We're* so happy." My eyes get moist. I try to blink away the tears, but they roll down my cheeks anyway.

—*You got lucky with parents like yours. Not everyone gets to be the light of their father's life. Gus must hate you for that.*

Parents don't pick favourites. At least, mine didn't. I'm not answering that.

"I remember this day now, I do. It was after picture day at school."

Dad adjusts the bolo tie around his neck, loosening it as he sits down. He pulls Hazel up onto his lap and gently spins the chair so they both face the window. I watch them—us—looking out onto the river. There is sunlight along the water. Waves slowly and quickly tumble over the rocks and sand of the riverbed. He points to the water's edge.

"He's telling me the story of how the pickerel got his scales."

Nanabush is quiet, but I know he's listening.

Dad's baritone is soft, but it still fills the room. "The sunlight and the colours of the leaves of the trees used to love dancing along the water. It was the most beautiful sight to watch light and leaf as they twirled with the river. They fell in love with their reflections along the glassy surface. They wanted so badly to look like that always, so one day, together, they leapt from their places in the sky and the earth and dove into the water. But sunlight and leaf could not live in the water. They could not swim. It was then that the pickerel—not a pretty fish to look at, but one who was hearty, proud, and an excellent swimmer—hurried to rescue them. He swam, his back fin moving back and forth with power and grace, and he caught sunlight and leaf just as they had given up. He told them that he would carry them for as long as they wished to live in the water. So happy were sunlight and leaf that they stayed with pickerel for days ever after."

I say the last words with him. "And to this day, pickerel wears the beauty of sun and leaf and river on his back."

Hazel beams up at her father. And Abe looks down at her lovingly. He brushes the long hair from her face, then looks back out the window.

"I used to love that story," I say. "I'd make him tell it over and over. Not because I liked the words or the images, but because I loved the way he told it. Even when he was just speaking, his voice sounded like a song."

—*We have to go.*

"I know." I turn away, squeezing my eyes closed, shutting Hazel and her father out. But I can't seem to get rid of them. Their images stay burned into my vision. I want to hold on to them until it stops hurting. But it does hurt. Will always hurt.

When I open my eyes, we're back in the cemetery. The colours here seem vivid, as if what I experienced wasn't real—couldn't be real. Sounds from the main road seep through the surrounding trees. Cars and trucks go by. Life continues as usual. Nanabush is looking at me from his perch on my father's headstone. My hand is still resting on his feathers. I move it, bring it up to my face, wipe my cheeks.

"I, uh, I heard someone say that my dad left them with a problem. Something unsigned that has to do with the quarry."

—*Anything else?*

"Yeah, another name. Someone called Gagnon."

—*All right. Good.*

Nanabush readjusts. He stretches his talons. He's getting ready for flight.

—*Go home, Hazel. You should talk to your mother.*

I nod and turn away from him. "All right."

He spreads his wings. I hear them, feel the rush of air as he takes flight. The feathers sound like silk against the sky. I go to move, but my legs give out and I'm on the ground, on my hands and knees. I dig my fingers into the grass, dirt quickly settling underneath my nails. I close out the world and shut my eyes. What I see are the silvery scales of a river fish.

✖ ✖ ✖

There's still light in the sky when I make it home. The sun is already beyond the horizon, leaving oranges and pinks painted across the clouds that hang in the air. It's distracting and beautiful. The light puts the trees and sloping, shingled rooftops in silhouette, their soft, angled lines marking their place against the sky. Our house is lit from the inside. The curtains are open, so I can see inside the living room as I walk up the long drive. I can see Mom amidst the forest of plants in the sitting room. She's got her eyes fixed on the book she's reading. I take a moment to look at her while I'm far away and unseen. Is she upset from our talk earlier? Did my outburst hurt her feelings? I can't be sure. Mom's face is unreadable beyond her clear investment in what she's reading.

I stand there as the sky gets progressively darker and the shadows start to take me. This must be what it's like for Nanabush. Observing without being seen. I can see why he likes shadows. The street lights flicker to life, spilling an almost antiseptic fluorescent light onto the highway and the end of the drive. It feels like the searchlight of a prison on my back. I march, reluctantly, expectantly, up to the house.

It's unlocked, as always, and the light's on in the hallway. I shut the front door as noiselessly as possible to try to keep the space between Mom and me a moment longer. It makes noise all the same. I take off my shoes, leave them at the door. I take off my jacket, hang it on the clothes tree. I take a deep breath to get my bearings and calm myself down. Even if everything is fine, I can't help but be worried. Two steps and I'm in the doorway of the living room, standing at the bottom of the stairs. Easily, I could turn and hurry up to my bedroom, avoid speaking to her altogether. My weight shifts, my foot angles, I start to pivot.

"Hazel."

Exhale. Walk into the room.

Her arms are open and I easily move into her embrace. I lie on the couch beside her, cradled in her arms. She rocks me back and forth. She sings a lullaby. I don't cry. I don't apologize. I don't say anything at all.

And somehow, we're okay.

10

I REMAIN, SIR, YOUR OBEDIENT SERVANT...

Joni pushes open the door to the conference room and I stop in my tracks. My jaw drops—which feels like something out of a movie, but it's my honest-to-god reaction. Spread across the extra-long table is a terrifyingly large assortment of banker's boxes, each of them labelled in their own unique way. The one consistency I can spot is that each box is still in decent-enough shape to be classified as a box, although a few are bulging out from severe overcrowding.

"It'll be good for a little bit, I tink, me. You just let me know when you need more space, eh?" Joni says, placing her hands on her hips as she surveys the room before looking at me.

"You mean I've got the whole room to myself to sort through boxes?" I reply.

Joni laughs and rubs her chin with the back of her hand. "If you get chrew more dan one box today, I'll be *real* impressed."

Confusion must be plain on my face because Joni claps me on the shoulder.

"Don't look so scared! You'll be fine."

"Should I have brought some luggage? A pillow? Maybe a blanket? By the looks of things, I'll be living here now."

Waving away my questions, Joni walks into the room and reaches for the lone box-less folder sitting on the table. She motions for me to stand next to her as she flicks it open. "Okay, so! This here's a list of all dem terms and tings you need to know to understand dem letters."

I put down my coffee Thermos and bring the paper closer to look it over. "What does *ultimo* mean?"

"It's an old-timey way of saying 'last month.' And *instant* is their way of saying 'this month.' You'll see dat all de time." When she places her hand on my shoulder again, it feels less like a gesture of confidence and more like it might be pity. "You good now? I tink you are."

I give her a small smile and shrug. "Yeah, I guess."

"Dat's de spirit. Give me a shout if you need anyting," she says as she turns to walk out of the room.

I'm already studying the page of definitions as her footsteps fade. I pause when I realize I need some clarification. "Wait, you mean, like, literally?"

"Yeah, I'm just down the hall, me," she calls.

"Oh, okay." I resolve to walk down to her office if I need her. Shouting feels like pushing the limits of a proper work environment.

Sighing, I let my arms flap to my sides as I look back at the enormous wall of work in front of me. I move to the far end of the table and pull over the box marked "1." I take off the top and reach for a folder. The first document I pull out, ink-splotched and water-stained, is covered in the worst handwriting I've ever seen. It's like a doctor wrote the whole thing and assumed they'd be the only one looking at it. I can hardly make out the words. It might as well have been written in another alphabet. For all I know, it probably is.

If my job is to organize these boxes of documents into an easily accessible system, then what category am I supposed to put *this* illegible mess into?

Miscellaneous. That's a good choice.

I set the letter aside and gingerly pull out the next one. Right away, I deflate. Same mess, different handwriting. This is going to be the longest few weeks ever.

I should have brought more coffee.

¤ ¤ ¤

The clock above the door doesn't tick; the second hand just swoops around the face smoothly. It's practically noiseless. I've been watching it for nearly five minutes now. In one more minute, it'll be 2:00 p.m. My head feels heavy as it rests on my hand. I've got my elbow propped up on the table and I'm slumped forward. My chair is pushed back far enough so that my body is nearly horizontal against the tabletop. Looking at these letters, maps, and treaties has left me exhausted. And it's only been an hour since I came back from lunch.

I've organized documents across the long table in a haphazard chronology. I think I've sifted through about four dozen different sets of papers since I started this morning. Sometimes, the dates can span close to a hundred years from the same box. Not that that means anything. From what I've seen so far, certain correspondence spent decades trying to sort out one issue. I found a stack of letters about the misplacement of a fence that went on so long, the original property owner died before it was resolved.

When I agreed to this job, I assumed that the problem was with abundance. But it isn't just the amount of backlog, it's everything. It's all a complete mess. Joni wasn't kidding when she said she needed someone to do her busy work. I know that she and Mom meant well when they decided this would be a good way for me to spend my time instead of moping around the house, but this is, well, it's something else.

Usually a first day of work is simple and straightforward. A day that plants a seed of motivation in a person, so they feel excited, ready to come back tomorrow and the day after. But today? Oof. I feel like I've been hit over the head by one of these boxes and then beaten senseless with a bunch of letters from 1867. Probably a complaint about property or dogs or corn. There's no end to what people write in to Indian Affairs about. Indian Affairs, on the other hand, sends back pretty much the same set of replies. Usually along the lines of "Tell the Indians no and resurvey their land to make it smaller. Sell their lumber and set up a church. xoxo Indian Affairs."

The throbbing between my eyes that's been going on for the past hour is making it hard for me to see. I've read the same letter over about five times and I am still confused if it should be filed under "land disputes" or "petty-fence-building."

I reach out and tug the banker's box I'm working through closer to me, tilting it so I can see inside. Most of its contents are spread out on the table in front of me, save for the two folders taking up space at the bottom of the box. With a tired sigh, I pull out one of the folders and peel back the cover. I grab the first letter and start reading out loud in a last-ditch attempt to keep my eyes from falling shut.

"Date says, *March 12, 1910. Ste-Marie des Oblats. Dear sir, I write to you in reply of your letter from 24 ultimo wherein following the survey completed by the Ferguson Group, the potential of a mining development within the boundaries of the Spirit Bear Point Indian Reserve was presented.*"

My interest spikes for the first time all day, the paper in my hands gaining a sudden weight. I scoot forward, using my feet to wheel my chair closer to the table. I get so excited that I end up staring at the words in their swirling script for a few moments before I can pull myself together.

The letter is from the Indian agent assigned to our region, Joseph Côté. I've already come across so many letters by him that I don't even need to see his signature to know it's his work. His penmanship is of the elegantly atrocious variety—so pretty that it's practically illegible. Thankfully, the earlier hours I spent trudging through documents like this one have trained my eye enough to be able to read it without too much trouble. If I squint, somehow that makes it easier.

I write to inform you that the call for bids has produced two potential business candidates who are willing to invest in the venture. The first is the Ottawa River Mining Corporation, a company that is highly experienced with holdings in both the River Desert Agency and the Ottawa River basin. The second is a local company headed by one man, Philippe Gagnon. His company, Gagnon et Fils, is surprisingly successful given its size. Each company has proposed that a mining quarry be dug in order to harvest the profitable silver ore buried therein. Both companies have submitted adequate proposals detailing the budget and timeline of the venture. I have enclosed both the letters of introduction and pertinent following details.

I look forward to your response and decision.

I remain, sir, your obedient servant,

Joseph Côté
Indian Agent, Sagi'idiwin Agency, Québec

I take a second. Digest the contents. Gagnon. That name again. Is this the same man Reggie was talking about? That can't be right. This letter is more than a hundred years old. I look back up at the top. Who is this addressed to? I lean closer to the paper to make out the looping strokes of Côté's handwriting. The first line of the address reads, "Lawrence Wright. Deputy Superintendent General of Indian Affairs." Wow, these men just love making their titles as long as possible. His acronym, DSGIA, almost takes up as much real estate as the whole title.

The letters in this folder are all attached with one of those brass pins, so I have to fight delicately to get them out without causing any damage. Somehow, the correspondence from the Ottawa River Mining Corporation and Gagnon et Fils survives my mediocre attempt at a safe retrieval. The paper scrapes against the pin when I lift it up and stare at the swirling, inky writing.

March 8th, 1910
Ste-Marie des Oblats, Québec

Dear sir,

I write to you to introduce myself and answer the call for bids issued on 14 ultimo regarding the proposed silver mine on the land of the Indians of Spirit Bear Point. My name is Philippe Gagnon and I am the director of the Gagnon et Fils construction and mining operation in the town of Ste-Marie des Oblats, which lies one and a quarter miles west of the Indian settlement. It is my belief that the Department should consider my bid for the development of the open pit mine as we are local, hardworking, and have an established relationship with the Indians. My wife is of Indian blood being a half-breed herself. As such, I know the hardiness of the Indian people is ideal for work in construction and mining. My proposal includes the employment of strong, reliable Indians.

I await your quick reply and acceptance of the Gagnon et Fils proposal.

Yrs truly,
M. Philippe Gagnon
Director
Gagnon et Fils ltée.

There's something about the way this Philippe Gagnon writes that reeks of desperation. As if, all these years later, the parchment still carries the same greasiness that its author used to write it. I don't think I can blame him, though. After all, he's trying to get his company a chance at a huge project that could bring all kinds of money and opportunity to the area. And going up against what appears to be a major company must be difficult. Maybe he's got his employees' best interests at heart? Or maybe he's concerned with the town's welfare? Even still, I can't get on his side. Not with knowing that somewhere down the line, someone with his last name is going to force a deal with my dad. Besides, the pressure of his writing changes a lot: some lines are saturated in ink and others are hardly legible. I remember reading that that's an indicator of instability.

Gently, I put the letter down and move on to the next, from the Ottawa River Mining Corporation. Already this one is clearly better. A banner at the top states the company's information. They've even got a logo and slogan, "From Rocks to Riches!" in a beautifully penned script. The letter seems elaborate and somehow simple all at once. It must be the way its author has phrased everything. Or maybe I'm getting that feeling because Gagnon's slimy letter is fresh in my mind. Whatever is making me think it, I have no doubt that it'll be this corporation that wins the bid. Indian Affairs would be foolish not to choose an obviously viable company to put their investment behind.

March 4th, 1910
Ottawa, Ontario

Dear sir,

It is my pleasure to introduce the Ottawa River Mining Corporation as an option to you in your most recent call for bids to develop the region surrounding the Spirit Bear Point Indian Reserve. Our company has been in business for nearly thirty successful years. During that period, we have accumulated holdings in the River Desert Agency, the Ottawa Valley, and as far north as Fort William.

Should you choose our corporation for your investment, we vow to bring our own machinery and highly skilled workmen to complete the quarrying of the mine in a quick and orderly fashion. Having worked with the Indians before, we are already well versed in how they view the land. As such, we will work with care to avoid disrupting them while we extract the valuable silver ore. In the past, we have found that the Indians have been reluctant to allow a Canadian business onto what was once their land, so we feel that giving them a say in naming the mine shall be sufficient compensation.

My associates and I look forward to your reply.

Yours truly,
Mr. George Gideon
CEO
Ottawa River Mining Corporation

"Duh, choose these guys," I mutter as I put the letters down on the table.

I peek into the box and pull out another folder, hoping that these documents are next in the chain of communication. Now that I've found mention of Gagnon, even though this one is long dead, I need to find out more. The trail can't go cold here. Not yet.

Grabbing the first letter in the stack, I catch sight of the date. It's too far back and the letter is about a shipment of flour that's gone missing. I toss it aside and move on to the next one. The papers crumple slightly when I fold back the cover page to read what's underneath. This one is written in a different hand than the first three I read. I glance quickly down at the bottom of the page to see Wright's signature, but the handwriting doesn't match the letters I read this morning. This one must've been written by one of the departmental aides or his secretary. Guess a man like Wright doesn't always have time to pen his own letters. His schedule was already packed with taking away Indigenous rights and limiting and cutting our lands. I scoff and grumble a few curses at the past DSGIA before I start reading.

April 10th, 1910
Ottawa, Ontario

Dear sir,

I am writing in reply to your letter of 12 ultimo regarding the surrender of territory by the Indians of Spirit Bear Point to quarry the land for a mine by the Ottawa River Mining Corporation. The land reserved for the Indians must be surrendered according to the current Indian Act. In order for the surrender to be valid, there must be assent by a majority of the male members of the band of the full age of twenty-one years, at a meeting or council thereof summoned for that purpose according to their rules, and held in the presence of the Superintendent General, or of an officer duly authorized to attend such council by the Governor in Council or by the Superintendent General; Provided that no Indian shall be entitled to vote or be present at such council, unless he habitually resides on or near and is interested in the reserve in question.

Following the surrender, the land will belong to the Crown and the sale can move forward. The land is suited for such a mine, and it would be a viable investment for the Crown to provide the territory for the Ottawa River Mining Corporation. It is in the best interests of the Department and yourself that you hold a council to complete the surrender.

I remain, yrs,

Lawrence Wright
Deputy Superintendent General of Indian Affairs

Eagerly, I flip the page over, hoping for more. But there's nothing. Twice in the past few minutes. I can't handle this up-and-down hope and disappointment. I set the letters down next to me and stand up, letting the chair roll away into the wall. There has to be more to this somewhere. The box is nearly empty, but that does little to quash my hopes of finding the reply. A small part of me wonders if Nanabush would be of any help if he were here. He'd probably find it right away and then make a big deal about how amazing he is. Thinks he's so smart, that bird brain. Riffling through the letters, I finally catch sight of what I'm looking for.

The page is yellowed with age but in perfect condition otherwise. Sitting untouched in an unopened box for who knows how many years probably helped with the preservation. I read it standing up, too interested and excited to bother pulling my chair back.

April 29th, 1910
Ste-Marie des Oblats, Québec

Dear sir,

I acknowledge receipt of your letter from 10 instant with reference to the surrender of Indian lands to the Crown by the Indians of Spirit Bear Point in order to allow the Ottawa River Mining Corporation access to the territory to begin operations on their silver mine.

Several attempts have been made by myself and other councilmen from Ste-Marie des Oblats to reason with the Indians. They cannot be made to see the good a mine would bring to the region. As of 23 instant, the Indians have banded together to form blockades around the land earmarked for development. The Ottawa River Mining Corporation will attempt one last bid toward an amicable surrender before they pull their investment.

May I request your advice on this matter? I look forward to your quick reply.

I remain, sir, your obedient servant,

Joseph Côté
Indian Agent, Sagi'idiwin Agency, Québec

Of course Côté bands together with men from town. Ste-Marie des Oblats has always had a rocky relationship with Spirit Bear Point. The quarry has probably had a big part in the past and present disputes. Any bridges of communication and co-operation we build together are quick to fall apart thanks to long-standing prejudice from both sides.

The reply letter is short and straight to the point. Something I wasn't expecting from a department like Indian Affairs.

May 3rd, 1910
Ottawa, Ontario

Dear sir,

I am writing to acknowledge your letter of 29 ultimo regarding the quarrying of a silver mine by the Ottawa River Mining Corporation on the territory of the Indians of Spirit Bear Point Reserve.

The Indian Act is quite clear in regard to the surrender and sale of Indian land. It cannot be allotted for the Ottawa River Mining Corporation without a legal surrender by the Indians. If there is no surrender, the company may not use the land to their benefit without consequence. It is the recommendation of the Department that this matter be abandoned and revisited come the election of a new council of chieftains.

I remain, yrs,

Lawrence Wright
Deputy Superintendent General of Indian Affairs

Questions begin to settle in the space between my eyebrows. If they weren't allowed to dig, then why is there a quarry? Especially one that's clearly been operational at some point or another? Everyone around here knows the story of the old quarry. It was built quickly, almost like it showed up overnight. Before long, the mine was open and they were pulling silver from the earth, Red Man and White Man working side by side. Everybody wins for a while. Then bad things start to happen. The sort of bad things you can't ignore, so the whole thing closed. That's it. End of story.

But this correspondence muddies the water.

Slowly, I put the letters back onto the table and stare across the room into the eyes of a medicine woman in a painting framed on the wall. The artist was careful to craft her face with meticulous detail, to the point that her wrinkled skin is tree bark. The blanket around her shoulders is a deep red, with embroidered flowers and fringes made of tanned leather. It's funny that I've been in this room all day and this is the first time I've noticed the painting. She looks sad. Abandoned. Hmm, no. Wrong word. Displaced.

"You have any ideas why there's a quarry when there clearly shouldn't've been one?" I ask her. Part of me expects her to answer. What's left of the rational, logical part of my brain knows she won't. Paintings don't talk to me. Birds, on the other hand . . .

I comb my fingers through my hair and start the arduous process of running the names of potential information holders through my head. Joni knocks on the door. I glance over, give her a tired smile and a wave, and she comes inside the room, leaving the door open, so the sounds of the offices around the conference room trickle inside.

"So!" This is a standard greeting from Auntie Joni. "How'd it all go?"

I rest my hands on the table. "I started to sort things by year but then got the idea that maybe it's best done by topic and then year within that as a subdivision. Which worked for a while, until I realized there needs to be more specific categories for the topics."

Joni laughs and her old smoker's lungs wheeze. She coughs slightly, but she's still smiling. "Dat sure sounds right to me. I guess you'll be stuck in dat one box for the next week or two. If you get a good-enough way of sorting. Magine dat's a tough ting to figure out?"

"That's an understatement if I've ever heard one."

"Ah well, you have as much time as you need. We have enough funding to keep you as my assistant for all of fall and probably a good chunk into the winter." She tugs on the golden cross around her neck.

"Winter? Wow, that long?"

Joni gives me a look I recognize from my childhood as her way of saying, "As if now." She laughs again. "Already thinking of quittin' on me, you?"

"What? I . . . no. That's not what—"

She waves her hand at me as if swatting away a particularly bothersome fly. "Ehn, I'm just joking with you."

"Right, sorry."

"Sorry?" She says it incredulously, looking at me overtop her glasses as they slide down her nose. "You apologizing for not getting a joke? You been in the city and away from your people too long. Losing dat sense of humour we got."

"No, I don't think I could ever lose that. No matter how much time I spend away from the Rez."

Joni folds her arms across her chest, then clicks her tongue. "Always come back though, eh?" She fixes me with a knowing stare.

"Is that a request?" I observe her curiously.

She nods. "I tink being back here is gonna be good for you. You know, my mom used to tell me stories about how coming back home after a time away can heal you as much as any medicine. She said there was someting in the water, in the earth, dat could take away your hurts. 'Our People are like trees with deep roots,' she would say. 'We can't be touched by the frost, no matter how hard it tries to dig down into the ground. But if we don't keep ourselves watered, the whole tree will wither. So, come home, and come home often. Drink deep from the waters of the earth and you will be healed. You heal yourself and your People with every drop of *nibi* you drink.' Nice way with words, dat one."

I smile at Joni. In that moment, I see her as she must have been back then. Young and gentle with the drive to explore the world beyond the few square kilometres that we call home.

"Mm-hmm," I say softly. "She was right about all that too." That's why I came home in the first place, I think but don't say. Besides, I'm not so sure if it was the right decision after all.

She lets out a long sigh. "Anehways, it's four thirty, you can head home. Just leave the room like this. There's no meetings planned for a while, so the room's all yours. Tell your ma I said hello."

"I will." Don't know why she never tells her herself. Mom's got a cellphone like everyone else. Doesn't take much to send a text.

Joni walks out and I look back down at the table.

"Oh, shit." I should have asked her about the quarry.

When I rush out into the hallway to call after her, she's already gone. With a sigh, I turn back to the conference room. There are papers in piles everywhere. And now that I have something specific I need to find, the whole task is somehow even more daunting than before. But my drive to discover the truth has ignited a slow-burning fire in me. One that, if left untouched, will completely consume me. So, I need to know everything. I need someone to tell me what I'm missing. Fill in the blanks.

Mom might know. Only, things didn't go so well the last time we tried talking about Dad and the quarry. Maybe she's not the right person. At least, not right now. There must be someone else.

Then it hits me. I know just who to ask.

I reach for my phone from my back pocket and move to sit down. The vinyl padded chair I've spent most of the day in makes a satisfying hiss as I slump into it. I press my lips together as I scroll through the messages screen, looking for my brother's name. He's near the bottom of my recent texts, meaning that our conversations haven't been recent at all. The date on the last messages we sent is August 17. Today is September 12.

I start to type out a text message to Gus: "Hey, Gus. It's Hazel. Remember me? Your sister? Yeah, quick questio"

Nope. Backspace and delete all of that.

"Hey, bro. Need a favour. Think you can help me out?" That's rude. I didn't even ask how he is. That's a no too. Also *bro*? What the hell is wrong with me? Backspace, backspace, backspace. Every time I try to type something, it comes out all wrong. This shouldn't be so damn hard. It's just my brother. I have literally known him my entire life. This is strange because of him, though. He's all weird now. Dad dying really did a number on him. He's cold, brilliant, and sad. Reminds me of Nanabush. Just less of a complete jackass.

This is so dumb. He's my *brother*. I'm going to call him. Quick and painless.

He doesn't pick up, but I hear his voice all the same.

"Hey, you've reached Gus Ellis. Actually, you've just missed Gus Ellis. But leave me a message and I'll reach you."

Beep.

"Hey, Gus. It's me, Hazel. How are you? I hope you're good. I'm good. Um, and Mom's good. Wow, okay, guess I'll just have a conversation with your voicemail. Um, but 'kay, to the point. I'm working in land claims with Auntie Joni and I found these letters about the old quarry. Need your expertise on it. Um, yeah. Call me back."

It's days before I hear from him.

11

TENSE

The living room is pleasantly quiet while Mom and I both enjoy a Saturday indoors, reading. I'm covered in a fuzzy blanket with a book on my lap. One of the windows is open and a chilled breeze is blowing in, making the blinds move back and forth, the plastic lightly clapping together every time the wind picks up. The weather doesn't usually match up so perfectly with the change of season, but this day is an exception.

Books always remind me of Mom. The reason there are books in almost every room in our house is because of her. Some of my earliest memories are of her reading. When I was growing up, we had this little ritual, she and I. The first Tuesday of every month, the bookstore in town would get a new shipment, so we'd drive there together and pick out something new to read. Or we'd try to. There wasn't always something good. But that didn't matter. The best part was the time we spent together. Even when I'd come back from school during the summer, we'd make the trip out there. When Dad got sick, those visits became less and less frequent. First, they were every other month. Then once every four. And finally, after Dad was moved permanently into the hospital, our ritual stopped. We've never talked about starting it up again. Doesn't seem right. We aren't the same people we were before.

My phone starts ringing and vibrating, and the sudden sound startles us both. Mom half shouts, "Je-*sus*!" and nearly drops her book. We both laugh off the sudden excitement, and I look down at my phone.

A picture of Gus's face stares up at me. His dark eyes are gleaming as they look away from the camera. His smile is broad, mischievous, proud. Gus looks just like Dad when he smiles. He's got his hair in two long, tight, shining black braids. His face is darker than normal, tanned a rich, deep golden brown from weekends spent in the sun on the powwow trail, grass-dancing. Tucked carefully under his left arm is his newly framed degree. He's in a suit and wearing a bolo tie in the shape of a bear with turquoise eyes—a gift from Dad.

The picture is from his university graduation day. One of my favourite days. If I ever had to pick a memory that brings me real happiness, I think I'd choose that one. The four of us were all in Ottawa. His graduation was at three in the afternoon. He didn't have to be there until two, so we had time to grab lunch. My parents loved making a show of any of our accomplishments, so they told him to pick anywhere to go and eat. No limits. We'd go out for lunch now and an even bigger dinner later. Anything for the young Native man graduating with highest honours. So, Gus, being Gus, asked Mom to make fried bologna, boiled potatoes, and creamed corn. A real nice lunch of "Indian steak." His words exactly. Mom laughed and scolded him, but she found a grocery store that knew what she meant when she asked for a huge half-moon chunk of bologna with the wax still on it.

We had our glamorous lunch together and then walked from Gus's tiny one-bedroom Sandy Hill apartment to the National Arts Centre to watch my brother cross the stage. The hall where we all gathered was richly opulent, filled with red velvet, dark draping curtains, and gold filigree. The ceremony itself was ridiculously long, mostly thanks to the honoured guest speaker giving her full speech in both official languages. Dad fell asleep and snored a little, but I woke him when it was time for them to call Gus's name. When they did, both of my parents let out classic war cries, startling the very proper, very old, very White people seated next to us. I, being fifteen, was mortified. But I'll always remember the way they looked at each other as they laughed and cheered with pride for their son. That glance is what I picture when I hear anyone talk about real love. Gus lifted his fist in the air when he heard them. And even I joined in the whooping then.

After the ceremony, Gus found us out on the crowded front lawn that opened out onto the Rideau Canal. He came to me and hugged me first. He stuck one arm around my shoulders and pulled me in. Then, only for me, he said, "Little sister, you're gonna get your day like this one. And then we'll all cry out like warriors for you too."

Just as he leaned back from the hug and we grinned excitedly at each other, my mom's camera flashed. That moment frozen in time. My brother and I, equally proud to call each other *tcinedagan*.

I pick up the phone. "Hello?"

"Nice to know you're still shit at leaving messages."

My eyes roll up toward my brows and I shake my head, even though I know he can't see me. "It's good to hear from you too. Kinda thought you disappeared for a while there since you took your sweet time finally getting back to me."

Mom watches me as I push the blanket off and move to walk through the living room on my way toward my bedroom. She waves to get my attention and mouths, "Who's that?" while pointing with her lips to the phone in my hand.

"Been busy."

"You are just a ray of sunshine, you know that?"

In the background, I hear Mom say, "Oh, it's Gus," before letting her attention wander back to her book.

I head upstairs to my bedroom and shut the door. Closing the door means it'll start to get warm and stuffy in here, but I don't mind. It's not like I expect Mom to listen to our conversation, but I'd rather she didn't catch me asking questions about the land. I step over a crumpled pile of laundry to sit on my bed.

"Your message said something about that stupid quarry?"

I sigh. Does everyone in my family hate the quarry? With Gus, I think it's because talking about anything that has to do with Dad is hard for him. Hating everything is easier. He'll never admit to it, but it's close to the truth.

I mean for my voice to be gentle when I speak, but it just comes out irritated. "What's your problem with it? You know, sometimes I feel like I'm the older one, not you."

"What's my problem with it? It's a damn burden, that's what. Dad left it to us knowing full well it would only ever be a total fucking mess. Have you had to deal with Heath yet?" His words are biting and his voice is lilting in the condescending way he's developed since he left home.

"Not directly, but yeah, I heard him talking about it the other day."

"Greedy bastard has wanted it for years. What did he say?"

Gus is crankier than usual. When he gets in moods like this, it's hard to talk to him. He can be a real ass when he wants to be. I consider ending the conversation now, saving myself the trouble. But if I do that, I don't get any of the answers I've been hoping to find.

"Hazel, what did he say?"

"Stop saying my name like that."

"Like what?"

"Like it tastes like something you want to spit out."

Gus pauses. He takes an exasperated breath. When he apologizes, I hear a trace of the brother I knew growing up. His voice softens, emotion touching its edges. He sounds tired. "I'm sorry. It's been the worst week. I shouldn't be taking it out on you."

He's caught me off guard. I'm used to our conversations being battles. This sounds too much like a truce. "Uh, yeah. It's not very nice of you."

"Okay, so tell me about Heath then."

"This was, like, almost two weeks ago now. I don't really remember. But he was all in a huff. His face goes so red, oh my god. He looks like a moulting walrus—all pink skin and white whiskers. It's so weird."

Gus laughs. "Ah, he's still got that same moustache, I take it?"

"Yeah, it's bigger than it used to be."

"Impressive."

"I don't know about that. He's starting to look like a puffy Hulk Hogan."

"Also impressive."

"Yeah, I guess. Anyway, he was in the Band Office when I was there and he was shouting about not getting the quarry—"

"Not surprising."

"Said something about the Council making excuses and whatnot about why they aren't giving him the rights to open it up again."

Gus clicks his tongue. "It's not their decision. If the land was Dad's and now ours, then it's not like the Council can even move on that. They'd need to talk to us."

I sink back into the pillows on my bed. "Okay, I have questions about that. How is there even a quarry if the land is still in our name?"

"Shady deal after shady deal after shady deal."

"But I thought the Ottawa River Mining Corporation went ahead and dug it out? They seemed legitimate enough."

"What job are you doing up there and how do you know about that company?" The genuine confusion in my brother's voice annoys me. He would know the answers to those questions already if he cared enough to stay in touch.

"I'm a casual hire for the Lands and Memberships department. Sorting out old boxes and stuff. I found a bunch of letters about the start of the quarry the other day."

Now he's interested. "Who wrote the letters?"

"Indian agent and some guy named Philippe Gagnon and then . . . Oh, I don't remember the other guy's name, but he works for the Ottawa River Mining Corporation. And a few from the DSGIA's office."

"Lawrence Wright?"

"Yeah, him."

"Are they original letters? Shit, Haze, that could be super important stuff you're looking at."

"I know," I snap. But I didn't know they were as vital as Gus is making them out to be. "Can I get back to my question now?"

"Holeh, she's cranky too."

"You keep interrupting me. Of course, I'm cranky."

"Gwan den."

"Thank you." Gus always slips into Rez talk when he wants to lighten the mood. It's nice to hear. Reminds me of old times, when talk was easy between us. I smile and relax. "'Kay, so. I was saying that that company started a mine and then they had to stop. I read in those letters that there wasn't an actual land surrender. Now, wouldn't that be all kinds of illegal for them to keep going? Like, trespassing?"

He doesn't answer right away, and I can hear him thinking in the silence. "It's trespassing. But that's a big deal. If that *did* happen, then there should be some evidence or a paper trail. Is there anything else about this in those boxes?"

"Something about the mine not being able to continue because the Indian agent couldn't get the people to surrender."

"Yeah, but there's a mine."

"There's a quarry."

"Same fucking thing. I'm hanging up now."

"No, no! Gus, wait! Okay, I'll stop, I'll stop."

"Good. Jesus Christ, it's annoying when you correct everything I say."

Pushing myself off my bed, I walk over to the window and lean against the varnished wooden sill. The leaves are starting to turn. Fall always comes so much earlier up here. I used to think that there were only two months of summer, which was an obvious side effect from being in school. Still not convinced, though. The leaves are green until the autumnal equinox and then it's like they can't get to the ground fast enough. Then it's only a short few weeks until snow and cold and the long dark that is a Northern winter. I set my eyes on a pair of chickadees flitting in and out of the evergreen trees in our front yard.

"What am I supposed to do? It's sounding like this shit is serious."

"It *is* serious. You know that the Rez never made any money off the mine? Nothing. Not even a nickel."

"How is that even legal?" I can't believe what he's telling me. What's more, I can't believe I didn't know sooner.

He laughs humourlessly. "It wasn't. But the thing was the Band got payment that kept them all quiet. I spent a good chunk of time a few years back trying to figure all this shit out and I got nowhere. Jesus, you work a few days at that place and you find a bunch of original letters. Hey, tell me, you find anything else signed by that Gagnon guy yet?"

"Do you mean Philippe?" I ask. "The guy who owned the local company?"

"Yeah, him."

The casual way Gus mentions Gagnon irks me. How do I reply? Do I tell him what I heard at the Band Office? Should Gus know about the deal Dad made? Maybe he knows already. My bedroom suddenly feels stuffy, boxed in. I need air. My lungs start to burn.

I gasp.

"What?" Gus says, concern clear in his intonation.

"Nothing, it's nothing. Sorry."

"Sounded like someone walked over your grave."

Nervous laughter is all I can give him until I catch my breath. "His name came up a few times."

"I'm convinced he's the one behind it all. The mine, the money, the lies."

"I don't know. They never went forward with his company's bid for the mine. How could he be involved if he wasn't ever chosen to have a part in the whole thing?"

"Oh, I see," he says, as if he's realizing something. "You haven't found out yet?"

"Found out what yet?"

"Gagnon? Yeah, he might not have gotten that bid outright, but he gets the mine eventually."

"How the hell did he manage that? Côté didn't recommend him for the job. His letter was so slimy and desperate. He said that he'd get 'reliable' Indians to work for him! I might not have worked in this field long, but even I know that's colonizer talk for saying they won't be drunks."

"Or that they'll get off the couch and work. I'm sure that's what he wanted to say."

"Ugh, sick." The two birds I've been watching aren't playing after all. It looks as if they're fighting. They keep darting in and out of the same patch of needles. The smaller bird seems panicked, little feathers puffed out and ragged. "Gus, can you just tell me what you know, please?"

"Right. That Gagnon guy? Once the government changes from Liberal to Conservative, he gets hired on as Indian agent for our whole area."

"What? How?"

"Friends in the government." Gus's words have that edge to them again. Colonial talk like this always kills the Indian in his voice. "Have enough connections and you can get anything you want. Gagnon wanted that mine, so his buddies helped him. Guess there's something to be said about camaraderie, huh?"

"That can't have been legal? You can't just make a job for someone who isn't right for it." I sound like I'm pleading for a different answer. I hate desperation.

"They had the power. They could do anything they wanted. You think the government is gonna listen to a bunch of disenfranchised Indians crying for help? When has that ever worked out for us, huh?"

I don't know how to answer him.

He exhales harshly into the phone, and the sound makes me jump. "Look, I gotta go now. I have plans with some people from work. Let me know if you find out any more depressing shit. You know how that thrills me."

Gus hangs up.

The little bird is pushed from the tree. The bigger one takes its place and calls out triumphantly.

◘ ◘ ◘

Coming back to work after talking with Gus has been disappointing. Every document makes me angry even if it doesn't have Gagnon's now familiar messy signature on it. I am so sick of this conference room. The colour of the walls, the smell of the vinyl chairs, the smoothness of the lacquered laminate tabletop. Everything. I am sick of every damn thing in this room—even the artwork. The painting of the old Indian woman that I used to find so beautiful with her dark, sad eyes, now just frustrates me.

I remember thinking that there was only a knowing sadness in her expression, but I was wrong. There's more there. The lines around her eyes are like a silent laugh behind the hurt. The determination and hardness in her gaze asks—no—*demands* that you look at her. *See* her. She is staring her colonizer right in the face. Last week, this revelation had me thrilled, my little red fist in the air. Her painted power reassured me. Gave me permission to dig deeper. Mine for gold, not just silver ore. And for a while my passion renewed. I went through box after box of correspondence. Read every letter, every census, every enfranchisement request and found nothing. I am officially stuck.

Dead in the water.

And now the painted *gôkom* mocks me. I'm tired of her. Two days earlier, I tried moving across the room, but her eyes follow me. Sitting with my back to her does no good either because I can feel her gaze on me, like the heat of a fire warming through my clothes and skin until my bones crack from the weight of her stare. So now I've settled with sitting across from her, but this place is still uncomfortable. Conference rooms are supposed to be filled with living, breathing people. And here I am stuck with nothing but dead words and rotting paper for company.

The table is covered in an overlapping layer of yellowed paper and aging manila folders. Like almost everything I've come across so far, the documents are a mismatched collection spanning nearly a century. Some of the pages are finely dressed in looping ink and embossed seals, while others are harshly splattered with the punctuated formality of a typewriter. The letters penned by machines have become my fast favourites, because they're the easiest to read. Yet they get me nowhere, since the mine closed before the first typewriter made its way to our lonely slice of Indian Country. So my days are spent in search of that telltale, forward-leaning scribble bearing the hastily scrawled signature of M. Philippe Gagnon.

With as little effort as possible, I let my hand fall into the box closest to me. I fish around and grab a folder, nearly giving myself another paper cut. The folder flops open when I drop it onto the table, and I lean forward, my eyes absently gazing over the contents. I gasp so hard and fast that I choke on my own spit.

Joni's voice comes in surprisingly loudly from down the hall: "You okay down there, Hazel?"

I cough until I can get control of my voice again. "Fine, thanks!"

But I'm not. I've found the letter. The one with those two all-important words following Gagnon's name: *Indian Agent*. Just like Gus had said. I read the letter over and over until the words become etched in my memory.

January 13th, 1912
Ste-Marie des Oblats, Québec

Dear sir,

You knew this day would come. My friends in the government are more than happy to relieve you of your position. I look forward to taking over and improving upon whatever you might have accomplished.

Sincerely,

M. Philippe Gagnon
Indian Agent, Sagi'idiwin Agency, Québec

I feel sick. The same man who spoke of taming the Indian savages with hard labour was suddenly the one in charge of our welfare. Leaving us with only the Indian Act to protect us. This is why the quarry exists, despite the roadblocks. Rules mean nothing to a man who can rewrite them. He's left his mark carved into the landscape, dug deep into the earth.

I stare at the letter until the words blur. Even though I knew this was coming, it's still hard to accept. I can't look at it anymore. I toss the letter back, slamming the folder shut as if to put distance between Gagnon and me. My first impression of this man was right. He's only looking out for himself. His mocking, self-satisfied tone is enough to prove that. If this wasn't an important document, I'd tear it to shreds myself. Briefly, I entertain the idea of photocopying it so I can do just that, but it's not worth the effort. None of this seems worth it.

I look down at my palms, covered in tiny red lines. These paper cuts are my battle scars. I turn my hands over and study the pale blue of my veins. My hands look older than I do. Touching the past will do that. Balling them into fists stretches the skin taut over bone. I hold them like that until my knuckles turn white.

Tap. Tap.

Beak on glass.

When I open my fists, the blood rushes to my fingertips. I

wiggle my fingers and bend my wrists to get the feeling back. The skin darkens red and then returns to pale brown.

Tap-tap. Tap-tap-tap.

Sighing, I haul myself to my feet and take the two steps toward the window. It makes a whooshing sound when I lift it open. Nanabush pecks at the screen until he can push his beak through. With a satisfying *zip*, he slices a hole through the mesh. Cool air flows in behind him.

He soars around the ceiling once before landing on the back of one of the chairs. His talons dig into the cheap vinyl and poor padding, leaving clear marks. For a second I'm concerned that someone will notice, but it's nothing a little duct tape can't fix. The chairs aren't much better off even without the claw marks.

Nanabush readjusts his wings as he settles down. He looks at me with those grey eyes, and instantly I know he knows how upset I am.

"Indian agent. Gagnon became the goddamn Indian agent." My voice is thick with frustration. "That's how he got the mine. He just gave it to himself!"

—*Men are predictable. They haven't changed in thousands of years. This news isn't shocking.*

Exasperated, I drop my hands to the table. "How are you not bothered by this? This is disgusting. Wasn't it enough taking all our land in the first place? No, they had to do it again and again and again."

—*What are you going to do about it?*

"What the hell *can* I do? It's not like a handful of letters is going to get us the land back. I can't mail these in to the prime minister and tell him we were robbed. There's not enough proof here. Besides, all that letter says is that he's taking over. There isn't a mention of the mine. I don't even know that he did anything wrong. At least not obviously." I take my head in my hands and sink into one of the chairs.

Nanabush hops down onto the table. His feet click across the papers and I worry that he might rip something important. Slowly, I raise my head. I watch him for a moment. He's looking over the letters I have strewn across the tabletop. It's weird watching him read. Human intelligence in an animal is unsettling. He's completely invested in reading each document. When he finishes one, he reaches down with his beak and tosses it aside to read the next one underneath. But why?

"Nanabush?"

He croaks but keeps reading.

"Why do you even care about this?"

That catches his attention. He stops hopping about and brings his gaze to meet mine. His head twitches to the right twice and then once to the left as he blinks. When he behaves like this, he could be any normal crow.

"The quarry. Gagnon. My dad. Me. All of this doesn't seem like it matters, or it shouldn't. I know the Seven said you had to come and help me. But all this shit has only made me more upset."

—*Those stuffy old coots said it was important for both of us, so here I am.*

I lean my elbows forward on the table. "Did they say anything about the quarry?"

—*No. Not exactly.*

"'Not exactly?' What does that mean?"

He shifts his weight from foot to foot, adjusting the fold of his wings.

—*They told me to find you. Find your dad. And they said I would understand when I saw an exchange marked by a joining of hands. Cryptic as usual. You can't trust old gods.*

"What does *that* mean? Hands coming together seems more like a union than an exchange." But even as I say that, it comes to me. "A handshake, they meant a handshake."

—*Are you sure?*

"Yes, I'm sure. I'll prove it to you." I stand up quickly, pushing the chair away from me. It thuds when it hits the wall.

—*Handshake. Why didn't I think of that? I guess you spend enough time with wings, you forget that arms don't all end with feathers.*

I reach out for him and he quickly hops away from me, looking offended. "No, come back. You need to take me to the past. We have to find the handshake they talked about."

—*You think I can go back whenever I want without a destination? I'm not some runner you can send to find whatever you're looking for.*

"Search engine."

—*What?*

"We have a name for that now: search engine. But that doesn't matter. Let's just go."

—*I need something to link me. If you want me to find something I wasn't there for, you need to give me a proper link. I can't just search the memories of whomever I want.*

I pause with my hand outstretched. The distance between us is small. "Use me. Use the name Gagnon. We seem to be important in all of this, so let's find out why."

He looks skeptical. The doubt reads plainly on his face as he blinks at my hand. Nanabush weighs the thought in his mind before he inches closer, letting me feel the cool silken black of his feathers.

—*I don't know if this is good for you. Humans aren't supposed to move through memory like I do. There's a reason you can only go back when you're dreaming.*

"I don't care. Everything about the present hurts. How can this be any more damaging?"

He nods. And then his eyes turn milky white. There's a breath like the pause before an honour beat on the big drum and then everything around me fades. That feeling of falling and flying pitches my stomach as Nanabush tugs me along after him. I see this experience for what it is this time. Not blindness, but the blur of memories as they move past us. Like white light before it hits a prism. Everything occurring at once at a speed that can't be perceived by the human eye. Then we crash into the glass and the colours spread out, each wavelength travelling at its own speed so they can be seen as they exist on their own. Individual. Only here, it isn't light. It's time and memory.

There's a change in the way I feel the skin around my body, and I know we've found what we're looking for. It's coming up. Prism.

Crash.

Scatter.

Pick one and focus.

We're at the quarry. I smell water and rock. I know that scent. I've grown up with it. But I shouldn't smell the water on stone or feel the moisture in the air. We can't have gone very far back. I take a few steps until I'm at the edge of the drop-off. I look down and see the glassy blue at the bottom, brilliantly clear even here. It looks so familiar. Almost as if this moment could have been only yesterday. Nanabush lands on my shoulder. I feel his talons but they don't hurt me.

"Are you sure this is right?" I ask.

—Yes. This is where it happens. But move from the edge. I can't save you if you decide to jump.

"I'm not going to jump." As I step back, a few rocks shift and fall. The water ripples when the stones break the surface, but I can't hear anything. It takes a big object to make a splash.

I can see Dad taking offence to the very idea that he would go back on his word, but he forces down the indignation. "That's correct. You have my word that I'll proceed with the land transfer as soon as I get my own paperwork in order. Then it's a matter of arranging the lease and your payment. Once we get that all together, this mine will be yours."

I stop breathing. My mouth goes dry. What is he doing? He's giving the mine to this man. He's handing it over. How can he do that? Numbness starts to move through my limbs. A weight settles on my chest and shoulders and I start to gasp for air. The scene in front of me wobbles off-kilter as I shake my head. No. No. No.

"What about the backlash? You said that many of your people would be divided by this. That they would worry about the environment. Is that going to be an issue?" Gagnon motions to the trees surrounding the quarry as if they stand in for all the damage that will be caused by his desire to reopen the mine.

"There'll be those who say that we're hurting Mother Earth, but they'll be wrong. This mine is important for the community. We need the money to help us build a future. Once they understand the jobs and the growth that'll come to the region because of the work we do here, they'll get it and back off." Dad gives Thomas a reassuring nod. "You leave that part to me."

"All right, Abraham. You have me convinced." He crosses the space between them and pauses with his hand outstretched. "We have a deal."

The smile on my dad's face is so genuine, it feels like a slap across my cheek. He takes a hand from his pocket.

No. He can't do this. There's a reason this mine hasn't been reopened. What is he doing? This isn't right. He can't sign it over to this man. Doesn't he know what will happen? I can't watch. I don't want to see him do this. I start to backpedal, moving as far

Watching the tiny waves, I feel dizzy and weak in my joints. I'm suddenly painfully aware that it's a very long drop.

—*I think we're early. The pair of them should be by soon.*

"Who is it?"

—*It's best if you wait and see.*

"Best for who? Me? Or do you mean you'll enjoy it more to watch me find out?"

—*Wait.*

Footsteps approach from the old truck road. There are voices too, but they're too far for me to hear what they're saying. I turn away from the quarry and watch the clearing for whomever it is I'm waiting on. I can only assume Gagnon will be here. But the timing still has me confused. I shake the thoughts from my head and take Nanabush's instruction to wait.

The raspberry bushes at the mouth of the trail rustle as Dad pushes his way out into the open. He's older than the last time I saw him. Thinner too. His hair is grey. It's pulled back into a tail at the base of his skull. It's shorter. His face is lined and there's something sad about the colour of his eyes.

"What the hell?" I mumble. "This wasn't that long ago. I can tell just by looking at him. Look at the way he's trying to catch his breath. He's sick."

This can't be more than two years ago. That tired look on his face. He's going to wear it from now until the day he decides to die. My eyes sting.

I go to say something else, but Nanabush quiets me. He nods to the bushes as another figure emerges.

This man I don't know. He's young, especially next to my father. Somewhere in his mid-thirties, maybe? He's dressed well in a navy blue suit. It's tailored. His hair is cut short, and even in this faded colouring, I can see that it's light brown. He's fair with blue eyes. When he straightens up after leaving the bush, he stands taller than my tired father. The smile he gives to the old man is warm and sincere. He is too nice.

"Are you all right there, Mr. Gagnon?" the memory of my dad asks.

I look at Nanabush. "What? No. That's not right. Who is that?"

His talons grip my shoulder and I go quiet.

"Yes, I'm fine. Thank you for asking." The clear honesty in his voice bothers me. He laughs gently. "I guess I'm not quite dressed for this sort of hike."

Dad laughs in reply. "No, sir, you certainly are not."

Gagnon raises his hands in front of him. "Please, call me Thomas. If we are to be partners, we should try to be friends. I don't want any of these formalities. Besides, I feel like I should be calling you 'sir.'"

"That's a dig at my age, isn't it? Ah, well, it's better than 'old man.'" Dad sticks his hands into the pockets of his jeans.

The friendliness between them is unsettling. Why are they so nice to each other? Doesn't Dad know who this guy is? Who his family is? What they did?

They walk along the open space between the forest and where I'm standing at the quarry's edge. Their shoes crunch on the rocks, Dad's worn trainers and Gagnon's shiny oxfords. Thomas slips slightly as he walks on the loose gravel. I smile.

"This is it. Big chunk of land. There's lots of water down in the pit, which I'm sure you're aware of already. Don't know how you plan on taking it out, but I guess that's your decision to make once you get started on the whole operation—" Dad gets cut off by a barrage of coughing. He tries hard to fight back, but it keeps coming. He holds a hand up when Thomas tries to offer help.

I want to run to his side. I want to scream at him to go to a

different doctor. Seek another opinion. Tell him that th[...] he's coughing isn't because of some cold, but something[...] a home inside his lungs. Eventually, he gets the coughi[...] control, but his voice is weaker when he speaks agai[...] about that. The wet air here always gets me coughing."

"It's not a problem. If you're sure you can continu[...] am on board." I would have expected this man to hav[...] Québécois accent, but there's hardly a trace of it. His [...] impeccable.

Dad nods. "Oh yes. I'm okay. That way we came i[...] old road the trucks and other big equipment used to use[...] out about half a kilometre down the highway. Pretty ov[...] but it wouldn't take too long to clear-cut through it."

Gagnon takes out a pen and pad and starts jotti[...] notes. He walks away from my dad and moves to the edg[...] where I'm standing with Nanabush on my shoulder. I lo[...] closer at him. He's handsome. There's no denying it. [...] people are hard to hate, but I'm sure I'll find a way.

"I have a few ideas of how we'll drain the pit, but th[...] to be run by our engineers. Rest assured, we'll do this [...] wouldn't want to do anything that would disrupt the [...] ity." Gagnon continues to write. I try to see what he [...] paper, but his handwriting runs in the family.

Dad smiles. "That's what I like to hear. That's [...] important thing, you know. That our communities a[...] by the development. Things haven't always gone our v[...] past, but I want to change that. You and I will change t[...]

Gagnon returns the smile, and I'm bothered by t[...] ity of it. "Yes, I think we will. Now, I know that you [...] me anything in writing yet, as you said earlier. But am [...] assuming that you won't back out on this deal?"

Watching the tiny waves, I feel dizzy and weak in my joints. I'm suddenly painfully aware that it's a very long drop.

—*I think we're early. The pair of them should be by soon.*

"Who is it?"

—*It's best if you wait and see.*

"Best for who? Me? Or do you mean you'll enjoy it more to watch me find out?"

—*Wait.*

Footsteps approach from the old truck road. There are voices too, but they're too far for me to hear what they're saying. I turn away from the quarry and watch the clearing for whomever it is I'm waiting on. I can only assume Gagnon will be here. But the timing still has me confused. I shake the thoughts from my head and take Nanabush's instruction to wait.

The raspberry bushes at the mouth of the trail rustle as Dad pushes his way out into the open. He's older than the last time I saw him. Thinner too. His hair is grey. It's pulled back into a tail at the base of his skull. It's shorter. His face is lined and there's something sad about the colour of his eyes.

"What the hell?" I mumble. "This wasn't that long ago. I can tell just by looking at him. Look at the way he's trying to catch his breath. He's sick."

This can't be more than two years ago. That tired look on his face. He's going to wear it from now until the day he decides to die. My eyes sting.

I go to say something else, but Nanabush quiets me. He nods to the bushes as another figure emerges.

This man I don't know. He's young, especially next to my father. Somewhere in his mid-thirties, maybe? He's dressed well in a navy blue suit. It's tailored. His hair is cut short, and even in this faded colouring, I can see that it's light brown. He's fair with blue eyes. When he straightens up after leaving the bush, he stands taller than my tired father. The smile he gives to the old man is warm and sincere. He is too nice.

"Are you all right there, Mr. Gagnon?" the memory of my dad asks.

I look at Nanabush. "What? No. That's not right. Who is that?"

His talons grip my shoulder and I go quiet.

"Yes, I'm fine. Thank you for asking." The clear honesty in his voice bothers me. He laughs gently. "I guess I'm not quite dressed for this sort of hike."

Dad laughs in reply. "No, sir, you certainly are not."

Gagnon raises his hands in front of him. "Please, call me Thomas. If we are to be partners, we should try to be friends. I don't want any of these formalities. Besides, I feel like I should be calling you 'sir.'"

"That's a dig at my age, isn't it? Ah, well, it's better than 'old man.'" Dad sticks his hands into the pockets of his jeans.

The friendliness between them is unsettling. Why are they so nice to each other? Doesn't Dad know who this guy is? Who his family is? What they did?

They walk along the open space between the forest and where I'm standing at the quarry's edge. Their shoes crunch on the rocks, Dad's worn trainers and Gagnon's shiny oxfords. Thomas slips slightly as he walks on the loose gravel. I smile.

"This is it. Big chunk of land. There's lots of water down in the pit, which I'm sure you're aware of already. Don't know how you plan on taking it out, but I guess that's your decision to make once you get started on the whole operation—" Dad gets cut off by a barrage of coughing. He tries hard to fight back, but it keeps coming. He holds a hand up when Thomas tries to offer help.

I want to run to his side. I want to scream at him to go to a different doctor. Seek another opinion. Tell him that the reason he's coughing isn't because of some cold, but something making a home inside his lungs. Eventually, he gets the coughing under control, but his voice is weaker when he speaks again. "Sorry about that. The wet air here always gets me coughing."

"It's not a problem. If you're sure you can continue, then I am on board." I would have expected this man to have a harsh Québécois accent, but there's hardly a trace of it. His English is impeccable.

Dad nods. "Oh yes. I'm okay. That way we came in was the old road the trucks and other big equipment used to use. It comes out about half a kilometre down the highway. Pretty overgrown, but it wouldn't take too long to clear-cut through it."

Gagnon takes out a pen and pad and starts jotting down notes. He walks away from my dad and moves to the edge near to where I'm standing with Nanabush on my shoulder. I look a little closer at him. He's handsome. There's no denying it. Beautiful people are hard to hate, but I'm sure I'll find a way.

"I have a few ideas of how we'll drain the pit, but they'll have to be run by our engineers. Rest assured, we'll do this properly. I wouldn't want to do anything that would disrupt the community." Gagnon continues to write. I try to see what he's put on paper, but his handwriting runs in the family.

Dad smiles. "That's what I like to hear. That's the most important thing, you know. That our communities aren't hurt by the development. Things haven't always gone our way in the past, but I want to change that. You and I will change that."

Gagnon returns the smile, and I'm bothered by the sincerity of it. "Yes, I think we will. Now, I know that you can't offer me anything in writing yet, as you said earlier. But am I right in assuming that you won't back out on this deal?"

I can see Dad taking offence to the very idea that he would go back on his word, but he forces down the indignation. "That's correct. You have my word that I'll proceed with the land transfer as soon as I get my own paperwork in order. Then it's a matter of arranging the lease and your payment. Once we get that all together, this mine will be yours."

I stop breathing. My mouth goes dry. What is he doing? He's giving the mine to this man. He's handing it over. How can he do that? Numbness starts to move through my limbs. A weight settles on my chest and shoulders and I start to gasp for air. The scene in front of me wobbles off-kilter as I shake my head. No. No. No.

"What about the backlash? You said that many of your people would be divided by this. That they would worry about the environment. Is that going to be an issue?" Gagnon motions to the trees surrounding the quarry as if they stand in for all the damage that will be caused by his desire to reopen the mine.

"There'll be those who say that we're hurting Mother Earth, but they'll be wrong. This mine is important for the community. We need the money to help us build a future. Once they understand the jobs and the growth that'll come to the region because of the work we do here, they'll get it and back off." Dad gives Thomas a reassuring nod. "You leave that part to me."

"All right, Abraham. You have me convinced." He crosses the space between them and pauses with his hand outstretched. "We have a deal."

The smile on my dad's face is so genuine, it feels like a slap across my cheek. He takes a hand from his pocket.

No. He can't do this. There's a reason this mine hasn't been reopened. What is he doing? This isn't right. He can't sign it over to this man. Doesn't he know what will happen? I can't watch. I don't want to see him do this. I start to backpedal, moving as far away from this as I can. But I see their hands meet. They shake.

I slip off the edge.

I feel myself falling. I'm screaming. Then there is hot pain in my shoulder as Nanabush digs in. Everything blurs until I see only the burn of white light.

The conference room comes back into focus. I'm breathless, staring up into the blinking fluorescent bulbs lining the ceiling. My heart hurts as it knocks against my chest. Nanabush's claws are still in my shoulder. Emotion starts to pool inside my eyes, but it's cut short when I hear the sound of a fist rapping crisply on the door frame. I spin around. The bird slips into the shadows.

Joni is standing there with that same happy perma-smile that she always wears. She's leaning into the room slightly, her right shoulder coming around the metal frame. "Hazel, sorry to bug you while you're workin' over here. Phew, looks like you were workin' hard! Dat focus on your face ever intense."

"Hi," I manage.

"I was just showing our new business investor around the Band Office, and I figured now would be a good time to introduce you two since you're back here working anehways. Give ya a break from the papers at least!" Joni steps into the room and a man comes in after her.

I already know his bright eyes and kind smile.

"This here is Thomas Gagnon. He's the director of a company dat wants to do some development here on the Rez. He's gonna be working with me and those O&M boys on some tings." She puts a hand on his shoulder and then motions for him to walk over to me.

I don't move closer.

"Thomas, this is Hazel Ellis. She's kinda like—oh, what's that fancy city word I always hear in dem movies—my intern! Yes, dat's it. Working away on these old files back here." Joni keeps smiling. I wonder if her cheeks hurt when she gets home after a long day of work.

"It's nice to meet you, Hazel." Thomas extends his hand. Everything about his demeanour is welcoming. There's an eagerness in the way he holds himself.

I don't like it.

His smile falters slightly when I leave his hand hanging in the air between us. My shoulder aches with pain, but I don't react.

"Perhaps we will get a chance to work together down the road," he says.

"Why?"

He hesitates, tugging on the hem of his suit jacket as he straightens up. "We have a mutual connection in Joni. Our paths seem to connect."

"They do seem to do that."

Joni finally clues in to the tension that is quickly settling in the room. She clears her throat and awkwardly claps her hands together to get our attention. "We better keep on going in dis office. It's almost quittin' time and I want you to meet everyone. Let's leave little Hazel to her work."

Thomas leans back and then starts to follow Joni out of the room. He pauses in the doorway and gives me one more glance. "Your father was a good man. I am sorry for your loss."

His words crash into me and move right through me all at once. I can only stare at him in reply. He pulls the door shut behind him, and I'm left in a growing quiet. The pain in my shoulder feels worse.

There are six punctures beneath my collarbone and two on my back.

I bleed.

12

ONADOTÂN

Falling into the shadows, I feel my feathers melt away as if they are nothing but an old layer of skin. I shed my wings, trading them for the hands I so dearly missed. The beak in front of my lips breaks away, and I take in a gasping breath. I exhale and inhale, over and over. It's hard work trying to fill human lungs with a crow's breath. My eyes feel the same, but they see differently. Everything is both familiar and frustratingly foreign. Remembering how to use this body is like humming only the melody of a song. It is half-started, half-finished. Incomplete because I cannot find its ending. Or maybe it's the beginning I'm missing?

Pushing my body up, I can see where I've slipped from this time. I see the four walls of the conference room Hazel has been chained to these past few weeks. Days? Time is a hard concept on this side of the Wheel. Here, in the Anishnaabe world, it matters. Hours, minutes, and seconds carry a weight and an urgency. Not so in the Spirit World. I should try to get used to it. After all, half of who I am is tied to the people on this side. And what I want—getting what I want—is tied to the fate of this place. Or so I've been told. I've been lied to before. But I don't think that's the case this time. Someone like me, someone who lies as much as I do, can tell when it's happening to them. I can smell deceit from miles away. So, no. I don't think that I should doubt what I've been told. The Seven aren't known for dishonesty. Quite the opposite. It's sickening. Hard to like people who only ever tell the truth. There's kindness in lying. The same cannot be said about candour.

It's been an eternity since I've felt the proper heaviness of four limbs; I can't get my head and my body to connect. I wait. Give myself more time. I take the opportunity to look back up at Hazel. From down here in the shadows, it looks like she's moving in slow motion, like seaweed in the undercurrent. I should not have left her alone—not after what happened. But what choice did I have? I can't risk being seen in a place like that. A crow has no reason to be among people. No one would invite a carrion-eater into their home.

That man is still there. What was his name? Thomas. Yes, that's it. How boring and dull. Not surprising. A name a family gives a child when they have a legacy to uphold. I don't doubt that there has been a wealth of Thomas Gagnons before he decided to come along.

There's no real reason for me or Hazel to hate Thomas Gagnon beyond the sins of his forefather. We're forced to tolerate him. Stand in the same room as him. Breathe the same air. Hazel is tense. He says something to her before he finally leaves the room. I can't hear what it is. There's blood blossoming like a poppy on her shoulder from where my talons sunk into her skin. I warned her it would be dangerous. Memories leave marks, the kind that may never heal. I said I wouldn't be able to save her if she fell.

I lied.

No, it was a half-truth. I thought what I was saying was correct. Honestly, I didn't think I'd be able to save her. I wasn't sure if she'd need saving. The memory wasn't hers to begin with, so I didn't think she was in danger of getting lost in it. Even so, that wasn't a risk I was willing to take. Not with the Seven breathing down my neck. That and I couldn't just let her fall into the unknown without trying to do something. Nobody's that heartless.

Hazel's image starts to blur around the edges before she disappears entirely. Everything around me starts to fade to that familiar nothingness of the other side. There is always darkness before the Spirit World welcomes anyone. Then, slowly, it begins to take shape. A glow starts on the horizon. It builds until everything around me is bathed in a haze of twilight. Or is it dawn? I can never be sure. But time doesn't matter here.

What matters is that there is always light touched by darkness. Ink drops in a glass of water.

The Spirit World is vast. It stretches out farther than anyone has ever explored. Men like Columbus and Cartier and Champlain would shame themselves if they ever tried to find new worlds here. This place extends beyond the reaches of the imagination. And yet, every time I come through, I always end up in the same village. The same tiny winter camp in the middle of the bush. There is fresh snow on the ground that glitters in the low light. The evergreens and birches at the edge of the wigwams are silhouettes against the sky. The camp is asleep. It always is. Only one fire is going. The Sacred Fire burns brightly, illuminating the hides of the great teepee at the centre of the clearing. Smoke billows around the poles and climbs even higher into the starry expanse above. I can hear voices from inside the teepee. I don't need to hear their words to know that they're talking about me. A trickster like myself always makes for good conversation.

I stand up, stumbling on these unfamiliar legs. Inside my moccasins, I wiggle my toes to try to remember how to walk. As a crow, all my time on the ground is spent hopping—not the most dignified way to get from place to place. My bones ache as I force my old body to move. How ridiculous I must look. Face lined with age while my legs wobble like a newborn calf.

The snow crunches beneath my moose hide. It feels good to have the ground meet my feet like this. There's a safety in knowing you can run— across an open field, through a forest—one that I'd forgotten since being trapped inside that other body. I missed the solid strength of being human. People seem to think that birds have freedom, that flying is the ultimate expression of a soul unbound. It's a pretty image. Incorrect, but pretty nonetheless. Having been bound to a form that only finds freedom by spreading its wings and taking to the sky, I can say with some authority that flying is little more than a novelty. One that I would gladly trade at any moment for a good, strong pair of hands.

Ah, hands.

How I have missed them.

I spread my fingers, crack my knuckles, clench into a fist. This is real freedom. Anyone who says otherwise has never had an itch they physically could not scratch. A beak can only do so much.

I move toward the great teepee, feeling small, even in this body, as I get closer. The hide is painted with footprints from each of the animals in creation. An overwhelming mass of paws, claws, and hooves covers the entire tent. But they cannot all be seen at once. Creation magic means that each group of animals pledges loyalty to one of the Seven. Crawlers to Tabasenimidiwin, swimmers to Tebwewin, four-leggeds to Manadji'idiwin, winged-ones to Sagi'idiwin, hunters to Sôginijiwin, two-leggeds to Gweyâkwâdiziwin, and the prey to Kaye Nibwâkawin. When their leader speaks, the creatures go walking.

I stand at the edge of the teepee, close enough that I can run my fingers along the hide. I trace the pointed claw-prints of a bird as it walks across the tent. I keep my eyes on the tracks until they disappear from view. Sagi'idiwin must be speaking. Their voice is quiet, so I cannot hear what they say. The long-toed footsteps of birds and other fliers make their way up and down the teepee, dancing in a round.

The power of the Seven used to send fear through my bones like a cold rain in the icy depths of winter. Was I bound to them like the others of my kind? For years, I cowered in their presence, darting into the shadows to avoid the power and might of the Seven. Until I learned that I was different than the others at their command. After all, was I not made of the very same clay as the Seven? I shared their blood, diluted though it was by mortality. I am at once of the Spirit World, the house of the Seven, and of the world of the People. I answer to none but myself because there are no others like me. Nanabush's fealty is to Nanabush alone.

Or it was.

That was when I was happy to live between the doorways—coming in through the East and leaving through the West as I pleased. I was of both worlds, so I lived between. Never truly mortal, so never bound by death. Yet not a pure being of the Spirit World, so chained to life. I thought I had won. That I had cheated.

Forgive me. I was young and foolish. I was not yet weary or worn thin. I hadn't known that I would one day grow tired of never being able to rest. How could I know that one day loneliness would grow in me like a sickness?

I run my fingers along the tanned leather of my buckskins. The bone breastplate on my chest feels heavy. Feathers weigh nothing. I wear them like skin. Clothes and jewellery feel like shackles. The wigwams that dot the camp are dark. Their owners must be sleeping. I let my gaze follow a seldom-used trail to the outskirts of the circle. There, covered in black furs, sits the wigwam I call my own. No smoke rises from the hole in the roof. It has been empty for some time. Seeing the dwelling abandoned hurts almost as much as being chained inside it. The Seven kept me there for years behind a door of birchbark and blood. I had meddled with their world too many times to be trusted on my own, so I was to be kept on a leash.

And so it would have been if Hazel hadn't let me out. When she crossed through the Western doorway and came upon the camp of the Seven, they were so enraptured in their own affairs, they failed to see her as she stumbled into my wigwam and set me free. The moment I felt the cool night air against my face, I thought I had escaped. But the power of the Seven runs deep, and they had found a way to keep my body from me. I remained bound to them but out of their reach on the human side of the doorway. And so, we made a deal.

Help the girl. Help the People. Earn my freedom.

Simple enough. That's how it appeared. I found Hazel quickly. Convincing her I was there to help proved to be much harder. Truth be told, I'm still not sure of where I stand with her on the matter. Each day that I worked to help her, I was closer to what I wanted. My body and my life.

The forest around me shifts in the night breeze. The naked birch trees sway and groan, so they sound as if they are speaking. At their roots comes low breathing and breaking twigs as black and brown bears trudge through the forest. They guard the camp and the way back into the world of the People. I am being watched. No matter how much I accomplish, I am still not trusted.

Being in my body is a gift, I know that much. How I've earned it is harder to figure out. I know that I'm not anywhere close to helping Hazel. She is still broken, maybe even more so now that I've shown her the handshake at the quarry. Yet, here I am. I'll hear all about my performance the second I step foot inside that teepee.

I walk around the great teepee until I am right outside the door. I'm so close that I can hear the flames of the Sacred Fire crack and spit. The hair on my body stands on end as I start to tremble. Pathetic. I hate that after everything, I fear them. Powerful beings holding me hostage is worthy of some ill will, but fear makes me angry. Cold sweat and a creased forehead. Lines on my face that make me older than I am. Makes me miss my feathers. Almost.

The footprints on the skin of the teepee fade as the voices fall silent. The wind picks up, blowing through the camp, making the door of the tent billow, spilling the firelight onto the snow at my feet.

A voice like thunder, Sôginijiwin, speaks.

—Come inside, Trickster. It is time we spoke.

13

ALONE

I look like shit.

I have been standing in front of the mirror in our bathroom for nearly twenty minutes. The door's shut even though Mom's not home. I need the extra buffer between "in here" and "out there." I'd hate for her to come back and hear my pathetic sobbing. Still, if she does, with the door shut there's no invitation to come and try to fix me. What would I tell her if she asked me what was wrong? That I know what Dad did because I went back into his memories with a magic crow? Mm-hmm, that'll go over well.

My eyelashes are dewy and sticking together like spider legs. My eyes are red, puffy. Grief. Ragged on my face. There's a throbbing pressure behind my forehead that has me pushing it into lines. Not only do I look sad, I look angry too. Completely ridiculous. Wish I could get that Iron Eyes Cody single-tear-down-my-cheek look. But no. Real tears from real pain don't look pretty. Snot-filled, gasping breaths, wailing—that's grief.

I touch the red stain on the back of my shirt. Guess today was a bad day to wear white. The fabric is torn from where Nanabush sunk his talons into me. If I ever doubted he was real, now I have my proof. Eight bloody marks on my right shoulder. But I'm lucky I got away with just that. It could have been worse. I assume. Nanabush disappeared before I could pull the broken pieces of myself back together. I didn't get to ask him. Next time we find each other, it'll be the first thing I say.

Slowly and carefully, I peel the shirt off my body, let it crumple to the floor. Exhaling, I gather my dark hair to one side and reach for the bottle of clear liquid. The alcohol burns when it hits my skin and I wince. The disinfectant makes the puncture marks along my collarbone and on the back of my shoulder bleed again for a moment. The red stands out against my beige skin. I watch it trickle along me before wiping it away. I have no idea how to bandage this, so I settle on cut gauze and medical tape. It holds, so it'll do for now.

My phone chimes the second I step out of the bathroom. It's Mom saying she's gone into town to grab a few things and she'll be home later with dinner. Chinese food, my favourite. Me and a lot of people here. I don't know what it is, but Indians love small-town Chinese food. Give us a buffet with some properly crispy egg rolls and we're happy.

This is good news. I have time to get myself together. Get my story straight. Hide this bandage. Hide the hurt on my face and in my heart. I want to ask Mom about the quarry. Ask her if she knew what Dad had been planning all along, but I know she'll cry and then so will I, and nothing will get done. Besides, I'm sick of crying. It hurts my head.

I take a few steps down the hallway with the intention of going into my room and into my closet for something to cover this mess, but something stops me at the doorway to my parents' room. No, Mom's room. That's who it belongs to now. Or that's what she's been trying to tell herself to make the sting of loneliness go away. Too bad Dad's still everywhere, even if she rearranged the furniture.

I move into the room, dragging my fingers along the deep mahogany of the sleigh bed. It's cool to the touch. Comforting. I walk to the far side of the bed and sit down, facing the wardrobe that used to belong to my father. In a way, it still does. It's full of his things. The doors creak when I pull them open, and I'm greeted with a collection of faded striped button-down shirts and warm sweaters in deep hues. A smile tugs on the corners of my mouth, but I can't feel the warmth that usually comes with it. I spot the shirt he was wearing that day at the quarry. Looking at it brings a sour taste to my mouth. I expect to feel angry, but instead I'm sad.

Despite the emotions wrestling inside me, I take the worn blue sweater and pull it over my head. The fabric is soft against my skin thanks to years of wear. The sleeves hang loose and baggy around my wrists and over my hands. The sweater dwarfs me, makes me feel small—like a child. If only I could get back to that. How does Nanabush do it? How does he step back in time, in memories, at will? As if it's as easy as looking at a photograph. More than that, how does he stay in the present? If I had that power, I'd stay back there. Happy forever.

Didn't he tell me that I was different than the rest? I'm able to move through memory alongside him. That sets me apart. Does it mean that there's something inside of me that's waiting to wake up?

I close my eyes and try to shut out the sounds and smells around me. Breathe in. One, two. Breathe out. Three, four. Again and again, until I can feel myself settling into a mindful silence. A quiet humming creeps into my ears. I feel like something is pulling on the edges of my body. I can smell a fire burning, the scent of sweetgrass and cedar. Then the house creaks, settling as the cold autumn air blows against it, and my eyes are open. I'm too aware, too awake, for this to work. And maybe too eager? Did I feel that change or is someone outside burning old leaves and wood?

I dig the heels of my hands into my eyes, rubbing until stars explode in my vision. Slowly, everything comes back into focus.

The top of Dad's wardrobe is still covered in things that Gus and I made him over the years. A duct tape wallet that he used for months before it started to fall apart. Two painted handprints with each of our names scribbled messily overtop them. A key chain that I beaded back in grade eight. There's a picture of me and Gus in a frame of coloured Popsicle sticks. Gus has a rat-tail and I've got one of those awful mushroom cuts. Dark times.

Seeing all these snippets from our lives makes me want more. He must have other things kicking around in here. Maybe in the junk drawer of the dresser. I tug it open and find what I'm looking for. I consider going through the stuff piece by piece, but that seems ridiculous when I could empty the whole thing out onto the bed. Papers and photographs fan out across the floral duvet. The pictures catch my eye instantly, so I gather them into a little pile and flick through them.

The ones that he decided to keep for himself seem to be picked completely at random. Sometimes, they're not even in focus. But I guess Dad had his reasons. Maybe the photos made him smile.

I gather everything up, carefully place the pictures on top, and cram the drawer back into the dresser. Just as I get it shut properly, an envelope slides out and onto the floor. The edges are soft. It's been opened and closed a number of times. Inside, there's a letter in Dad's handwriting. It's addressed to Mom. He must've written it while he was in the hospital.

February 4th, 2015

Nora,

There won't be a word said in this letter that you don't already know. I talked to the doctors yesterday and they didn't have good news. Said I should start thinking about what happens after I'm gone. I told them to go to hell in Anishnaabemowin, so they didn't understand what I'd said. Told 'em it was an old Nish blessing that's been said to their folk for years. Wasn't a full lie.

But even if I don't like what they said about me dying, they're right about me needing to think about what happens next. You know I don't wanna go, Nora, but it's looking like I'm gonna have to. I don't want some slick White man in a suit coming in here, getting his lawyer stink on everything, so this letter will have to do.

The house is yours, along with everything we put in it. We built that thing together, so it's only right that you take over after me. You do what you want with my truck. Sell it, maybe. Put some of the money aside for Haze and Gus. Whatever money I got left in my name goes to you too. Buy something nice. Maybe take a vacation?

The land goes to the kids. Whatever happens to that quarry, I want them to finish it. They'll know what's right for them and for the community. It's okay if they think I did wrong at first. But they need to think about the future. Invest now and there'll be something for everyone later. Elders always say that Mother Earth provides for us. That mine sure will.

I guess that's pretty much it. You think of anything else, tell the suits I say it's okay. You've always done right by me. Don't see how that'll change once I'm not around.

Thank you for the years you gave me. They were the best of my life. Tell the kids I'm proud of them and I love them too.

If what they told us growing up is right, then I guess I'll see you again someplace else.

Until then,
Your Abe

He died a week later.

Mom knew about his plans for the quarry. She knew about Gagnon and she knew about the mine. When I asked her about him in September, she told me she had no idea who he was. The phone call with my aunt makes sense now. She said something about a deal. This was it. The same deal Reggie Lee and Brian Howard were talking about weeks ago. Did everyone know?

I guess some part of me should be glad that Mom and Dad didn't have secrets after all, but all the lying is hard to see past. Why didn't she think it was important to tell us the truth? And what the hell was Dad thinking?

Elders always say that Mother Earth provides for us. That mine sure will.

That's not what they meant, Dad. Respect. Honour. Humility. Boring into her already broken body to take what isn't ours—it's not right. That quarry shouldn't even be there. Our land was stolen from us. How can selling it off to the highest bidder be what's right for us?

I can't get away from this mess no matter how hard I try. I hate that missing him doesn't feel the same anymore. It hurts. Stings bitterly. I want to stop feeling this way. Lost and completely helpless. I can't stand it. But I have no one to turn to. I can't bring myself to spend any more time trying to fix this.

This is where Nanabush should come back in. He should be knocking at the window. But he isn't. No one is here to help me. It's just me.

Alone.

The front door opens and shuts. Keys hit the table in the hall. Mom calls out to me.

"Supper has arrived!"

How long have I been up here?

I clear my throat. "Okay, I'm coming."

I carefully fold the letter in half and slide it into the back pocket of my jeans. I shuffle into the hallway and then down the stairs. Mom's in the entryway, juggling a large brown bag in one hand and four smaller plastic ones in the other. I reach out and take the food from her.

"Thanks, kid. Get it all out on the table, will you?" She moves past me and into the kitchen to unload the groceries.

I nod and head into the dining room, start unpacking. She's in a good mood. I could ask her about the letter. Demand to know why she kept all of this stuff from me for a whole year and a half and why she's still lying. But why bother? I don't want to hurt her. If she thought I shouldn't know, then maybe she had a good reason. Anything I ask will only leave us both exhausted.

Mom comes into the room with plates and utensils for us. "You just wake up from a nap?"

"No," I say. "Didn't nap, but I'm definitely tired."

"Go to bed early tonight. Makes a hell of a difference when you get a whole eight hours, you know."

"Yeah, I'll try that."

She sits down and starts opening the aluminum containers. Steam hovers an inch above the collection of noodles, rice, and vegetables. "Oh, I saw your friend Mia at the restaurant. She was there with her little girl and her mom. That Emmy is getting big. And does she ever look just like Mia!"

"Yeah, better that than her dad."

"No kidding. Imagine having to look at your ex every single day? Yikes. Anyway, how was work?"

Awful. Weird. Heartbreaking.

"It was fine," I say, digging my fork into my fried rice. "I, uh, met Thomas Gagnon."

ni KAREN McBRIDE

Mom flinches and her fork misses the chow mein and slams tine-first into the plate. She exhales and looks across the table at me. "Oh?"

"He's working with Joni and Operations and Maintenance on some new projects. Auntie Joni said he's an investor or something. You know him?"

Her lips straighten into a line. "I do. Owns a business in town. His family used to do work around here. You know, I think his great-grandfather or something used to be Indian agent. No one liked him. Thomas is a nice kid, though."

"Kid? How old is he?"

She shrugs. "Mid-thirties?"

"So how do you know him?" I push the rice around on my plate.

"I don't know him, not really. Your father did."

"What was his business with Dad?"

She shrugs. "Unfinished. Which is probably why he's in talks with the Band now. I wouldn't worry about it, kid."

I nod but stay quiet.

"I think you should call Mia tomorrow. Maybe get out of the house. She told me she's free all weekend." Mom's back to her normal self now that she's changed the subject. "You're about as gloomy as this rainy weather we've been having."

"You saying that I'm cold, damp, and smell like dead leaves?"

"Only when you haven't showered. It's not constant."

"Bully."

She grins. "Love you."

"You know, I wonder about that sometimes."

I don't though. But I don't know how to do this on my own. Nanabush, where are you?

I turn my face toward the window, but all I see is rain.

⋈ ⋈ ⋈

188

Mia lied about having a completely free weekend. While her daughter is away, she's been roped into helping her cousin gather materials for a ceremony tomorrow. So, naturally, I'm roped into doing it too. I let Mom know that I'll probably be gone for most of the day. As I head out the door, she simply waves her hand at me and doesn't look up from the book she's reading. Honestly, I'm impressed that she even heard me.

The rain from yesterday has settled into the ground, making the air smell like crisp, earthy decay. I breathe it in, let it fog out. The sun lights up the reds and oranges of the maple trees so they glow like fire in the cold morning. I slide into my car and slam the door shut. I turn the key and the engine rolls over. Hot air blasts from the vents, but it takes me a long time to get warm. I text Mia to let her know that I'm on my way to pick her up and then pull my gloves on so touching the steering wheel isn't so painful. The cold reaches my fingers anyway.

Mia lives across the reserve from me. In truth, if I could cut across the quarry and then the river, I'd end up right in her backyard. But I can't travel as the crow flies, so I have to take the long way around, which means driving through Ste-Marie des Oblats. The town lies just over two kilometres away from Spirit Bear Point. A curved, tree-lined stretch of highway peppered with one-level vinyl-covered houses in a variety of colours connects the two settlements. Right in the place where our territories connect lies the cemetery where both French and Algonquin share the same earth. As I drive by, I search the trees outside the graveyard for any sign of Nanabush. Nothing. The brilliant light of day makes shadows for him to hide behind.

The sign for Ste-Marie des Oblats is unnecessarily pretty. It's hand-carved wood with a decorative painting showing a pale woman dressed in blue holding her hands out to a group of people with equally pale faces. In the back of the crowd around Ste-Marie herself, the tips of feathers hovering over brown skin are visible. The Natives in the painting are enchanted with the glowing woman in front of them. To be fair, so is everyone else, but the Indians look especially transfixed. When I was in high school, this guy from my grade, Alex, vandalized the sign. He spray-painted a speech bubble over the Nishes that said, "Get off our land!" It was a whole ordeal. Cops from town and the Rez were involved. The SQ demanded that Alex's family pay for the damages and the restoration fees. Our cops said the sun would eventually make the paint fade. Alex ended up getting away with community service as long as he promised to write up a very heartfelt apology. The town angrily accepted and repainted.

The main street is packed with old houses that all lean toward the church at the far end. The church itself is a monument of dark brick and light wood that sits like a beacon at the head of the lake. It looms over the edge of the mouth of the river where it opens into the bay. When the river is high in the spring, it nearly reaches the edges of the building, sending water into the basement. It's flooded so many times that everyone calls it the Oblates' Well.

I drive to the end of the street, heading directly toward the church, then turn right past the first of three chip stands and continue through the town. I search the tree branches in the park across from the post office as closely as I can without driving myself off the road, but still no sign of him. I need to remind myself that it's only been a day. I have no idea what Nanabush went through to save me from falling into the quarry. He must need time to recover. A voice in my mind starts to selfishly cry that he said he was here to fix me, and that now is a time when he could be earning his keep. Doing his damn job. But, no. It's silly. Foolish to depend on someone like him. I should be able to fix myself.

I cross the bridge and come to a stop at the one big intersection in town. There isn't anyone else around, but I stay at the sign. Left leads down to the boardwalk, the river. Straight is the quickest way to get out of this province and into the next one. Most people look at it as the only road out of this place. As if leaving the Rez behind is as easy as driving west into the sunset. That ending has always been reserved for the cowboys. Indians end up in the dirt. I stare ahead, longingly. Wishing that I could drive off back to the city where my life used to be. When I didn't have to worry about old gods and dirty deals and dead dads.

I turn right down the poorly paved road toward Mia's place. I have to swerve onto the other side of the road and back again a few times to avoid potholes that are big enough to swallow a kid or small dog. Back here, away from the town, the roads belong to the Band. Naturally, it's all bush and gravel. Not for lack of funding, though. Part of me thinks that it's a conscious decision to remind anyone passing through that it's wild out here in Indian Country. Living up to our title of Keepers of the Land. Though it wouldn't hurt to get some trimming done once in a while.

Mia's already outside the house when I pull into the driveway. Since I've known her, she's lived with her parents. They're all right, stricter than they need to be. Mia had Emmy when she was just seventeen, so I guess they saw that as a failure. Teen pregnancy meant she'd be chained to the reserve forever. Doomed to a life hovering above the poverty line, living from week to week on welfare and family allowance. But Mia refused to let that happen. She finished high school, applied to a local college, and got herself a certificate in office administration. She has a job on the Rez now, answering phones and fixing schedules. Sounds like success to me, but I'm not sure if it's enough to convince her parents that she overcame any odds.

She comes around the car and taps the back of it, signalling for me to open the trunk. I watch through the rear-view mirror as she tosses a blue tarp into the back. Mia slams the trunk closed and moves to open the passenger side door. She plunks herself down into the seat, her hands around a travel mug of hot coffee. There's sleep in the corners of her eyes and her hair is gathered into a messy nest on top of her head. She grunts a greeting to me.

"Hell-uh," she says.

"Ho, she's tired too, that one."

"It's friggin' early," she says as she brings the mug to her lips. She curses when the too-hot coffee burns her tongue.

I snort. "You're the one who picked the time."

"I can still complain," she says, eyeing me sleepily. "Cripes, it's friggin' early."

"What the hell's the tarp for? 'Magine it looks like we're planning to stow a body or something." I put the car in reverse and back onto the street. I start driving back toward the highway even though she hasn't given me a destination yet.

"A body! I guess! What kind of ceremony you tink we got planned?"

"Well, I don't know, me. Don't know what weird shit your cousin's into nowadays."

Mia laughs. "Robby? Not a ting more than usual."

"Yeesh, I don't know if that's comforting."

"Ehhhnn, I'm just kiddin' around." She looks over at me and grins. "Tarp keeps your trunk from getting dirty. We need a lot of cedar for a sweat. Now, go on and head back toward your place."

"My place? Are you serious?"

"Yeah, it's got the best access to the quarry."

Any hint of a smile falls from my face. "Why are we going there?"

"Best place to find the medicines in the wild is by that quarry."

"Why didn't you tell me that we were going there in the first place?"

She's straightened in her seat and is looking right at me. "Because you get all weird whenever anyone mentions that place. I didn't want to give you the chance to say no."

"There's got to be other places we can get what you need."

"No. Not unless you feel like driving an hour to Lac Fournier at seven in the morning? Suck it up. It's just a place like anywhere else." Mia readjusts so she's looking out the front again. She sips her coffee. "Geez, you're uptight first thing in the morning."

I want to fire back at her. I want to tell her that going to that place is going to be harder than it's ever been before. But how can I do that without explaining everything? The dreams, the crow, the journeys into the past, the handshake.

I exhale. "Sorry. Must be a side effect of being stuck in an office not talking to anyone for weeks on end."

I drive back through town. This time, there are more signs of life. Townsfolk are up and about finally, heading to one of two diners for a cup of burnt or weak coffee and the morning gossip. The sparse crowds are an unbalanced mix of Indian and French. Not surprising, since most people on the Rez choose to drive twenty minutes to the next town over for their coffee to avoid the threat of having to speak another language.

In total, it takes about five minutes to drive from Mia's end of town to mine. To me, the time rushes past and I'm already counting my breaths to try to calm myself. I pull into the driveway and park next to my mom's truck. There's a stream of hot air coming from the back corner of the house that tells me Mom's doing laundry.

Mia slams the door a bit too hard. She looks out in the direction of the quarry and then back at the car. "There's no way we can get closer, is there?"

I shake my head. "No, we can't use the old road. And the bush is too dense back in there to get the car close to it. Besides, if I drove on the lawn, my mom would scalp me."

"Holeh, real violent right away too."

"Mom's serious about gardening."

"No kidding. Okay, okay. Leave the car where it is, den." Mia sips her coffee again as she starts walking toward the back of the house. "Your mom loves gardening as much as you say, then there must be a wheelbarrow here somewhere?"

I follow her, sticking my hands in my pockets. My hair brushes along the back of my neck, tickling my skin, so I pull it over to one side, letting it drape down the shoulder with the marks, which are hidden beneath my jacket. "I think so, me. Probably somewhere in the shed. One sec."

The metal door to Mom's gardening shed is rusted. It's painfully difficult to open. You have to hold it at a certain angle, pushing up slightly while also pushing forward to get it to slide. It takes me a couple of tries, but I get it, stumbling as it screeches open. All her tools are neatly arranged inside. Everything from gloves to shovels to what looks like a brand-new leaf blower has its place. Makes it easy to spot the wheelbarrow. I step inside, grab it, and awkwardly back out.

"You're gonna have to shut the door." I nod toward the shed.

Mia steps to it. "'Kay den, but you gotta hold my coffee."

"I'm sorta in the middle of the last favour you asked me. Can't hold the coffee if I'm holding up the wheelbarrow."

"Then put it down. It's got legs."

"Oh, right. Duh." I take the coffee and steal a sip while Mia goes to shut the door. I can't help but cringe and complain. "You drink this so sweet. What's the point of it?"

"Caffeine."

"This might as well be pop or something."

"Gets the job done. You don't like it? Don't drink it." She grabs two pairs of shears and carefully places them in the wheelbarrow.

I give her my best unimpressed look. "Are you serious?"

"What?"

"Were you prepared for this errand at all or was the plan to just use all my shit?"

"I brought the tarp, didn't I?" She grins and takes the coffee from me. "Besides, this is your mom's shit."

I lift the legs of the wheelbarrow so I can start pushing it as we walk. "Right, right. Well then, you're pushing this thing back once it's all full of cedar."

"Ugh, fine. Guess that's only fair."

Mia and I head toward the far end of the lawn. The cut grass slopes downward to a ditch that's half-filled with water and dead leaves, the sunlight making it look like shattered glass. We carefully lift the wheelbarrow over it and begin our awkward trek through the trees toward the quarry. The forest floor is littered with yellow, red, and brown leaves that give the air warmth even though our breath fogs into the space between the trees. We don't talk much save for the occasional curse when the wheelbarrow gets stuck in the mud. Bird calls echo in the air above our heads. I hear crows, but Nanabush's voice is silent.

The path in front of us opens up to the clearing. I keep walking, focused on our destination, but Mia has stopped. When I realize that she isn't next to me, I stop and turn to her, placing the wheelbarrow down and shaking the weight from my arms.

"What's the matter?" I ask.

Her nose wrinkles as discomfort tugs her eyebrows together. "You don't feel that weirdness? It's like . . . like a humming? Thrumming? Something, anyway."

I shake my head. "No, I've never felt it. My mom says the same thing about this place. She doesn't like how it feels."

"You're really okay?" She's looking at me with her eyes wide. I nod.

"Hmm, weird. Maybe I'm overreacting then," she says, spinning around slowly as she takes in the perfect circle. "Hey, I ever tell you the stories about this place?"

I shake my head. "Nope. These new ones you picked up?"

"Robby heard a good one at the last sweat he went to. Up in Longlac a few months back," she says, walking over to where I'm standing in the middle of the clearing.

"Ah, they're legit, huh?"

"As legit as they come." Mia takes a long drink of coffee, then places the empty mug in the wheelbarrow. She wipes her mouth with her thumb and takes a deep breath. "There are four doorways, one for each stage of life. You enter through the Eastern door, walk South through adulthood, and then you leave through the Western door, heading back into the Spirit World."

"What happens in the Northern door?" I ask, squinting at her when the sunlight beams onto my face. I shield my eyes.

She shrugs. "The Northern door is Spirit Country. Like something that happens behind the scenes of a play. Our spirits go back to the world where they were born, they grow and they learn, and then, when they're ready, they come back through that Eastern door again. So, I guess no one really knows. That's the truer answer."

I mumble, "Bet Nanabush could tell me what happens."

"What?"

"Nothing. Keep going. Sounds like you're building to something."

She looks at me a bit longer before she says, "When we learned about the Medicine Wheel when we were growing up, they told us that the four colours represented four directions, medicines, doorways, peoples. But it's more than that. There are stories that talk about the doorways like real places. Things that exist in the real world—*this* world."

"How could anyone know that?"

"They don't. That's why they're stories. Legends." There's a smile on her face as the wind picks up and blows the loose strands of her hair around her. "Kinda like believing in magic. It's fun, isn't it?"

I scoff. "I'm not sure about that anymore."

"Don't be jaded," she chides. The light catches her dark eyes, brightening them until they're like amber glass. "G'tchi Manitou put the doorways on the edge of both worlds—the Spirit World and ours—so that we could easily move from one to the next when the time came. Like little beacons."

When she talks, the air around us seems to glow like it's waking up. Wind weaves through the long grass, making it rush like waves on the shore of a lake. Mia pauses and bends down to run the palm of her hand along the grass, the morning dew leaving shining traces of moisture on her skin. Her voice is soft when she continues.

"They say the doorways look like hoops. The same kind we use to make our dreamcatchers, our Medicine Wheels, and our drums. The same kind that I dance with at powwows." There's a big grin on her face.

"Ehhhnn, you show-off," I say, reaching out to nudge her with my hand. "Just had to mention you're a hoop dancer too."

She bats her eyelashes at me. "Show-off? Me? Never!"

I roll my eyes and shake my head as I take a few steps into what feels like the exact middle of the clearing. I stand still and think about Mia's story. Weigh the thought of doorways in my mind. I stare straight ahead, watching the way the trees shift with the wind. "You think this place is a doorway?"

"That's what the stories say. An opening *in* to and *out* of the Spirit World. I mean, it makes sense, don't you think?" Mia's beside me, looking at me. "Why else would there be such a perfect clearing like this one? It would explain the weird feeling in the air. Bunch of spirits coming in and out of the other side might make for one hell of an energy traffic jam. Make this place feel uncomfortable."

"I'm sure there's a rational and logical scientific explanation for the weirdness. Probably something that has to do with the Earth's electromagnetic field or whatever." The theory makes sense, but I'm more inclined to believe Mia's version. Spending the past few months hanging out with a trickster god can have that effect on a person. I keep talking. "I read that somewhere. Changes in the field can make people feel all kinds of things. Nausea, dizziness, even tasting copper."

"Sure, I guess," Mia says, picking up the wheelbarrow and pushing it forward. "Whatever you want to call it, this place has power. There's no denying that. Come on. Let's go and get that cedar."

She trudges forward, struggling to get the wheelbarrow through the grass and damp earth. I turn away from her to look back at the path we took into the circle. It's almost impossible to find the entrance. The trees that border the clearing all look the same dressed in their coloured leaves. Black ash, balsam poplar, and sycamore surround this place like sentinels. The patterns look like they are intentional. I can almost see the hand of the Creator who put them here. An ornate frame around a door, marking it as a place of importance. I close my eyes. Blood pulses in my ears. Even and calm. Drumbeats. The sounds of the clearing fade away to static and then to nothing.

Murmurs. Whispers. I hear seven voices speaking at once, but I can't understand the language. I hear footsteps crunching on snow. I feel the cold of winter's nighttime air. The tall figure of a man begins to take shape. He's walking toward me, to the centre of the circle. I can almost see his face when my eyes shoot open.

"Hazel?" Mia is looking at me, her eyebrows disappearing into her bangs. "You leave the planet there?"

"Just needed a second. Zoned out a bit, eh?" I blink a few times, trying to make sense of the world around me. I feel disjointed, uneasy. Like I went someplace else. Only, I didn't make it. Not quite. I clear my throat and turn to walk with Mia. "You get that wheelbarrow stuck?"

She scrunches her nose. "Yeah, but I got it loose. That's how I noticed you were still back here. No one was making fun of me."

I laugh. "Sorry to leave you hanging."

"It's okay," she says with a shrug. "Everyone needs to space out from time to time."

We leave the clearing, navigating our way through the rest of the forest until we step out onto the rocky ledge of the quarry. The raspberry bushes that I was sent to harvest are a collection of long branches armed with tiny thorns. The brambles make a natural railing to stop anyone from jumping off at this point. My gaze finds its way to the edge a bit farther up. No barrier lies there. Only a few small stones and ragged patches of green moss stand between the edge and a drop into the cold water below. I think of how it must feel to break the surface. I touch my right shoulder, timidly running my fingers along Nanabush's marks. The skin throbs beneath my touch.

"To think we used to come here all the time when we were kids," Mia says, looking out at the quarry. "How the hell did we not get in trouble? I mean, if Emmy wanted to run along this road, I'd lose my shit."

I turn to her, happy to look away from the edge. "We got in trouble all the time. We just always came back. And eventually we learned how to come here without our parents finding out. Give a kid an obstacle and they'll find a way around it."

She laughs and rolls her eyes. "Oh god, don't say shit like that. I'm going to turn into one of those helicopter parents. Don't let me, okay? The second you see me buying one of those kid-leashes, you slap me."

"Deal."

"You agreed to that *so* fast. I'm insulted."

"Obviously, you have permission to slap me if I do the same," I say, walking up the old road to where the cedar trees are. "Even if it's years and years from now."

Mia mulls it over for a second and then nods. "Deal. And don't you think I won't remember this, Ellis."

I wave a hand dismissively at her. "Yeah, yeah. Come on, it's going to take us all day to get enough cedar to fill that barrow if you keep blabbing on like that."

She joins me at the height of a small hill. From this spot we can see the quarry in all its glory. The sun hasn't quite made it high enough to light the old mine yet, so that much of the stone and water still lies in a shaded darkness. Mia's part of town is almost visible through the yellow and brown half-shed birch leaves. Collecting the branches is hard work that requires a dedicated eye and touch so that we never take more than what we need, and leave the tree intact and able to grow again. We spend a silent ten minutes cutting off cedar branches, adding each new piece to the growing pile.

Mia's the first to break the silence. "So what's the matter with you?"

I glance over at her, careful not to get myself as I cut off another branch. "What do you mean?"

"You have this hurt-bunny look on your face." She looks at me, her expression drooping for a second before going back to normal. "Like that."

"I don't look like that."

"It's not that obvious, but it's there."

"When you say it like that it sounds silly," I grumble. "*Hurt bunny.*"

She tosses another two branches into the wheelbarrow. They rustle the rest of the cedar, sending the clear, earthy scent into the air around us. "I don't know how else to describe it. It's like you look fine at first glance or whatever, but underneath the smiles and the jokes, you're just *sad*. What's the matter?"

She's right. It's unseen and unnoticed to the untrained eye. But my grief is there just beneath my skin. Now that she's pointed it out, I feel my face relax and settle into that familiar frown. It's a sadness that tugs on the corners of my lips. Like there's a weight on my mouth, keeping it from lifting into a smile.

What do I say? How can I tell her the truth of what I'm feeling without telling her everything? I can't do that. I'll sound crazy.

Even if I have Nanabush's bloody signature on my shoulder, it'll never be enough to keep her on my side. If I tell her the truth, even if she believes me, I know she'll never look at me without pity or fear again.

The call of a songbird echoes across the quarry's expanse from somewhere in the surrounding forest, resonating around us. The birds twitter happily, taking no notice of the two friends standing in their wake.

"I'm just sad all the time." The honesty in my words makes me feel like I'm whimpering. This is the most truthful I've been to anyone who doesn't have a beak for a mouth. I avoid looking at Mia. "Being here is harder than I thought it would be. Everywhere I go—home, work—I'm surrounded by my dad, or what's left of him."

Mia stops snipping at the cedar so she can keep her eyes on me. Her gaze feels heavy. She doesn't say anything, but I can feel her urge me to continue. She knows I'm not done talking. There's more I need to say.

I rub my lips together to keep them from trembling, but already my voice starts to shake. "It's all too much. Like there's a big part of me that'll always be missing. I'm terrified. I'm going to be this broken person for the rest of my life. And I can't . . . I can't fix anything. Ever since I came back here, things have been falling apart. It's like I don't know who I am because I don't know who *he* was."

I've dropped the shears. My face is in my hands, but I'm not crying. I'm starting to get used to this reaction. Pain and wet eyes, but no real tears. It scares me if I think on it too long. Like I can't cry just for the sake of missing my dead dad anymore. The memory of him is tainted. Maybe it'll be like this forever. That what I've learned about him, his beliefs, will be all I remember. That I'll forget the man he was to me and to Gus and only ever remember the man who sold us out.

Next to me, Mia stiffens up. She's bad at handling emotional reactions. Which is why we only ever talk about our feelings through jokes. Quickly, I move my hands, rub my nose, and stand properly. I wipe the moisture from the corners of my eyes and look over at her. I give her a small smile to try to calm her down.

"That the answer you had in mind?" I say it with a hint of awkward laughter.

She visibly relaxes and laughs a little herself. "I thought you might go down that emotional road, so I was basically ready to deal with it. But feelings, ugh, awkward." She moves back to her work. "I'm shit at advice—real advice. I could say all the nice stuff that people say. 'Oh, your dad loved you and he still loves you, blah blah blah.' But I know you don't want to hear that. Instead, I'm going to tell you one thing."

I look at her expectantly.

Her eyes go big with seriousness. "Come. To. The. Sweat."

I bend down to grab the shears and try to turn my attention back to the cedar-snipping. The thought of it makes me nervous. Sweats are about truth and healing. I don't know if I'm ready for either of those things. But what other options do I have? "All right."

"Ah! Yay!" The excitement in her voice makes me smile. "I'm so pumped to have you there with me! You're not going to regret it, I promise."

I know she's right. I give her a nod, even though my mouth feels like cotton. Already I wish that I could take it back. Willingly shutting myself up in the dark with the ancestors seems like a bad idea considering I've spent the past few months working with the trickster they kicked out of the Spirit World. And yet that very same trickster has left me helpless. I thought I could count on him to find me whenever things got tough. That's how it's been so far. I mess up, discover things, and he comes for me. But now, nothing.

That's when I realize what I need to do.

This time, I'm coming for him.

14

THE SWEAT LODGE

The next day, I'm sitting on the edge of Mom's bed as she rummages through her closet. She has changed the bedding since I was in here last. Now the bed is sporting a bright red and orange Navajo-style print. Mom loves anything Indian, even if it's not her tribe. She's like the Indigenous Peoples' cheerleader. Her thinking is that if she's buying it, there's a market for it.

I'm in here to get help with my wardrobe for tonight. Apparently, I don't have the right clothing for the ceremony, so Mom's decided to take charge. Being in here is strange. Almost like I'm revisiting my crime scene. I can't help but glance at the drawer in Dad's dresser where I found the letter. It isn't in there anymore. I've got it in my room, hidden inside a book about Indians being in the wrong places at the wrong time. Figured it was a fitting spot for it. Mom hasn't noticed that it's gone. Or if she has, she hasn't asked me about it. I wonder if she knows that I know and is avoiding the conversation just like I did. Why throw salt on a wound that's starting to heal?

"I can't believe you're going to a sweat," Mom says, her voice barely audible from inside the closet. "It's been ages since I've been to one. I almost wanna go too, but I know that it's better for you to be there with your friend. 'Magine it'd be weird if I was sitting there next to you. Heck, I'd feel so old with you and Mia in there and with Robby Littleduck conducting it too! Time flies. Look at all of you, adults allasudden."

"Robby's not conducting it, it's just his lodge. Mia said he's asked an elder from Blanche River to come down to do it."

"He still single?"

"How should I know?"

"Because you used to have a huge crush on him when you were a kid. Thought you'd be well aware of his relationship status." I can't see her, but I can hear her grinning in the way she talks.

"What? How'd you know?"

"Maternal instinct."

"Oh my god, Mom." But now she's got me wondering. Robby always has been kind to me. Don't think the timing's right, though. I fall back against the bed, roll over onto my side, and rest my head on my hand as I watch her.

Her long black hair is pulled back into a tail at the base of her neck. She's got a beaded clip holding it together. The clip is beautiful, all turquoise and orange beads like a river at sunset. I recognize it as one she bought at the big competition powwow down south last summer.

She pokes her head out to answer me or to come up for air. "Elder's name is Bonneau or something, right? I've heard he does a real good sweat. Something like eighteen Grandfather stones were in his last one." She whistles lowly. "You better be ready for a hot one, kid."

"You used to go to these all the time?" I ask.

She nods, pushing hanger after hanger aside. "Oh yeah. Your auntie and I loved them. But, if I'm being honest, sometimes I'd just go because I needed a facial and I wasn't in the best financial shape to afford it."

"Mom!"

"What? The ancestors understand."

"I'll be sure to ask them when I'm in the lodge tonight." I say it as a joke, but part of me wonders if the opportunity might actually arise.

"Do you know if many people are going? Here, take this and try it on over your jeans." She tosses me a black skirt with an elastic waistband and a trio of orange ribbons around the hem.

I shake my head as I push myself up off the bed and shimmy into the skirt. The fabric is smooth and cool against my hands. The skirt goes nearly to my feet, hitting below my ankles. I tug it up a bit higher. "How the hell do you not trip when you wear this? It's so long and you, well, you're not a giant."

"I used to just wear it for ceremonies and things like that. Never for dancing. Could you imagine? God, I'd be patting down the grass more than a grass dancer before Grand Entry." She laughs at herself.

I laugh too, but I give her an eye roll anyway. I tug at the waistband, stretching it out in front of me. "It's nice and comfy. If it's been good enough for you for sixty-some years, then I guess it'll be fine for me tonight."

"Hey now. It's not that old. I got this beauty in the seventies."

"Pardon me. Forty-some years, then."

"Ugh, that doesn't sound much better. Sah, kid, you're making me sound old!"

"If the shoe fits . . ."

"Hi-yah, you're bad, you!" She rolls up another skirt in her hands and whips me with it.

I laugh, then plunk myself back down on the bed. The skirt fans out around me, blending in perfectly with the bedding. "Do you still go to ceremonies?"

She folds up the other options she offered me, carefully placing them on their respective hangers. "Not so much."

I lean back onto my hands. "Why not?"

Mom shrugs, then turns to force the hangers back into the closet. "I don't know. It's been almost two years since I last went to one. I haven't felt like going much."

"That long?" I look down into my lap and busy myself with a loose thread on the edge of the skirt. Quietly, I ask, "Is it because of Dad?"

She steps out of the closet, reaching back behind her to grab her hair. She brings it over one shoulder and combs her fingers through it. "Yes and no. I mean, on the one hand I stopped going because I wasn't up to it anymore. I go to big things, powwows and stuff like that. But full-moon ceremonies aren't me. I know I shouldn't be that way. I'm supposed to be one of the elders now, but I don't think that title fits me. I probably have things I could teach or pass on, but right now it wouldn't feel right. I mean, it *doesn't* feel right."

"Why not?"

"Can't fix other people when you're not fixed yourself."

"What do you mean?"

She shrugs. "Takes time to get over the hurt your dad left us with."

She's right about that. Feels selfish even to try.

Mom takes a deep breath. "Once your dad went into the hospital, I didn't have time for anything else. I was there all the time, so whenever I got home or had a few hours to spare, all I could think about was sleeping. I got tired of everything. The constant fear, the smell of the hospital—hell, even the sound of the oxygen machine he was hooked up to started to drive me crazy. It was exhausting, and I don't think I realized how tired I was until after he was gone." Her eyes are wide. She looks like she wants to take back what she's said. "Not that I was glad it all ended the way it did. You know that, right?"

I swallow hard, push away the sadness, and give her a reassuring smile. "I know, Mom. I know what you meant. It must have been tough to do all of that on your own. I should have come home more. We both should have, me and Gus."

"No." She comes over to sit next to me, putting a hand overtop mine. "Don't you think that for one second. You came back as much as you could. Above all else, your dad wanted you to finish school and you did. He'd have been none too pleased if you skipped out on weeks of classes just to keep him company. I think he would've banned you from visiting if you tried that."

We laugh despite the hurt it causes to talk about him.

"Yeah," I say. "You're right. He would've went all Vice-Chief Ellis on me. Like that time I skipped class in high school. He was mad—no, no, he was disappointed."

"Oh yes, I remember that day. I tried to tell him it was part of being a teenager. That everyone should skip at least once." She giggles to herself at the memory. "He wasn't having any of that talk."

"You could have saved me from that whole month of being grounded?"

"I tried, kid. Your dad needed you to learn your lesson."

"Do you know what I did during that one class I missed? I got ice cream with Mia."

"Mia skipped too?"

"Um, yes. Her mom called you and that's how you found out I had been with her."

"Oh, yeah. 'Kay, I remember now, me."

"Don't know what good grounding me did, anyway. It's not like I ever went out."

"You never did it again, did you?"

"No, but that was more because I didn't want to have to deal with Dad's angry-slash-disappointed face again."

She smiles at me, crow's feet and all, and gently taps my hand. "Your dad was never actually disappointed in you. He was so proud of you and your brother. He still is. He'll always be proud of you." She places her hand on my cheek, holding my gaze for a moment, her eyes watering, before lightly patting my face and standing up. She turns away from me, but I see her wipe her eyes. "Come on. Let's get some food in you before you have to head out. I know you'll be feasting after the whole thing is done, but I don't want you sweating on an empty stomach."

¤ ¤ ¤

An hour and a sandwich later, I'm back in my car. Mia texted, asking me to pick up some strawberries because apparently there was a misunderstanding and her mom used the ceremony berries to make jam. It's not out of my way, so I stop to grab a couple of baskets. They're on the seat beside me as I make my way to her cousin's place. Luckily, it's across the road from her parents' house. She promised to meet me there, so we could walk over together. That way, I won't feel so out of place.

I pull into her yard and turn off the car. Now that the engine isn't running, I can hear my heart. For a moment, I let myself lean back in the seat, sink into the fabric. I push back against it, wanting to disappear. This will be good for me. Knowing that doesn't make me any less nervous. I tell myself one more minute and then I'll get out. So far, it's been five minutes.

I don't get to make that decision. Mia comes out of the house wearing a long red skirt and a sweater. Her hair is in two braids on either side of her face and she's holding a big wooden bowl. She waves at me. I wave back and unbuckle my seat belt. Grabbing the strawberries, I get out of my car to meet her.

"Hey. I got the berries. Didn't get a chance to cut them or whatever."

She smiles. "Ahn, that's okay. Robby's got a real good set-up behind his house. Basically, an outdoor kitchen, so we can do it all over there. Gives us something to do while we wait on other people to show up."

"'Kay den," I say as we start to walk together. "You look nice. Went for the old classic Nish look, eh?"

"Double braids are timeless," she says, smoothing down one of the braids with her free hand. "You brought an elastic, right? I mean, go for the hair-down look if that's what you want, but it's gonna be *hot* in there."

I point to my wrist. "Of course. I've always got a hair tie."

"'Kay, good. I was worried for a second there. Like, yeah, the point is to sweat, but you don't want to go overkill for your first one." Mia grins.

We walk across the street to Robby's place. His house is a modest little place with dark green siding and a front porch. He's got a bamboo wind chime hanging from the light beside the door. It knocks together quietly in the cold air. We move around to the back of the house, where the lodge is set up. The house sits on the top of a hill overlooking a huge forest of evergreen trees that stretch out until they reach the highway. The lodge is at the far end of Robby's property. It's not much to look at in its current state. A small, rounded hut covered in tarps. I imagine that animal hide was used in the past, but now opting for something slightly more sustainable is the best choice. Modernizing culture. Underneath the plastic, the hut's bones are cedar saplings, bent to meet in the middle. There's a door that faces East. The only way in and out.

To the side of the lodge is a Sacred Fire, its light brightening the cedar trail that leads from it to the Eastern doorway. Shadows spark and dance on the sides of the lodge in the flickering fire-light. Mia's dad is seated just outside the circle of rocks that mark the edge of the Sacred Fire. He's been there since dawn. As fire-keeper, it's his job to feed the fire and help it grow for the entire day. Inside the fire, the Grandfather stones are waiting. They've been seated in the flames since sunrise, building and holding the heat and energy needed for a sweat.

The chill in the air goes right through my jacket. I want to go and stand next to the fire, but Mia leads me over to the deck. Her mom is there already. She's busy at the barbecue, where she's got a bunch of vegetables wrapped in aluminum foil heating over the gas grill.

"Mom, Hazel brought some more strawberries. You got some knives we can use to cut them up?" Before her mom can reply, Mia's already grabbed two small paring knives from the counter.

"Why ask a question when you go and answer it yourself?" her mom asks without turning from the grill.

Mia looks at me. "She gets stressed when she cooks."

I nod along, but I know that her mom is just naturally abrasive.

Mia takes the berries from me, washes them, and then gives one container back to me. She hands me a knife and we both start cutting off the tops and slicing them into quarters. It's busy work, but I don't mind it. Gives me something to focus on instead of worrying about what happens once that door is closed and we're in the dark with the ancestors.

Robby comes out of his house. He's wearing a traditional rib-bon shirt that's almost the same colours as the ribbons on my skirt. Robby's tall with a neck that seems too long for his body. His dark hair is cut short, but he's been growing it out, so it looks slightly unkempt. He's a few years younger than Gus, but still three years older than me. The reason he's got a house is a sad one. Both his parents died in a car accident about five years back. After that, he lived with his grandpa until he passed away two years ago. I guess that's why he got so into culture. That much heartbreak needs some way to resolve itself. Robby gives us an awkward wave as he walks over.

"About time you made it over here. Coulda used you earlier. How long did it take you to do them braids, eh?" he says.

Mia rolls her eyes. "Not as long as it took you to pick out a shirt that conveniently matches Hazel's skirt."

I think he blushes. The sun has set completely, so the only light comes from the lanterns on the back porch. He looks down at his shirt and then at my skirt. Robby shrugs. "That's just a coincidence. But you do look nice, Hazel."

My mouth tugs up at one corner in that uncontrollable way it does when something gives me butterflies. I try to shrug off the compliment without letting the moment get too awkward. "Thanks. Nice of you to say."

He smiles and nods. Then things get quiet while we look at each other. I can feel Mia glancing between the pair of us. I just know she's wearing that smirk of hers. It must be killing her not to say something about the whole situation.

Robby clears his throat. "It's good to have you here with us."

"Yeah, Mia said it would be good for me to come. So here I am," I say.

"It *will* be good for you. I can guarantee it," he says. "Helped me a lot. Still helps me."

I smile. He's so open with his feelings. It makes me uncomfortable.

Mia's mom makes a disapproving noise, which we take as our sign to move out of her way and over to the lodge. Robby leads us along a narrow, packed-dirt path. Mia grabs the bowl full of strawberries and rests it on her hip as she walks alongside me. I bring my arms close to my body to try to warm myself up. Now that the sun is down, the air is much colder. Once we reach the fire, I happily unfold my arms and stick my hands out.

I look over at Mia. "Is there anything you'd like me to do? I mean, I don't know much about this stuff, but I can do easy things. Like hold stuff or whatever."

She shakes her head. "Nah, you're good. I just have to bless these berries before we can get started officially. Then I'll lead you through the first few steps. Ah, don't look so scared! You have a guide. It'll be fine." She laughs, then takes the bowl in both hands and turns to face East.

Mia quietly speaks a few words to each direction, asking for blessings, guidance, and abundance. When she finishes, she takes one of the heart berries in her hand and tosses it into the fire. She straightens up and wipes her hand on her skirt. "Gotta feed the ancestors. They get hungry too."

An older man comes to join us by the fire. His long white hair is back in a tail at the base of his neck. He's hunched slightly as he walks, his broad shoulders rolled forward. Despite this, he walks with a pride and dignity that makes him seem taller than anyone there. He must be the elder conducting the sweat.

"*Kwe kwe, Anishnaabes!*" he says brightly. His voice rasps when he laughs. He looks over the three of us and smiles. "Hoowah, looks like it's a young ones' sweat tonight. We expectin' anyone else?"

Mia's dad speaks up from his lawn chair next to the fire. "Should be at least one more coming in soon."

"Oh, yes, that's right. Robby told me that earlier."

"Hazel," Mia says, placing her hand on my shoulder, "this is Jack Bonneau. He's the conductor for our sweat tonight."

He shakes my hand. His grip is strong but soft. When he

smiles at me, his face looks like an old apple that's been left in the sun. "Everyone just calls me *Ananginini*. Means 'Star-man.' Don't know if the elders who gave me that name did so because I see heavenly good tings in everyting or if dey were sayin' my head's always up in the clouds. Ahn! Either way, I like it and it's a name just for me. Anehway! S'good to meet you, Hazel. Mia tells me dis is your first sweat?"

I wonder if the elder who gave him his name was also a fan of David Bowie. Dad would've made some kind of comment or joke about that to calm me down. Too bad he's not here.

"Mm-hmm," I answer.

"You're nervous, eh?"

"Mm-hmm."

"Ahn! Don't be! I'll take good care of all of yiz in dere. De scariest part is de sharin', and if you don't want ta do dat, you don't have ta. You'll come out of dere feelin' so much bedder." He walks around the fire and moves to sit in the lawn chair next to Mia's dad. They strike up a conversation about the stones and then move on to the latest hockey standings.

Star-man sits back into the chair, making himself comfortable. He looks like he's settling in instead of getting ready for the ceremony.

I turn to Mia. "Do you know who else is coming?"

She glances around the backyard and shakes her head. "Nope. Supposed to start soon, though. Whoever they are, they're pushing it."

I look at her skeptically. "Did you think we'd start on time, though?"

She laughs. "True. Indian time is real."

"Seriously. My mom is consistently twenty minutes late for everything. So much so that me and Gus started lying to her about when we had to be places."

"Oh my god, did that work?"

"Yup."

"I might steal that. My mom is bad for running on Indian time too. Can't take that lady anywhere. Least, not on time."

Talking with her like this helps me calm down, quiets some of the voices crying about claustrophobia and exhaustion. Robby's smiling but not participating in the conversation. The look on his face says that he's torn between wanting to talk with us and wanting to chime in about hockey. In the end, he moves to stand closer to the fire.

Lights shine from the driveway as a dark-coloured vehicle pulls into the yard. The car idles in the drive a moment before it's turned off. The white lights disappear and the barely visible silhouette of a person steps out of the car. Whoever it is sticks their arm in the air and waves in our direction. Everyone waves back even though we can't see who it is yet. That's what we do around here. Walk down the road and wave if someone honks as they drive by. Odds are it's a friend or cousin or auntie.

The fifth member of the sweat comes down the path and steps into the firelight. I gasp audibly, causing Mia to look at me.

It's Thomas Gagnon.

"What's the matter?" she whispers.

I don't get a chance to answer as Thomas and I have met eyes. He smiles at me. I don't know what to do, so I barely nod after I look him over. He's dressed casually in dark sweatpants and a jacket. I recognize the brand as something well-made but overpriced. His shoes, while practical, are white and designed for athletic work. He looks polished, professional.

Robby moves past Mia and me to where Thomas is standing somewhat awkwardly away from the circle. Thomas's face brightens as Robby reaches out to shake his hand. They exchange a few words before walking back over to where Mia and I are standing.

Robby introduces Thomas to Mia, saying something about knowing him from other cultural events. She smiles broadly when she shakes his hand, colour rising in her cheeks, and she laughs too easily when he speaks.

"And," Robby says as he motions to me, "this is—"

"Hazel. We've met already."

Thomas nods. "It's good to see you again."

"Mm-hmm." Seems to be my reply of the night. "What are you doing here?"

If he's caught off guard by the question, he makes no show of it. "Robby invited me. He said it would be good for me to see a ceremony like this."

"He's been coming to the different cultural events that I've hosted and organized for almost a year now. This is the first time a businessman like him has cared enough to be a part of our community," says Robby.

"I'm happy to be building bridges between Ste-Marie des Oblats and Spirit Bear Point," Thomas says earnestly. "I've always been an advocate for bringing our communities together. "We've spent too much time divided. And that's not the way it should be."

"You running for office or something?" The words tumble out of my mouth, but I don't regret saying them. "You talk like a politician."

"Geez, what's with the firing squad?" Mia says.

"What? I'm just saying."

Thomas laughs graciously. He acts like a politician too. "It's all right. I get that a lot. Sometimes I have a hard time turning off my work voice."

"Wow, your English is good," says Mia, sitting into her hip. "Are you actually from town or what?"

"I was here for the first few years of my life. Then my family moved to Ottawa and sent me to school in English. They wanted to make sure I was bilingual. Which is why I hardly have an accent."

"Hey, Hazel went to school there too!" Mia nudges me.

"Yeah, but university," I say. "That's different. It's not like we have the same life."

Star-man saves Thomas from replying as he gets up and comes over to greet him. "Mr. Gagnon! Our resident White Man for the evening, huh?"

"That would be me," Thomas replies, reaching out to shake the old man's hand. "It's good to see you doing well, Jack."

Star-man pulls him into an embrace, patting his back. "You too, *Wabi-Mahigan.*" He steps back from the hug and looks at the four of us. "I tink it's time we all got ourselves in de lodge, ahn? What yiz tink?"

Robby answers for all of us. "You bet, *Ananginini.* Don't want to keep you up too late."

Star-man chuckles. "Watch it now, Littleduck, or I'll make you sing lead on all the songs in dere." He rubs his hands together and then claps them once. "Okay, tonight we have two who are new to the sweat. *Minwa pijawok!* Welcome! We'll be heading inside de lodge shortly. I just want to give yiz all a little rundown of how tings are gonna go in dere. Tonight's sweat is gonna be about healing hurts—physical, emotional, spiritual. When we enter into a sweat lodge, we are givin' ourselves the permission to heal. Everyting dat happens inside the lodge is to help make ourselves better, safer, and so dat we can continue on living de Good Life.

"Now, we need someone in each doorway once we're inside de lodge. That'll decide how we enter. I'll be in the Eastern doorway. Robby, you go ahead and take the Southern doorway." He pauses, his eyebrows inching toward each other, the lines of his face curving in. "The Western doorway is rough. Shouldn't ever be given to first-timers. All the pain and hurt flows through it."

"I can do it," says Mia.

"It's a tough place to be," says Star-man. "Are you sure?"

"I'm sure. I've been in enough sweats to know how the whole thing goes down." Mia nods. "Besides, I got so much positivity in me that I'll be fine with whatever sad stuff you all throw at me."

"Good, it's good to have dat kinda fire," Star-man says. "Now den, you two can decide where you'd like to sit. I know we still have one more doorway, but it would be all right dis time if we left it open. Northern doorway belongs to the Spirit World anyhow."

Thomas and I look at each other. He speaks first. "I'll be okay with whatever you decide."

When he looks at me, I can feel my cheeks get hot. I clear my throat. "I'll go after Mia. Why don't you sit near Robby? Since you two know each other and all."

Thomas nods. "Sure. I'll come in last. Probably best since I'm the outsider here."

"Mm. That's true." I cross my arms and look away from him.

"Which means dat, Mia, you'll go into de lodge second after me," Star-man says. "Jus' be sure to leave a bit of a gap for de Northern doorway. What you'll all do is introduce yourself to de lodge. Say hello and your name. Den you'll crawl clockwise until you get to your spot. Now, it's gonna be real dark in dere, even with de door open, so try to give each other a heads-up if you tink you're gettin' too close. Don't want anyone to collide if dey don't need to."

Star-man turns toward the fire. Balanced carefully on two rocks just outside the firepit are two dark stone bowls. One is filled with tobacco and the other with cedar. Star-man takes a small bit of each medicine and places it in the palm of his left hand. He closes it into a gentle fist, placing his other hand overtop like a blanket. He shuts his eyes and prays softly. He speaks too quickly and too quietly for me to understand the words.

Mia leans close to me and whispers, "How are you not freaking out right now?"

"I am," I answer. "I keep worrying that this'll be the time I discover that I'm claustrophobic."

"What? No. Not about that. About *that*." She nods her head subtly toward Thomas and then brings a hand up to scratch behind her ear as if that could hide the suspicious motion.

"What about him?"

"Um, he's hot. Duh. And the way he keeps smiling at you and talking to you." She shakes her head. "It's like he's doing everything he can to get you to like him."

"It's not like that."

"He could be your John Smith."

"What? Inappropriately older than me and a guy from the group who forced their religion upon me and my People and then brought me back to England to die alone and childless?"

"You must be fun at parties."

"You know I don't go out. Besides, this guy's *wemitigòji*. Pretty sure John Smith was *anganeshà*."

"French, English, whatever, it's all the same. If you're not going to enjoy this, then I will." She looks Thomas up and down while he's busy talking quietly to Robby. "Nakoma's gonna get herself some."

"Oh my god."

Star-man finishes his prayer, opens his eyes, lifts his hands toward the rising moon, and tosses the medicines into the Sacred

Fire. The old man dusts his hands on his pants and then presses them against his back as he straightens up. "I'd like each of yiz to grab some tobacco and some cedar. Take de medicines in your hands and take a second to ask the Creator for help with what you want healed tonight. You don't have ta say it out loud or any-ting—tinking it is powerful enough. Den, when yiz are ready, you go ahead and trow dat handful into de fire. Send dem prayers up to G'tchi Manitou," Star-man says when he turns back toward us.

We do as we're told.

I'm not sure what to ask for. There are so many things I need help with these days that I don't know where to begin. Forgetting what it feels like to grieve—that would be nice. That's a big ask, and I know that the Creator must have bigger things to worry about than helping me tonight. I close my eyes.

Guide me down the right path.

I open my hand and offer the medicines to the fire. The tobacco and cedar catch fire and crinkle in upon themselves like a closing fist.

"An offer of tobacco and cedar to the Sacred Fire means dat it's time for all of us to enter into de lodge. Remember dat dis is a place of healing and welcoming de new and good tings dat are waiting for us once we come back out dat door." Star-man points with his lips toward the lodge, and we all turn our heads, follow-ing his gaze.

Mia's mom is standing in front of the door and on the other side of the cedar trail that leads from the fire to the lodge. Her long skirt grazes the toes of her moccasins as she sways back and forth slightly, her hands folded in front of her stomach.

"Give your coats and sweaters to our gracious chef. She'll take good care of dem," Star-man continues as he walks toward the lodge, sliding out of his jacket and tugging the worn ribbon shirt over his head. He turns to us, pointing to the ground as he steps out of his moccasins. "Oh, and leave your shoes out here. Make sure you're in de order we decided."

"Mia," I whisper, "does that mean everyone's practically naked in there?"

"Tsk, well yeah. It gets hot in there. Guys wear shorts or whatever, but they usually go topless. We gotta wear skirts and shirts, though. Can't be too indecent."

"Okay."

"What are you worried about? It's dark in there. Not like you have to stare at anyone's half-naked body. I mean, I wouldn't mind staring at *someone*." She nods toward Thomas and I roll my eyes.

Then the four of us awkwardly move around one another into a line. Thomas places a hand on my shoulder when he moves to stand behind Robby and me. Mia watches as he walks by. She smiles at him and tries to play with her hair, tossing one of the tight braids over her shoulder.

Robby leans in to whisper to me as we start to walk toward the lodge. "Think she's upset she volunteered for the Western doorway now?"

"You could still switch with her," I say.

"Nah," he says. "It's funnier this way. She can't flirt around if she's not right next to him."

"Probably won't stop her from trying, somehow. She's a pretty determined person."

"True. Betcha she'll start with her Pocahontas stuff."

I snort. "Oh, she definitely already has."

"If she starts using *mukluk* as a verb, then we'd better watch out."

"Ew, gross, Robby."

"What? I'm kidding, I'm kidding!"

"Still. Ever sick, that's your cousin."

I shake my head at him, but I'm smiling.

Star-man bends down, his old bones crackling like the fire at our backs. He pauses in the doorway and then crawls on his hands and knees into the dark of the lodge. Mia steps forward to hand her sweater to her mom. She slides out of it slowly, as if she knows that there are eyes on her. I sneak a glance over my shoulder, pretending to be interested in the Sacred Fire. Thomas isn't watching her, but he catches my gaze and gives me another of his charming smiles. I bring my attention back to the lodge, which is suddenly much closer now that it's nearly my turn to step inside. My nerves come back, my heart beating so loudly that I have to struggle to focus on what Mia says as she enters the lodge.

"*Kwe kwe, madòdison. Wâwâshkeshîkwe nidijinikaz. Màg dodem.*" Then she moves into the lodge.

I unzip my jacket and hand it over to Mia's mom. The night air turns my bare arms to gooseflesh. Standing at the mouth of the lodge, it seems smaller. Like it can't possibly hold the five of us. How close will we be inside it? How will I be able to breathe when there's no air and the roof comes crashing in on us?

"Go on," Robby whispers. "You can do it."

I nod, swallow hard, and then sink down onto my hands and knees. My hair falls over my shoulder, covering the bandage that's hiding Nanabush's signature. I open my mouth to introduce myself, my voice so quiet that it's barely worth calling it a mumble. "*Kwe kwe, madòdison.* Hazel *nidijinikaz. Migizî dodem.*"

It is blindingly dark inside the lodge, even with the light from the open door. I freeze, startled by my disorientation. Then Star-man's voice comes to me from my immediate right. He speaks softly so that he doesn't scare me. He tells me to crawl to my left along the wall of the lodge. I breathe in the cedar-scented air and move into the lodge. I reach out and feel the curved branches of the wall as I move forward. The packed earth is cool against my palms. I crawl, trying to picture the circle in my mind as I move so that I don't stop too soon. It feels like I've gone too far when I bump into Mia.

"There's lots of room in here. You can definitely scoot back a little," she whispers.

I smile and blush, feeling the embarrassment even though she can't see my face. "Right. Sorry. It's a lot bigger in here than I imagined from out there."

"Mm-hmm," she says. "One of the great things about the sweat. Makes you realize that even the smallest things can be bigger than they seem. Offer more than we expect them to."

"That's very poetic," I say.

"I know, right?" Mia says.

The doorway darkens when Robby kneels down. *"Kwe kwe, madòdison. Wàwàsamòg Kekinàmàgedji nidijinikaz. Màg dodem."*

I watch his silhouetted form until he blends in with the darkness. I hear him shuffle toward me. He stops a good distance away. I wonder if I've moved too far into the lodge? What would happen if I were to sit in a doorway? Probably nothing. I need to calm down. It's not like there's power here. At least, not the same kind that I've become used to with Nanabush. This is different. I'm here for myself. To try to heal.

And to try to find him.

Thomas follows Robby after taking off his jacket, shirt, and shoes. The light might be dim, but I can still tell that he's well-built. I don't know how he finds the time to work out between running his great-great-grandfather's crooked company and trying to take over my damn quarry.

Star-man claps his hands once to get our attention. "Okay, den! Everyone's in. Are yiz comfortable?"

"Hey," says Mia's dad, bending down so that he can peer into the lodge at Thomas and Robby. "Take the drums and the shakers. Yiz'll need them for songs."

"Do I pass them around?" asks Thomas.

Mia's dad nods. "Yeah, just keep giving things to Robby until I stop handing you stuff."

"Oh, okay," says Thomas. "I can do that. Here, Robby."

"Thanks," he replies as he takes the first drum in his hands.

The instruments are passed around the circle so that we each get one. I'm given a shaker. It feels like it's made from a tortoise shell. I go to give a few test shakes, but Robby's already handing me a bucket of water. It's cold to the touch and heavy. I hand it to Mia to pass down to Star-man.

"Okay! Looks like we are finally all set to sweat, ahn! Yiz are nice and ready, so it's time to bring in the *madònewàbik*—our first four stones. We welcome dis first group into de lodge wit warm greetings." The elder leans forward onto his hands so that he can stick his head out the door. He calls to the fire-keeper for the stones.

Mia's dad follows the cedar trail to the lodge as he brings the stones to us. One at a time, he carries them balanced carefully on a pitchfork. We greet each stone as it comes through the Eastern doorway and is placed gently into the hole dug in the centre of the lodge. The stones are so hot that they almost glow. The last stone splits in half, revealing its orange centre. Heat radiates off them and slowly begins to fill the lodge.

"We honour our four directions with dese first four stones. Each one represents a direction," says Star-man. "Take some of dat cedar dat we jus' passed around and sprinkle it onto the stones. Hullo, ancestors!"

The cedar lights up briefly before burning away.

Star-man calls out to the fire-keeper again, and three more stones are added to the glowing pile. The heat builds.

"Now we have seven beautiful stones in our lodge," continues Star-man. "Seven is an important number to the Anishnaabeg as it represents our Seven Grandfather Teachings. A lot, a lot of people like to tink dat dem teachings is like a religion and dat is wrong. You see, de way we choose to live our lives is by honouring those teachings. If we follow dem teachings, then we can say that we are living the 'Good Life.' Can anyone tell me what the Seven Grandfather Teachings are?"

"Honesty, respect, love, bravery, humility, wisdom," says Robby. He pauses and grumbles. "Dang, I can never remember them all."

"Anyone else want to take a crack at it?" asks Star-man. "Mia?"

"Beats me," she says. "Seven's a lot to try to keep track of."

"Truth," I say, turning my face toward the doorway, where I know Thomas is sitting. "The last one is truth."

"Dat's the one!" Star-man says. "Might even be the most important. Because without truth, dere can be no meaning. Now we welcome the Seven Teachings into the lodge. Hullo, Grandfathers!"

There's a chorus of greetings as we toss more of our cedar bits onto the rocks.

Star-man calls out to the fire-keeper one final time, telling him to close the door.

Seated where I am, almost directly across from the entrance, I watch as Mia's dad unravels the tarp and lets it fall over the doorway. The light is swallowed up immediately and we're in total darkness. The lodge feels like it's shrinking in on me. I open my eyes wider, as if that can somehow help me see. Beside me, Robby is breathing evenly. He sounds so relaxed. I close my eyes, try to take some control back, make it seem like I'm in charge of the dark surrounding me. My mouth is pasty and dry from the hot air. I wish I had something to drink. Everything starts to feel too close. I drop my hands by my sides, dig my fingers into the ground. There's pressure at the tips of my fingers as dirt settles beneath my nails.

Then the smell of the air changes. Wood. Earthy musk, sweet and warm. I open my eyes in time to see the cinders of bear root twinkle like stars on the heat of the rocks. The dying orange glow from the burning osha root brings light to the faces of everyone in the lodge before it fizzles out, leaving us all in complete darkness once more.

Star-man begins to hum as he throws water onto the rocks. They hiss and sizzle and pop as the water changes to steam, filling the air with its heat and moisture. Collectively, we breathe in deeply, letting the steam fill our lungs, and slowly we breathe out, exhaling with a sigh.

"Ho-kah," comes Star-man's gentle voice. "I want to start with a welcome song. If you know it, sing with me. But if you don't, dat's fine. Just listening is someting we people seem to have forgotten."

The sound of four drumbeats reverberates inside the lodge, sending vibrations into my chest. Star-man settles into a steady rhythm, and Robby and Mia join in. The drumming surrounds me and I close my eyes, letting the sounds and the heat of the air wash over me. Star-man sings the first line of the song, sending a call into the lodge. Robby and Mia join in to give the answer. Their voices sing in chorus. It's beautiful. But I hear something else. A hum beneath their clear, strong voices. Someone is speaking and it sounds like thunder.

¤ ¤ ¤

It was Sôginijiwin who called me in here, and now it is Sôginijiwin who I stand in front of. Even in my tall, two-legged body, I'm small. Dwarfed by the might of the Seven. Inside this great teepee, I know that I am not safe. There's something about the way they look at me that tells me so. Indifference? Yes, that's it. They look at me with an indifference that tells me that to them, I am "less than." I am not one of their charges, so they do not give me pity or true kindness. But I am also not one of their enemies, so they do not give me hatred or disgust. Right now, I am their tool, their weapon. Their way of reaching into the other side without having to go there themselves. Something they cannot do without some form of sacrifice. I have some power in this exchange. I'm the right hand of the Seven, after all. What can a hand do? It gives and takes. It can make a fist.

Sôginijiwin and the rest of the Seven are seated on a dais around the edges of the teepee. They sit with straight backs, tall and proud. Each of them is beautiful in a way that is neither female nor male, with hair woven from the night sky, and skin the colours of deep clay red, smooth fawn, and rich copper. They are dressed in ornately beaded and fringed cloth and hide. They radiate with a light that is both seen and unseen. As if looking upon them is like the image left inside your eyelids after staring at the sun. They are bigger than I am, inhumanly so, and they move slowly, like redwoods in a breeze. They are frightening and arresting. Like watching the rising of the dawn on a battlefield.

The ever-burning fire at the centre of the teepee sends smoke up into the air, dancing through the wooden poles that are the bones of the tent. The smoke weaves up and up until it reaches the starlit sky above. It isn't hot inside the teepee, but I can feel myself beginning to sweat. I hear the sound of distant drumming, but maybe that's just my heart.

"Why did you call me here?" I ask. "And why have I got my body back?"

—Are you not grateful to be in your proper home, Trickster? Sôginijiwin tilts their head and reaches long fingers up to adjust the white weasel pelt draped over their shoulders.

I raise my hands up in defence. "What? No, that's not it at all. I'm happy, but I know how you work. There's a reason I'm like this right now."

Gweyâkwâdiziwin laughs, a sound that rings high and true like a rainstorm on a lake. —It would appear we have become predictable. Nanabush, the Trickster, can see right through us.

"You don't make it hard to do, now, do you?"

A chorus of laughter. Together, they sound like a forest full of song.

—Why don't you tell us why you think we have gifted you with your body? Tabasenimidiwin folds their turquoise-and-silver-ringed hands in their lap.

"I've done my time and deserve to be back to my regular self?"

They laugh again. I suppose that was too much of a stretch.

"Okay," I say. I start to shift my shoulders slightly, a motion that normally readjusts my wings, folding them so they look beautiful as they rest along my back. In this body, the movement is a shrug. How boring. "That must be a no."

—It is fun to watch him. Look how he creases his brow when he thinks. The lines on his face all come together in one point, like water rushing downhill into the dirt! Kaye Nibwâkawin leans forward to point at me. Their beautiful face lights up with laughter. You are getting old, Trickster, to have lines like those.

"Among those on the other side of your doorways, these lines mean I've lived. I look wise."

The white paint adorning Manadji'idiwin's eyes makes their look of skepticism so much more potent. —And do you think that you have lived a life worthy of the wisdom your lines speak of?

I cross my arms in front of my chest. The bone beads of my breastplate are cool against my skin. "I don't think that I've had that chance yet, Manadji'idiwin. Let me try my hand at a real life and I'll come back with my findings."

Manadji'idiwin shakes their head. —You have not earned a body on that side of the Wheel, Trickster. I am not so sure that you have rightly earned that body on this side either. But that was not for me alone to decide.

Sagi'idiwin smiles and their face fills with light. It's distractingly beautiful. —The Seven have always come to decisions as one. Together, or not at all. You should be thankful that many of us desire to see you succeed and are proud of your accomplishments thus far.

"Pray tell, what are those?" I say with a smile that curls up my lips.

Tebwewin adjusts and the jingle cones lining their shoulders chime together. —Your work with noshis Hazel, of course. Though you have fumbled time and time again, you have proved that you are the owner of true persistence.

"You could go into specifics. Everyone loves a compliment, and you've been stingy with them lately."

—You step backward as quickly as you step forward, Trickster, *says Sôginijiwin.*

"You're asking me to play a guessing game with you until I figure out why I have hands again? A waste of time."

Manadji'idiwin sighs heavily and the sound is like a bough breaking. —A waste of time, indeed. You fail to see the importance of the task you have taken from us. I say that we have waited on your success long enough. We should send one of our own to do what is necessary for noshis and for the Wheel.

"Wait. What are you going on about?" This sounds serious. I haven't been told anything about the Wheel before. This whole time it's been all "Save Hazel, stop the quarry," but they've clearly been leaving something out. Bringing up the Medicine Wheel now seems odd, so I need to press for more information. I hope they don't give it to me in riddles. "How do you expect me to do the right thing if you keep things from me?"

—Because you do not tread lightly. You are like a bull in a

pen. Always charging, even if the smallest bird should step onto your grass. *Kaye Nibwâkawin brushes the tips of their scalp feather aside as they stare at me, a slow anger clear in their eyes.* You stomp and crash your way through all that crosses your path.

"That isn't true," I snap. "I have been very careful with Hazel."

Sôginijiwin's face darkens with rage and their voice booms like the call of thunder in the night. —You have taken her to places that Anishnaabeg should not go until they have passed through the Western doorway! Memory is no place for one of them.

Sweat drips down my cheek from my forehead. "You told me to find the handshake and I did. We both did. Not once did you tell me that I could not bring Hazel with me as we searched."

Manadji'idiwin frowns and runs their fingers down the deep-black bear fur adorning their braids. The motion is almost hypnotic. It returns a calm look to their face. —Nanabush, you were told to keep her safe. Sifting through her memories and dragging her along is far from safe.

"What choice did you leave me with? Stuck in a crow's body? Do you have any idea of the work I put in just to get that binòdjish to trust me?" I want to turn away from them, but they're all around me, and every way that I turn, I'm forced to stare down another set of angular features and strong, deep eyes.

—But are you not Nanabush, the Great Shapeshifter? Trickster of many faces? Do you not possess power beyond that of your mortal brothers and sisters? Surely, this task could not be too much for someone as cunning as you? *Sôginijiwin laughs, punctuating the mockery of their tone.* Nanabush, Trickster god. It would seem that you are little more than a tired, old memory.

They want to get a rise out of me. That much is obvious. But why? That can't be the only reason they've summoned me here. "That sounds like the pot calling the kettle black, as they say."

The group of them looks at me with confusion.

KAREN McBRIDE

"Creator," I say, exasperated, "you need to spend more time paying attention to what goes on outside of your little camp. If you can't understand a saying like that, then you're all poor choices to deal with Hazel."

—Do you mean that we have fallen into myth and stories like you? *Kaye Nibwâkawin says.* We may not be spoken to as we once were, but we will not be forgotten. As long as our People still sing songs and light their sage, we will be remembered. I would not ever go as far as to speak our names in the same breath as you, Trickster.

"And why not? I may not be your brother, but I'm as good as a cousin. First cousin, even," I say. "I am not less than you because I carry the blood of the Anishnaabeg in me."

—We have been through this again and again, *says Sôginijiwin.* You are a child of both sides of the Wheel. You live in the Spirit World and in the world of the Anishnaabeg. You must accept that you will never truly fit in in either place.

I might have heard this all before, but their words still sting. Like tearing through scar tissue. I breathe in and out. The air is hot as it moves into my lungs. "Tell me about the Wheel. Why would you threaten to take my task from me now?"

Sôginijiwin observes me, looking down at me from their seat. They place their hands on their knees and breathe out, sending a gust of air through the teepee. —You above all others should understand the importance of the Wheel. Do not take this news lightly.

"It's what separates us and them. Go on. You've got my attention."

—The mine will go forward.

"How is that possible? The deal between Abe and Thomas wasn't ever written down. The whole mine shouldn't be there in the first place. The land was never surrendered!"

Tebwewin raises a hand to silence me. —This truth you have found with noshis must see the light of the dawn. The time for that will be soon, but now it is the new mine that must be stopped. The wemitigòji is following in the footsteps of his great-great-grandfather. Already there are sticks filled with fire and smoke waiting to be lit. They sleep in beds inside the rock and they will soon be woken to send the water that is flooding the mine back to the river.

"This isn't right. How could they have done all of that so quickly?" I ask, trying to find clarity. "Hazel and I have only just found out about the handshake. Gagnon can't have had time to push forward without the proper permission."

—We do not see such trivial details. What we know is that rock will fall to fire, and when that happens, the Western doorway will be destroyed. *Gweyâkwâdiziwin's words bring silence into the teepee.*

The wind outside pushes against the hide walls. It picks up until it shakes the tent. The door blows open and carries with it the sound of soft voices speaking in a hot room. I turn to look outside and see the outline of five bodies seated around a pit of stones. They cannot see me.

The door falls shut, leaving me alone with the Seven once more.

¤ ¤ ¤

Star-man finishes the song with one final beat of his drum. The hide is stretched tight over the wooden frame so the sound resonates inside the lodge like a cathedral. Though he hasn't added any water to the stones since we first closed the door, the heat rises.

I bring a hand to my forehead to wipe away the moisture settling on my skin. But it's useless. You can't remove sweat with more sweat. I tug the fabric of my skirt out from under me so I can lean back on my hands without getting them covered in dirt and cedar.

"Ho-kah, dat's a nice song," says Star-man into the darkness. "Now, de first ting we do inside de lodge after de song and de stones and de water is talk. Since dis is a healing sweat meant to take away your hurts, we are gonna talk about anyting dat is causing your heart and spirit to be heavy. Like always, we begin in de Eastern doorway. Dat means dat Thomas, you're lucky number one! Remember dat whatever is said inside this sweat will be kept here. You speak your hurts out, and we will listen and we will take that pain away. Dis is a sacred and safe place."

There's no immediate reply from Thomas. I imagine he's sitting in silent fear. I know I am, but he must feel worse than I do. At least I'm one of the crowd here. He's the odd one out.

"Wow," he says. "Go first, huh? No pressure."

Everyone around me laughs.

I guess I should have too. I should be more supportive. After all, Star-man said this was a safe place. Me being hostile negates that whole sentiment. And don't I want him to be kind to me as well? Fine. I shift slightly and turn my head to where he's sitting.

Thomas's voice cuts through the warm silence. "I don't quite know where to start."

"Most people find dat the beginning is the best."

"Okay, sure." Thomas clears his throat, the darkness making him seem closer to me than he is. "Hello, everyone. I, um, I'm White. I want to thank you for inviting me here to this ceremony tonight. It is an honour to be welcomed in your community and your culture. I know that it wasn't always this way."

He pauses and sighs. This is hard for him to say. I get it, though, I do. Sharing a part of yourself that is hurting feels like a confession. An admission of guilt and acknowledgement that there is something wrong with you, that there's a broken part that needs to be repaired or replaced.

"I meant to come here tonight and just be an observer. Someone who listens and appreciates from a distance. But I think there's more I should say. My family has a long and unfortunate history with your people. I know that things weren't always done the right way and there was suffering because of it. There's *still* suffering because of them. But I want you to know that I aim to fix those mistakes, the mistakes of my great-great-grandfather and all those who came after him. It's shameful that my past is what it is, but that stops with me. I want to change things. I *will* change things."

The passion in his voice is startling, bizarre. It should be off-putting, but I find myself feeling sympathetic. What he hopes to do, hopes to change, I understand. Righting the wrongs of a father certainly rings of unsavoury similarity. How different are we, Thomas and I? Are we actually on opposing sides in all of this? Maybe what he wants to do is the right thing after all?

Thomas speaks quietly and with an air of finality. "I want to build bridges, not burn them. Create a future that helps all of us."

There's a beat of silence before Star-man cries out, "*Semà!*"

I know that outside, the fire-keeper throws tobacco into the flames.

"Thank you for sharing, Thomas," says Star-man. "If you stay true to dat belief, den your path will be laid out before you. *Meegwetch.*"

Thomas says nothing.

Star-man addresses Robby next, inviting him to share in the talking circle. Robby starts talking, but I can't seem to focus on his voice. He sounds so distant now. I feel a chill at my back as if a breeze has swept in through the Eastern doorway and continued on behind me. The feeling only lasts a moment before the heat of the lodge comes back to me. I try to listen, pay attention to what Robby is sharing so openly and easily with all of us, but there are other voices murmuring. They sound as if they're behind me, so I turn to look for any sign of their owners, but all I see is the wall of the lodge. It's possible that there are people talking back at Robby's house, though being able to hear them at this distance seems unlikely. The voices sound different, as if they have a power to them. Something nameless. The back of my neck tingles even as sweat drips along my skin.

"*Semà!*" calls Star-man.

Shit. I've missed everything Robby had to say. But there's no time to feel guilty. It's my turn next. I have to be ready to say something. My mouth aches for something to drink. Fresh air. I want to leave. The lodge feels too small, shrinking in and closing around me. The temperature rises, sweat rolls down my fingertips and onto my skirt. Even in the dark, I can feel everyone's eyes on me. They've turned their heads. My face burns with embarrassment and panic.

Thump. Thump.

The door to the lodge is pulled open and cold night air rushes inside. I squint as the glow from the fire lights everything around us, though because it's far away, everyone is in near-silhouette. Standing in the doorway is Mia's dad. He's holding a large glass of water.

"*Kwe kwe*, fire-keeper!" says Star-man.

"Everything going well?" asks Mia's dad.

"*Enhenh*," Star-man says, patting his knees. "Ready for a drink and some more Grandfathers."

"Whatcha tinkin'?"

"Five more. One for each of us sweaters in here."

Mia's dad whistles lowly. "Okay, if yiz are good, den I guess you'll be good." He hands the glass of water to Thomas. "Pass that around so everyone can have a sip."

"Geez, you can relax a bit," Mia says, tapping my left hand that's balled into a fist, knuckles white.

"Oh." I look down at my hands and quickly release them. Blood shoots back to my fingers uncomfortably. "Wow, I didn't even notice."

"You that stressed about having to talk next?" she asks. Her face is lit all along her left side as she turns to look at me.

"Yeah, I guess. Feelings aren't my favourite topic," I say with a nervous laugh.

She leans back on her hands and readjusts to scoot forward. "No shit."

Robby pokes my arm. "Hazel?" He hands the glass of water to me.

"Thanks." I drink more than I should, then hand it to Mia. "Do I *have* to share? I don't think I'm in the right mood to talk everything out. Don't the ancestors have a sixth sense to thoughts and stuff?"

She shrugs and sips from the glass. "I don't know. I mean, probably? You don't have to pray out loud all the time and they're supposed to hear you then too. I'm gonna tentatively say yes. They gotchu."

"Okay, good."

Our attention is called back to the Eastern doorway as five more Grandfather stones are brought into the lodge. Already, the heat rises higher and higher. Star-man thanks Mia's dad as he lowers the door, closing us all in the dark once again. The sound of water as it sloshes into the ladle seizes our attention before the now-familiar hiss of steam as the water comes into contact with the rocks. It is so hot now that the air presses against our bodies, wet and steaming. We're stuck like statues seated around a dead fire.

Breathe in through the nose. And out through the mouth.

"Hazel?"

"Yes?"

"It is your turn to share. Would you like to?" Star-man's words are gentle.

I can tell that he wants to hear from me. Wants me to participate properly in my first sweat. Get that real Anishnaabe experience. But I can't. There are too many places for me to start with this story. It's depressing as hell. I've already lived through all this pain and I don't want to push it on these people. Especially not with Thomas here. He's at the root of my new problems. Or are these old problems that have wriggled their way back out of the dirt? It isn't just Dad's death that haunts me, hurts me. It's all the things he left behind too.

"No," I say, flatly and without emotion. "Sorry. I just . . . not now."

"Ah, dat's okay," says Star-man. "Sharing can be hard. It is a hurt too, just like everything else we have to deal with and everything that we ask for help with. In time, we get the courage to speak our truth. But only if we are ready. Dat, in itself, is a gift. *Semà!*"

"*Meegwetch, Ananginini,*" I mumble.

Elders always talk in riddles.

Star-man claps his hands once. "Haaah, now den. We break at every doorway, but tonight, I tink, we should sing another song before den. And, Mia, if you're okay with it, I'd like to hear from you before we open the door again?"

"Yes, okay."

"Good, good! Okay den! Let's get dem drums up and shakers ready." Star-man runs his open palm in circles on the hide of his drum. "This song I learnt from a medicine man up North. It's called '*Manidò Makwa*,' which means 'Spirit Bear.' And the bear in our culture, he's the healer. The one who is strong enough to take the hurts away and carry dem safely away for us. If you know the song, join in, sing strong. And if you don't, that's okay too. I can sing for all of us here. Ho-kah, here we go."

He strikes the drum four times, clearly, letting each beat ring out before beginning the next. When he sings, I close my eyes and feel myself sinking into the song. Each beat is the beat of my heart, and each word speaks for me. His voice is low, shaking with age, but beautiful. The lodge seems to fade away as I lean back and let the song take me.

A rush of cold, dark air. Feel like I'm falling, flying, drifting. My body feels too solid. Wants to be lighter. Star-man's voice is far away from me, as if I am moving backward and into another place. Legs ache, tell me that it's time to stand. The literal, logical side of my mind is screaming at me that I'll hit my head if I try that—the lodge is too small, the roof too low. But I know I need to. I place both of my hands firmly on the ground beside me and push myself up. My shoulders lift to my ears, cringing in anticipation of the pain and embarrassment, but it does not come. The smell of the bear root dims and is replaced by the scent of a burning fire and the bite of cold winter air. I open my eyes.

At my feet, snow glimmers in the moonlight. The world is a collection of blues and blacks. The sky is a blanket of pitch with holes punched in it. Stars dance in the dark expanse, disappearing into the brilliant green and turquoise of a waving aurora. Wigwams stand silent in the village around me. A pine and birch forest, boughs reaching up into the sky, guards at the edge of the camp.

There are footprints leading farther up into the village. I turn around to follow their trail with my eyes. There, atop a small hill, sits a giant teepee lit from a burning fire behind the animal hide. Smoke billows from the hole in the top of it, twirling around the great poles. There are voices coming from the teepee. Seven, and one more that I know well.

I know where I am. What this is. I've been here before, only back then I took it for a dream. I was mistaken. Where I am is real, and it is precisely where I want to be.

This is the Spirit World.

15

THE DOORWAY

The wind picks up, howls, tosses my hair over my shoulders and around my face as I walk, step over step, toward the great teepee. The moccasins covering my once-bare feet are a deep tan, their toes adorned with beaded roses. Beneath me, the snow crunches. I pull the bearskin shawl draped around my shoulders tighter, bracing against the chill of the winter air. I'm dressed in beautiful skins, decorated with intricate beads and porcupine quills. There are crow feathers in my hair. My spirit is finely dressed and ready for a ceremony. Ready for what lies beyond that painted doorway at the top of the hill.

As I get closer, the voices become more distinct. I recognize them as the same ones I heard the first time I stumbled into the Spirit World. Now, I know them to be the voices of the Seven. Speaking at once, they sound like a hurricane. The closer I get to the teepee, the louder and clearer their voices become.

—*The time to act must be now,* comes a voice like an ancient oak, Manadji'idiwin. *We have waited too long for this Trickster to complete the task he has stolen from us.*

Sagi'idiwin speaks next. —*Rushing in with anger will not solve this problem. The mistake is his and his alone. He must be the one to fix it.*

—*Mistake?* Gweyâkwâdiziwin says, outrage clear in their voice. *The mistake is not his but ours. We did not act. We failed noshis before the Trickster even passed through the doorway. Letting him escape was our misstep.*

—*You are too kind to him, Gweyâkwâdiziwin. He chose to rush into her world. His choices are what have led him to this point. No one but he is responsible for his failure.* Harsh words from Sôginijiwin. With a voice like thunder, they speak the loudest.

"I'm supposed to just stand here while you all say terrible things about me?"

Nanabush.

I knew I would find him. I used to think people were ridiculous for saying things like "Whatever it costs" and "I'd do anything," but now that I've crossed into another realm to find my bird-friend, I can relate.

There's something different about his voice. The way he's speaking sounds comfortable, relaxed in a way that I haven't heard. There's a natural smoothness to his words, a lilting rhythm that tells me he's happy. Well, almost. He'll never truly be happy.

I inch closer to the teepee but stop outside of it. Moving one step to the side of the door, I crouch down and settle in to listen further. I want to know what they're talking about. Of course, I want to be able to see them for myself, but that's a temptation I have to resist. The moment they lay eyes on me, they'll rush me out of here. Anishnaabeg aren't supposed to be on this side of the Medicine Wheel when we can still walk the forests and plains of Turtle Island. There's only one true way to be welcomed here and I'm not ready for that yet.

—*Enough,* says Tebwewin, bringing silence to the room. *Have we not given Nanabush our word? Thus far he has upheld his end of the bargain. By stealing the right to complete his task, we would be all but declaring that our word means nothing. This cannot stand. We owe the Trickster the right to finish that which he has started.*

Bargain? So what, Nanabush struck a deal with the Seven?

The wind picks up and moves the doorway of the teepee aside, so that I can see in. At first, I can only see the back of a man in black buckskins. I recognize him instantly as Nanabush. He's standing with his arms crossed, silvery black hair hanging loose down his back. There are inky feathers in his hair, held in place by silver beads. This is what he looks like?

"Tebwewin, I knew there was a reason you were my favourite," says Nanabush. "If you give me a bit more time, I'll get the job done. I'll fix your broken noshis."

—Hush, Trickster. You might have me on your side, but the might of the Seven lies in our shared thought. You must convince all of us that you are ready for the challenge facing you, Tebwewin answers.

"How am I to do that if so many of you doubt me?" There's honesty and the pain of rejection in his voice.

—You must stop talking about this task as if it means nothing to you, Manadji'idiwin replies.

"That's not it. That isn't how I see it."

—And yet you have not succeeded at anything. Noshis is in pieces and soon the doorway will be as well, Manadji'idiwin huffs and the sound is like the clacking of tall, bare birch trees in a strong wind.

Nanabush groans in exasperation. "What more do you want me to do to try to fix that mess of a girl? You think you can hold my freedom hostage with riddles and half-truths just because you want me to put a crying girl back together?"

He's such an asshole. Even here, in front of a group of immortals, he's the same pompous piece of work. This is why kids throw rocks at birds.

—He does not listen. He chirps and chirps and chirps, jumping at every chance he can to talk about himself and the deeds he has done. In his eyes, every breath he takes is worthy of applause. Kaye Nibwâkawin's honeyed voice sounds exhausted.

"That isn't true," says Nanabush. "I can do many things while holding my breath as well."

There's a chorus of annoyed grunts and tuts.

—*I say he does not deserve what he desires*, Sôginijiwin rumbles. *He should remain a crow for eternity.*

"A sense of humour would make dealing with you much easier."

—*Perhaps you have worn us out, Trickster? Or perhaps you are simply not funny?* Sagi'idiwin says.

"Now that's just plain mean, Sagi'idiwin."

He turns toward the door. My breath catches in my throat, and I press myself up against the wall of the teepee to hide from view. I nearly lose my balance but catch myself, dig my hands into the snow to find the ground. Nanabush keeps talking. He hasn't seen me.

"What else do I have to do to prove to you that I am desperate for my body, my life, back? I saved her from the quarry, didn't I?"

I shift, straining my neck to try to see farther into the tent. But there's a glow of light that makes it impossible to catch sight of anyone else.

Tabasenimidiwin speaks. —*Ah, the answer to the first question asked by you when you arrived here.*

"What?" says Nanabush. He turns so I can see his profile. High cheekbones, long, pointed nose, copper skin with red paint beneath his eyes. "You mean the reason I'm in my body right now is because I saved Hazel from falling into the water?"

No one answers, but the change in light must mean that they've nodded.

—*An act of true selflessness is one of the most powerful*, Tabasenimidiwin says, soft and soothing. *It may be that you are finally learning what it means to be mortal.*

"Selfless? You . . . you think that was selfless?" Nanabush's voice is high and strained. He sounds nervous, offended. He laughs awkwardly and without humour. "That was me trying to cover up the mistake I made. You think I meant to save her? No, I was saving me. I've always just been saving *me*."

Why is he talking like that? Like I mean nothing to him. After everything we have been through, I am still nothing. A silly little girl, broken into pieces that she can't figure out how to put back together on her own.

Tabasenimidiwin laughs like a fall breeze. —*It took all your hard-earned power to stop her from falling into that abyss of nothingness, did it not? You could have let her fall. She would have found her way here, and we would have welcomed her spirit into our house. We would have held it warmly before guiding her back to where she belongs.*

"You mean, I *didn't* have to save her? I wasted everything I had on her?"

Wasted? I'm something to be thrown out with the trash. Saving me from a spiritual death wasn't an intentional act of sacrifice, but a mistake. An obstacle in the way of his path toward a body? He's selfish. Stupid. But maybe I am too? Thinking that a Trickster like Nanabush could care enough about someone like me is idiotic. Embarrassing.

—*You did not, no. Yet you did so without thinking*, says Gweyâk-wâdiziwin. *You saved her because you wanted to. It was an act of kindness.*

"Kindness? No. An accident. Unintentional," Nanabush says coldly. "Besides, it was repayment. She saved me from this place, and now I've saved her."

The hurt I'm feeling quickly sours to anger. I reach up and tear the crow feathers from my hair. I stand, completely disregarding the risk I'm taking by showing myself, and pull aside the door.

I'm shouting when I say, "I guess that makes us even then!" But I'm cut off by my own cry. My eyes instantly water as a rush of brilliant light forces me to close them shut. Blinded by the radiance of the Seven, I turn away from the teepee. Stumbling, I fall to my knees, hands and arms sinking into the snow. My body feels weighed down. Exhaustion washes over me. I want to lie down right here. Curl into a ball, fall asleep. Sleep for hours, days.

Nanabush calls my name and I hear his footsteps behind me.

From a distance I hear someone call out, "*Semà!*" and I feel the strength to continue. I haul myself to my feet. The bearskin slides from my shoulders, falling into a heap on the ground.

"Hazel, wait! Please!"

No. I won't wait. Scrambling, I run as far as I can from the teepee. I ignore Nanabush and his pleading. I put as much distance as I can between myself and the group of immortals. I sprint toward the tree line. Branches scratch at me, leaving thin red lines on my face and hands. The undergrowth grabs and tugs at me like unseen hands trying to hold me back, but I keep running through the forest, the light fading until I'm enveloped in blackness. The air changes, heats up, makes it hard to breathe. In the distance I see five figures seated in a circle.

The sweat.

I crouch down as I get closer until I'm crawling on my hands and knees. There's a numbing in my limbs. The sound of my breathing gets louder. The push and pull of blood through my veins is like wind, like waves. I pause, sitting at my back. For a moment, I can feel the call of the Spirit World. I glance over my shoulder as a longing blossoms in my heart. If I stay, I can rest. This will all be over. Is that the right thing to do?

Then the outline of a man emerges from the trees and I know that I cannot stay. If he is here, then there will be no rest for me. I turn from him and reach out to embrace myself. The return is quick, painless. I'm falling, floating, and then landing, gently. My spirit and my body come together like one hand into another.

I gasp as if breathing for the first time.

The Eastern doorway opens.

Mia's hand is on my arm. "Welcome back."

"What?"

I can see her smile in the dim light from the distant Sacred Fire. She laughs lightly. "You made it through your first sweat."

"Oh," I say, trying to get my breathing back to normal. "Thanks."

"What do you think? Feel better?"

"Um . . ." I hesitate. "I learned a lot."

"Good. That's all you can ask for. Bet your skin looks amazing too. Oh, shit." She pauses, quickly covering her mouth with her hand. "Sorry, didn't mean to swear. But it looks like you ended up in the Western doorway. Dammit, I *knew* I moved too far over. Are you okay? That's a hard place to be for your first sweat."

I nod absently and then give her the drum and shaker that Robby has placed in my hands. I watch the instruments as they move around the circle and then out of the lodge.

Mia looks over at me with concern. "Are you sure you're okay, Hazel? You look like you've seen one of the ancestors with your own eyes."

"Seven, actually."

She snorts. "Is that so?"

"Well, I heard them. They're hard to see."

"Right," she says. "Okay, I think it's time we got you something to eat."

Mia turns and crawls out of the lodge. I shift and move to follow her. Outside, it is cold and clear. Stars hang in the sky above our heads. The heat billows off my skin and up into the night.

Mia waves at me to join her by the Sacred Fire. The flames seem dull and small after seeing the fire of the Seven. She picks up two bowls, one filled with cedar and the other with tobacco.

"Here," she says. "Take a bit of each and then offer it to the Fire."

"What do I say?" I ask.

"You don't have to say anything."

"Am I supposed to think something?"

She laughs. "You don't have to think anything either. It's an offering. Throwing it into the Fire is thanks enough."

"Okay."

I take a bit of each medicine and place it in my hand before stepping toward the Sacred Fire. I pause. There are words I should say, proper thanks that I should give. I should be grateful for the healing, the help that the sweat has given me. But I don't feel fixed. I feel worse. Alone. I say nothing and throw the medicine into the fire. The cedar and tobacco curl and blacken.

I turn my back to the flames and join the others.

Robby and Thomas are standing together on the deck. Robby is gesturing animatedly as he talks about the sweat. "Can't believe it got so hot. How many Grandfathers did we have in there?"

Thomas pulls his shirt back on. The sweat on his skin shines in the porch light. "I stopped paying attention when it got too hot to breathe easily."

Robby claps him on the shoulder. "And you still survived!"

Thomas laughs. "I'm going to count that as an accomplishment."

"You should," replies Robby.

Thomas shrugs, but he's blushing. He smiles at Mia and me when we approach. "That was something, eh?"

"Mm-hmm," I answer coldly.

Robby hands me a towel. "Here."

I take the towel from him, wring it in my hands. Mia's mom peeks out from the house. She calls Mia and Robby over to help set up the feast. They head inside, leaving Thomas and me alone on the deck. I busy myself with dabbing the sweat on my neck. Thomas clears his throat to get my attention.

"It felt good," he says, "to leave all of that back in the lodge. Don't you think?"

He's watching me expectantly. He wants me to carry on, say something else. I focus on wiping the sweat from my forearms.

"Are you okay? You didn't say anything during the sweat." Thomas has lowered his voice. "Was it because I was there?"

I look up at him swiftly. "What? No."

"I just thought that maybe because of my history with your father, you might feel awkward talking about him."

"Maybe I'm not ready to talk about him. Doesn't mean you have anything to do with it."

"Oh." Thomas shifts his weight onto his back foot so he can lean away from me slightly. He crosses his arms, then rethinks the posture and stuffs his hands into his pockets. He doesn't know where to look, so he turns away from me.

I sigh. "Sorry, that was mean."

"No," he says. "It's all right. I was prying."

"Still," I say. I can feel the conversation slipping away. Silence ebbs in the cracks in between us, so I quickly speak up. "I'm glad the sweat helped you. It had to work for someone."

He looks back at me, offers me a smile. "Thank you. Shall we go and join the others?"

"Yeah, we should. Feast is the best part, after all."

I want him to go on ahead, but he waits for me. Reluctantly, I walk beside him as we move into the house. I stop on the threshold as Thomas politely holds the door open for me. I take one last look at the Sacred Fire. Part of me expects to see a crow flying from the lodge, but nothing comes. It lies empty. I step into the house and Thomas follows after. He pulls the door closed, shutting out the light from the fire and the choir of whispering voices just beyond.

¤ ¤ ¤

The day after the sweat, I go to work and try to act like everything is okay. I do my best to smile and chat with Joni, but it's hard. Too many thoughts swirl around inside me, pulling and pushing in different directions. Working with Thomas is part of her job, and I should leave it at that. Far too often I have to catch myself from saying a biting remark. It's not her fault. Still, I wish she would have at least talked to me about it. It's my damn land, after all.

The day goes by slowly, almost painfully. I do what I can to keep myself isolated until it's time to leave for lunch, and even then, I hide out in the conference room until I'm sure Joni's gone. I've stopped driving myself to work in an attempt to spend more time out of the house. So far, it's worked, but it eats away at my lunch break. Mom picks me up so that I don't waste too much time walking back to the house. We don't talk about the sweat or even about work. She knows I'm having an off day, so she lets me stew in my own silence. The only thing is, I think I need to talk. I want to tell someone what's bothering me. And when she pulls up to the Band Office again after lunch, I hesitate, holding the door handle. I can feel her looking at me with anticipation, her hands moving slightly on the steering wheel as she waits for me to make up my mind.

I look over at her, exhale, and say, "See you after work."

Mom nods. "You bet. Oh wait, no. I'll be gone. My bridge group is meeting up at five, so I gotta leave the house around four thirty to make sure I get there on time. But I'll leave the door unlocked for you."

"Okay," I reply. "I'll see you when I see you, then."

I slide out of the truck and shut the door without looking back. The rest of the day crawls by just like the first four hours did. I sort more boring files about road construction and water mains. Periodically, I take a break to stare out the window and watch leaves float to the ground. I force myself to ignore the treetops, tell myself that I don't want to see any more damn crows. It's getting colder. Fall is giving way to winter much faster than I would like. It hasn't snowed yet—that fact brings me comfort.

When the workday finally ends, I step out, exhausted, into the cool of the late afternoon. It's about 4:40, so the parking lot is empty. Cutting through the trailer park is the fastest way home. It's not something I'd do at night, but the sun, though low on the horizon, is still in the sky. Not that it's necessarily dangerous, but it gets dark as hell. The street lights are sparse around here. Guess that goes with the imposed low-rent lifestyle of the trailer park. Poverty looks better in the dark.

One of my best childhood friends lived in one of these trailers. When I was a kid, I thought it was cool that her house was so long. I remember reading about the Iroquois in school, so it didn't take much for my kid's mind to draw conclusions. Bonnie must live in a longhouse.

The trailer park has gotten more rundown over the years. Bonnie doesn't live here anymore. Her family moved when their application for a real house in town was finally accepted. When she lived here, every trailer was taken. Now there are a few vacancies. I doubt they'll be filled again, considering the state of most of them. The Band has plans to demolish the whole park in favour of a new housing development. Heath Whittaker's demands are being met after all. Wouldn't surprise me if he was still itching for the deed to my dad's quarry. Bad news, Heath, someone's already got their foot in the door. Take a number. Get in line.

A dog barks at me from the makeshift front porch of a trailer. The sound makes me jump, but I don't speed up. The little white dog keeps barking. I give it a wave and it wags its tail. I imagine that's what I look like when I'm trying to be menacing. Loud, yappy, mostly harmless. Bet that's what I looked like shouting into the Sevens' teepee. My face gets hot. How likely are they to remember the kid who threw a fit in their house in the middle of a private meeting?

The strained caw of a crow sounds above me. My pulse rockets. I look up and see a dark bird seated on the telephone wire. The dog keeps barking behind me.

—*Hazel.*

"No." I shake my head and keep walking.

—*Hazel, wait!*

"No."

—*Give me a chance to explain.*

"I can't believe you're going to make me say it again. No! I thought it was clear that I don't want to speak to you. Leave me alone, Nanabush."

He lets out a frustrated croak and I think I've lost him. Then he dive-bombs my head, making me scream and throw my arms into the air to cover myself.

"What the hell?" I straighten up swiftly and glare at him. "Are you crazy?"

He's hovering in the air in front of me. The wind created by his flapping wings gives me goosebumps. There's a look of indignation on his face.

—If this is the only way you'll talk to me, then yes, I'll be a little crazy. You have to listen to me. I've listened to you whine and complain so many times already that I think you owe me that much.

My mouth falls open slightly. "Oh, that's rich. I thought we were even? Pretty sure the way you were talking the other night made it seem that we're done."

He makes a noise that could be a growl of irritation.

—That was a joke. Trying to lighten the mood there.

"I agree with Sagi'idiwin: you aren't funny. Now get out of my way." I step to the side to push past him, but he moves quickly and stops me.

—What you heard that night wasn't the truth. I didn't mean those things.

I pinch the bridge of my nose and sigh heavily. "You sure sounded sincere from where I was standing."

A screen door slams shut, and both Nanabush and I turn toward the sound. There's an older woman standing on the porch with the barking dog. She's scooped him up into her arms and is now staring at me. There's a rush of air as Nanabush flies off. The woman keeps looking at me and the now empty air in front of my face. I don't smile as I turn away. She must think I'm crazy. I might have thought she was right a couple of months ago. Not anymore.

Once I've left the trailer park behind, Nanabush circles over my head until he's flying next to me.

—Hear me out, won't you? If I meant those things, then I wouldn't've come after you. Of all the tales you know about me, have I ever once made a point of admitting I was wrong?

I stop walking and think. "Tsk. No, I guess not."

—*Exactly.*

"You know, that's not a good thing."

—*Oh, I know.*

"Talk, then." I cross my arms and sit into my hip.

—*Not here. There are too many eyes. Did you see the way that gôkom looked at us? We can't risk that again. Unless, of course, you're happy to look insane?*

I roll my eyes and start to walk away from him.

—*Go to the clearing just before the quarry. I know you know the one.*

"Fine."

He takes to the sky and I watch as he flies off in the direction of the quarry. I consider heading straight home, leaving him to wait in the trees, but I know he'll find me again. He always does.

The setting sun paints the sky and grass in oranges and pinks. Clouds, spread long and thin, glow in the changing light. I trudge through the trees, pushing branches and brambles out of my path as I walk toward the clearing. The grass has yellowed and hardened, so that it crunches as I walk through it. The wind moves in and out of the clearing, sending dried leaves tumbling down like rain. I don't see Nanabush, but I know he's here. Somewhere on the edge of the clearing, clinging to the branches, on the cusp of my vision. I move farther into the clearing until I'm directly in the middle. I can feel his eyes on me.

"Hiding, huh? This is doing wonders for my opinion of you."

—*I'm not hiding. There isn't anywhere for me to perch out in the open. Come over here.*

I follow the sound of his voice to the far end of the clearing. Nanabush is sitting high in one of the trembling aspen trees. When I approach, he hops down to the lower branches so that we can be eye to eye. I stare at him, hold his gaze until he has to look away. Nanabush preens his feathers. He sighs.

—*You must be angry with me.*

"Mm-hmm."

—*What all did you hear?*

"That you think saving me was a mistake. You wasted your power. I'm a waste of time." I pause, take a big breath in to keep my emotions down. But my voice is small when I speak again. "You think I'm broken. Is that true?"

He doesn't answer me right away. Instead, he lets the silence between us grow until it feels like I'm standing across the clearing from him. I want to turn and walk away. What good will this conversation do? Will an apology take away the hurt he caused me?

—*No. It's not true.*

"Then why did you say it?"

—*I . . . it might have been true at one point. But I don't think so now.*

"I find that hard to believe." I stuff my hands into my pockets when the wind picks up and look in the direction of the quarry. "Look, it's like you said. Saving me from falling was repayment. I saved you by accident, and now you've saved me by accident. We're even. You can leave me be now."

—*No, that's not what I meant.*

"Why did you say it?" I shout. The wind dies down, making the quiet painful.

—*Because I had to!*

"You *had* to? What the hell does that mean?"

—*The Seven, they're unforgiving. If they decide that I'm the reason things are getting worse, then I'm the one who pays for it.*

"So you go ahead and drag me through the mud, saying shit like *I'm* the problem?"

—*They won't do anything to you. That's not their way.*

"Uh-huh, it's yours, though," I say, crossing my arms and shaking my head. "And for what? To get your regular body back,

259

so you can come in and out of all our lives whenever the hell you please? Don't think I don't know the stories. You come to our world and you mess everything up."

He croaks and flaps his wings twice to quiet me.

—*You think that what I am asking for is immortality? Don't you get it? I am sick of being a forgotten god. Do you know what happens to gods who go unremembered? They fade into nothingness.*

"And what does that matter to me? Go back to being washed up. Go be a god or whatever and live in the Spirit World and bother the Seven, because I'm done. I'm done being your scapegoat and your meal ticket and whatever the hell else people say to make themselves feel better about being used." I wave a hand in the air as I turn from him to walk away.

—*I want to die.*

What? I don't understand. I must have misheard. It's so grim. Fatalistic. How can he possibly want to *die*? The power to jump between doorways at will belongs to him alone. When I look back at him, he's looking down. The sadness and hurt are plain in his drooping shoulders. He looks different. Changed. Vulnerable.

"What do you mean?"

—*Not this second, but I want the chance. I want to be mortal.*

"But that would mean you would be powerless."

—*What good is power if there is nothing left for me to do? I am tired. If I am to be forgotten as Nanabush the Trickster, then I would like the chance to live as Nanabush of the People. The Seven have the power to give me my body and the life that I desire. I want to live as one of the Anishnaabeg so when that life has ended and it is time for me to come back to the Spirit World, I may finally know peace.*

"Hang on," I say. "Why would you need to die in order to go back to the Spirit World? I saw you there and you looked pretty damn content to me. And you can go there at will, can't you?"

He sighs.

—*Yes, I can. But as someone who is of both worlds, I can never find peace in either. Here, I am more than just myself. You people don't treat things that can't die very well. Cheating death scares you. Reminds you of your own mortality. And in the Spirit World, I am less than the other immortals because of my connection to humanity. I can never be accepted as one of them and can never be deemed worthy of their respect as an equal. I am treated like an errand boy, a lapdog, a pet. I'm stuck between both worlds. There is no place for me.*

Ah, yes. I know that feeling. Being an educated Indigenous woman is hard. At school I stuck out. Sometimes I was the only Native kid in the room. The second people found out I lived on a reserve, they'd look to me like I was the authority on all things Indian. But then coming back home is the same thing. Only here I am different because I am too "White." Go out into the White Man's world for long enough and somehow you lose some of what makes you Native. My degree might as well be my enfranchisement card. Little piece of paper that I can wave around to prove I'm not an Indian.

—*Please say something.*

I look at him and sigh. "Sounds like an overreaction to getting picked last in gym class."

He clacks his beak.

—*That's not what—*

"I know, I know. Geez, I thought you were supposed to be the immortal with a sense of humour."

He relaxes, lifting his head higher. His eyes narrow like he's smiling. Though I can't be sure. It's hard to tell when there are no lips.

—*So you understand?*

"Sort of. But just because I might empathize with you doesn't mean that you're off the hook."

—*I know. For what it's worth, I'm sorry. It has been a long while since*

I've had to look out for anyone besides myself. I've forgotten that words hurt as much as arrows and hatchets.

I breathe in slowly, purse my lips into a hard line. He's being honest, open. I can't berate him for that. Besides, I've been trying this whole "letting go" thing. First with Mom and the letter from Dad, and now with Nanabush.

"Next time I fall into the quarry, save me because you want to and not because you're trying to save yourself."

—*I wanted to save you, I did!*

I hold up a finger. "Nope, we're done talking about that now. Let's just move on."

He nods.

—*If that's what you want, then we can be done with it.*

The wind picks up again, moving through the clearing. In the distance, there are voices, indistinct. The moment becomes uncomfortable. I feel like I should hug him, but that's not an option.

"What are we supposed to do next?" I say. "I heard something about finishing the task you started. There must be more to do?"

—*We have to stop Gagnon from going forward with the quarry.*

"But how? Right now all we've got are a bunch of old letters and a handshake that we only know about because we went back through time to see it." I shift my weight between my feet, pausing to kick at a loose rock. "All of which adds up to nothing in the end."

—*I don't know. They weren't clear when they gave their orders.*

"Typical."

—*They mentioned something else though.*

He hesitates. Whatever he's trying to say must bother him deeply because he's starting to twitch and pick at his feathers. He lifts his head from his wing, blinks twice, then looks away to the right. He clacks his beak.

—*The mine is going to move forward.*

"What?" I feel like half of my time talking with Nanabush is spent in confusion. I say "What?" like it's my catchphrase now. "How could they possibly know that? It's not like they can see into the future. Oh god, *can* they see into the future?"

Nanabush shakes his head, puffs up his feathers as he inhales.

—*No, they can't. Not the way that you're thinking. It isn't some story-book magic with a crystal ball. When they're in jeopardy, they get glimpses of what's to come. It's heightened intuition.*

"How could the future of the quarry put them in danger? It's not like it exists in their world . . . right?" More confusion. I hate sounding like a parrot squawking back the same things over and over.

—*No, it's not there, but this place is.*

"Here? The clearing?"

He nods.

—*It's more than that, though. Haven't you ever wondered how such a perfect circle like this could exist in nature?*

The wind dies down again and the woods around us fall quiet, birdsongs silenced. The air shifts and I feel it thrum with energy. I close my eyes and everything changes. I see the night sky, stars twinkling, alight with a blazing aurora. The once-empty space is filled with the dark domes of wigwams. The great teepee stands like a monolith overlooking the camp. I open my eyes, the camp dissolves, and I'm looking at the clearing once more.

"The Western doorway. This is it."

—*Mm-hmm.*

"Mia's story. She told me that this place was a doorway and she was right. I can't believe it."

—*So you see why the Seven are so worried? If the mine is opened, there will be blasting and the rock face behind this clearing will crumble.*

"And completely destroy the camp." My heart beats faster. "What would that mean?"

—*The doorway would be destroyed in this world and the next. Then no one's getting into the Spirit World.*

"And nothing can leave." I whistle lowly, pushing my hands back into my hair. "That would be the end of the cycle."

—*Yes.*

"Couldn't they just rebuild? They're these great, all-powerful beings. Should be easy for them to fix."

—*Time passes differently in their world. What would take weeks on one side of the Wheel would be years or decades on this side. Imagine the loss that slippage would cause. Could you go on knowing that our inaction sent so many into the abyss?*

"You can't know that for sure."

—*What if your father had been cast into nothingness? Would you wish that on countless others?*

"You're awfully righteous all of a sudden."

—*Something I learned from you.*

I cover my eyes, then rub my face. "Well, shit."

—*This does leave us in a bit of a tough place.*

"Did they say anything else that could help us? Or was it all end-of-the-world-type stuff?"

Nanabush opens his beak to reply, but he's interrupted by the sound of shouting. We both look with terror in the direction of the quarry. Flocks of dark birds take to the sky. I stop breathing. We freeze.

There's a sound like cannon fire that cuts through the air and then the earth shakes. A rumble echoes across the open pit as the edge of the cliff crumbles into the water. Without speaking, Nanabush and I dash toward the sound. He flies alongside me as I sprint through the trees. The branches pull at my skin and clothes. I emerge from the forest and skid to a stop, dragging rocks and dirt with me. Everywhere I look are signs of construction. Huge lights rigged up to generators. A portable trailer. Yellow tape.

There are men in bright orange and yellow vests standing next to large dump trucks and other heavy equipment. They don't notice me at first, so I walk farther from the trees to look over the edge. Dust billows from the rocky overhang and hovers like a cloud above the pulsing water. The once clear, undisturbed pool is now dark with rock and mud.

"Hey! *Tu ne peux pas être ici!*"

The workers have spotted me and they're all pointing and moving in my direction. Anger and frustration rushes blood to my face. I don't run from these men, but walk toward them, stomping and with my hands in tight fists.

"What the hell do you think you're doing?" I call out, my voice breaking. "You can't do this!"

The tallest and widest man comes over to me. He's got a mess of a beard hanging from his chin and beady eyes that look at me with disdain and something that could be concern. He has a heavy French accent. "I don't know who you tink you har, but dis place his too danger-us for you to be 'ere right now."

"It shouldn't be, because you shouldn't be here," I spit. "Who gave you the right to blast?"

The men look at each other, confusion clear on their faces. One of them shrugs. They can't understand me, making this situation even more frustrating than it should be. My anger rises. I hear Nanabush croak from the treetops nearby.

"*Parlez-vous anglais? Non? Oh, merde,*" I say, my voice lilting sarcastically. "If only there was *some* way to tell you how pissed off I am without understanding the language I'm speaking!"

Another voice comes from behind the group of men. *"Qu'est-ce qui se passe ici?"* Thomas Gagnon pushes his way through to the front of the construction workers. His light eyes go wide for the briefest moment when he sees me. "Hazel? This is, uh, a surprise."

That damn honesty. I hate it. "That makes two of us. You mind filling me in on why you're blasting away here?"

Thomas turns to the men behind him. He says something in French and they back off.

"I'm sorry to hear that you didn't know this was happening today," he says. "But I can assure you that I've done this all the right way. Paperwork and all. I can show you, if you'd like?"

"What the hell are you talking about? You can't move on this place yet. You don't have my permission." My voice is shrill, shaking, though I fight to keep it under control.

He smiles, almost sadly, and looks down when he speaks. "Look, I don't mean this to sound as it does, but I don't need *your* permission. I've been working with Joan Kitchisabek over the past few months, and we discovered that this land was surrendered back in 1912. So there's no permission necessary for the mine to reopen."

I feel like the wind has been knocked out of me. I can't stop the hurt and confusion from showing on my face. "What? No."

He nods. "I'm sorry. I thought she would have at least mentioned it to you, seeing as you work together. But this land never belonged to you or your father."

"No. That has to be wrong. I've seen the letters. The project was halted because the people refused to surrender," I say.

"That's how it looked for a while, yes. But after further research, Ms. Kitchisabek and I found a survey from the time that lists the lot as surrendered. There's a parcel description that further corroborates this fact." He places a hand on my shoulder and I swat it away.

"Don't touch me."

"Sorry."

"You're not, though."

"What?"

"Sorry. You aren't sorry," I snap. "You're just like every other man out to take our land and resources. Destroy everything we have and leave us with nothing but holes in the earth. You are *just* like your ancestors."

That hurt him. His handsome face sours into a frown. "That's not true. Do you have any idea what a mine like this can bring to the people of both our towns? Jobs, money, resources. This mine could be operational for years."

I shake my head. "None of that matters. You have no idea what the cost of those few years will be."

"I'm going to have to ask you to leave. You're interrupting our work and it isn't safe for you here anymore." His patience has run out. He motions toward the old road that's suddenly clear now. How he managed to get all this construction done without me noticing only makes me more upset.

I have nothing else to say to him. I step back and we stare hard at each other for a moment more before I turn and head up the hill. I don't look back as I step into the forest. Nanabush is immediately by my side. He lands on my shoulder.

—*What do we do now?*

"We stop him. No matter the cost."

Nanabush flaps his wings and lets out a call that echoes into the darkening sky.

16

EVIDENCE

A chorus of voices calls my name, whispers it on the wind, lets it twirl and dance like a falling leaf until it reaches me. I let it tangle through my hair and caress my skin. It is a name I haven't heard before, but I instantly recognize it as my own.

—*Kotàganez-i Minisinòkwe.*

It sounds beautiful when they say it. My spirit answers, lifting my heart toward the sky, and I follow the sound of their voices into the camp. The snow glimmers in the greens and purples of the aurora hovering in the dark expanse above the tops of the trees. There is no moon tonight. The cold air smells of cedar, smoke, and sweetgrass. I pull the bear shawl tighter around me when the wind rushes into the clearing. There's a quiet, timeless beauty hanging in the air. Something that makes me want to stay. Step inside a darkened wigwam and start my own fire. Lie down and rest.

I hear my name again, their voices in harmony. They're calling me to them. I walk the trail in my moccasins until I'm outside the door. The teepee is lit, glowing with a radiance that is unique to this side of the Wheel. I reach out to push the door open, but something stops my hand.

"Hazel."

A singsong baritone from my childhood. I turn, drop my hand to my side, breath catching and eyes going wide. Dad is standing in front of me. He's tall and strong with hair braided on either side of his face. A bearskin shawl is around his broad shoulders, his leathers decorated to match mine with glass beads and porcupine quills. He holds open his arms to me and I run to him. He holds me as I cry, pats my hair and laughs softly.

"Shh, my girl. It's all right," he says. "Hi-yah, don't cry so loud. You'll wake up the ancestors, wailing like that."

I lean back from his embrace and smile, reaching up to wipe my tears away. "Don't worry. They're hard sleepers."

"Ah, that they are."

"What took you so long?" I ask.

"What do you mean?"

"To find me. I've been here many times and you've never found me. Not once." My words sound harsh, but my voice is gentle. "It's been almost two years. You could have at least dropped by to tell me you were all right."

He smiles and shrugs, the leather fringes of his jacket swaying. "I tried. You sleep harder than the ancestors."

"Not anymore," I say. "Why didn't you ask Nanabush for help? He always knows how to reach me."

"That old crow is more clever than I am. He's been here longer and he knows the ways of this world," Dad says. "Spirits like me can't talk as loudly as he can. Sometimes our voices are too quiet to be heard. Like speaking through a brick wall."

"The Seven always seem to get through, even if all they do is talk in riddles. It's exhausting." I glance over my shoulder at the teepee at my back. "I wish they would give me a break."

"I know, little one," he says, looking at me carefully. He surveys me with eyes bright even in the dim light. Concern creases his brow and he lowers his voice. "They haven't given you an easy gift."

I shake my head. "I don't think I'd call it a gift."

He sighs heavily. "What you are going through, it's my fault. *Gashkenindam, nidànis.*"

"*Kaye We'osimidj,*" I move to hug him again. "You thought what you were doing was right."

"It was a dream. I had hoped it would have been better," he says. "It was supposed to have been better. A way for us to create something for ourselves—something that would give us all a future. Money, strength, jobs." He pauses, sadness and regret weighing him down. "I only ever wanted more for our People. For you and for Gus."

"I'm going to fix it. I have to," I say, but my voice breaks and I feel the heat of tears in my eyes. "But I don't know how. I thought I had more time. Now I'm lost and I have nothing left to fight with."

"My little Hazel, you are much stronger than you know. Look how far you have come already." He moves out of the hug and starts to walk away from the teepee with his arm around my shoulders. "I saw the way you stood up to that boy in the fancy suit. You were so tough with that fire in your eyes!"

I laugh sheepishly. "I had no idea what I was doing. I was angry. I wanted to punch him in his perfect face."

"What a sight that would have been," he says. "I see why the Seven have named your spirit *Kotàganez-i Minisinòkwe.*"

"What does it mean?"

"Fierce Warrior-Woman."

I blush, raise my eyebrows as I look up at him. "Geez, seems a bit heavy-handed, don't you think?"

"Ah, maybe. But subtlety is not their way."

"Cool, though," I say. "Makes me sound like a superhero."

"Because you *are* one."

"Oh shush, *Kaye We'osimidj.* I haven't saved anyone yet."

"You're saving me."

"What?"

He stops walking. Dad steps in front of me and places his

hands on my shoulders, leaning down to look in my eyes. "By righting my wrong, you're saving me. I'm so, *so* proud of you."

I know I look goofy when I grin at him, but it's all I can do to keep from sobbing.

"And I know that it seems hopeless right now, like the colonizers have all the cards. But you have the fight in you. The strength of our People is behind you."

"But the land isn't ours. It never was. I don't have anything left to fight with," I say. "We are unarmed. Bows without arrows."

"When you run out of arrows, you throw the damn bow," he says with a laugh. "You are right. I promise you that you are right. You just have to look at things from the other side."

"Easy for you to say, you live over here."

Dad starts to answer me but stops. In the distance there's the sound of explosions, rock plunging into water. Then the ground starts to tremble beneath us. We both look down at the earth, watching the way the stones on the trail shiver and shake. Fear takes me, makes my stomach pitch and my hands go cold. The world is starting to disappear around us and I know that we'll be torn from each other. I look at my father and try to keep the gentle way he smiles in my mind. But then the earth shakes again, and Dad looks at me with urgency.

"You have to hurry. Time is running out. The next time they blast, they will cut a hole into the rock to drain the water. They think that sending it underground to the river will be safe and will happen without incident. But the clearing, the doorway, it won't hold."

Another set of explosions sounds and shakes the ground so powerfully that we nearly fall.

His grip tightens on my shoulders. "You have to go now."

"I can't leave you if this place is falling apart!"

"No, it's fine. This is only a vision of what is to come if the mine is allowed to continue. You have to leave, my girl," he says. The world seems to slow around us as he smiles. "I promise you, I'll be all right."

I throw my arms around him once more, memorize what it feels like to hug him, to hear the sound of his breath and the drumbeat of his heart. He places a kiss on the top of my head, then gently pushes me back. He looks at me one last time, holding my face in his hands.

"Don't leave me, please," I whimper. "I can't do this. I can't do it all on my own. Please don't go again."

"You aren't alone. I'm with you always."

"*Kaye We'osimidj.*"

I know we have to say goodbye. I don't want him to leave me.

"*K'zaagin, nidànis.*"

"I love you too."

The ground shakes violently as he steps back from me, holding on to my hand. Then everything stops. The world falls terrifyingly silent. I stare at Dad, wide-eyed with fear. He moves to let go, but I hold on tightly until the dark takes him from me. He fizzles out like bear root on hot stones. The camp falls to pieces as each light is blotted out. The sky darkens, the black shroud of night swallowing the spirit houses. I wrap my arms around one of the birch trees and close my eyes. The endless night comes closer and closer until I can feel it falling over me. I whimper, calling for my mother.

I wake up gasping, panting. I push myself up until I'm sitting. Soft, grey morning light from the window pools on the floor by my bed. I pull my knees into my chest.

Outside, it is snowing for the first time this year.

✠ ✠ ✠

I go downstairs, listening to Mom in the kitchen making a bunch of noise. I stuff my hands into the pocket of my sweater to keep warm. It's freezing down here. When I enter the kitchen, I see that she's got the patio door open and is rushing in and out. She's cursing politely, which is to say that she's repeating "Shit" over and over again as she carries plant after plant inside. They're covered in a velvet-soft coating of frost. Some have snow inside their pots.

"What's the matter?" I ask her when she trudges inside.

"Snow!" she says, placing an ivy down on the counter. As she tries to brush snow from the vine's leaves, she whines, "It's everywhere! Ah, shit, I don't think Cheryl's gonna make it."

"Cheryl?"

"My ivy."

"You named your plant Cheryl?"

"Yeah, doesn't she look like a Cheryl?"

"Uh, maybe?" I walk over to the counter to stand next to Mom. She's right, the ivy is looking pretty grim. Poor Cheryl.

Mom goes to shut the patio door. She shudders dramatically, then moves around the kitchen, inspecting each one of her plants carefully. "I knew I felt a chill in the air yesterday. I should've brought all my babies inside."

"It's early for it to be snowing, eh? Even for here." I shiver slightly.

"That's this *kòpàdiz-i* crow winter for you. The grass and the plants die before they should, and people like me are pissed the heck off," she grumbles.

"Didn't you say this was going to happen? I think you mentioned it back in August."

Mom grunts. "Didn't do me much good knowing it was coming, eh?"

She continues to fuss over her plants, moving back and forth between the group she has in the kitchen and the others scattered throughout the living room. She mutters grumpily to herself while she works. But beyond that bit of frustration at the state of the weather, she seems unbothered, completely fine. Does she know about the land and the quarry? She must. How could she not have noticed the sound of explosions and the way the earth shook?

"Did you know about the mine?"

That stops her. She takes a deep breath before she can look at me, before she answers me. "I did."

"You knew it was moving forward? You knew they'd be blasting the other day?"

The way she purses her lips tells me the answer even though she can't.

"Mom," I sigh, covering my eyes with my palms. "Why didn't you tell me?"

"I didn't know how."

"And you thought not telling me was the better option?"

Exasperated, she raises her arms and clenches her fists. "I don't know. What do you want me to say, Hazel? I'm sick of seeing you get your heart broken. Excuse me if I didn't want to be the one to do it this time."

I turn away from her. "Did you see the proof? Is what Gagnon is saying true?"

"Yes," she says flatly. "Joni showed me the maps earlier this week."

"This week?" I spin around to look at her. "You've known for days?"

She nods.

I exhale until I'm completely deflated. "And what? You're just okay with it?"

She makes another face, puckering her lips. "It's what your dad wanted."

"What he wanted was wrong."

"How can you know that?"

"I just do. And I know he knows his mistake now."

"You're only saying that to make this all hurt less. And that's okay."

"No!" I don't mean to shout, but I can't help it. It startles her and she leans back from me. I frown. "I know for real."

"How, Hazel? How do you know that?" Her voice rises to meet mine.

But I'm exhausted. Sick of fighting. I don't want to push Mom away. Shaking my head, I sigh deeply and give myself a chance to get myself under control. My mouth goes dry and I know that my body is telling me to cry, let go. Nothing comes. I'm tired of tears. I'm saying, "I can't," over and over until Mom's got her arms around me. I easily sink into her embrace, let her support me.

"I dreamt about Dad," I say into her red flannel shirt. I grip the back of it, bunch the fabric into my hand. "He told me then. He said he was sorry. And I know he is. He's sorry, Mom. He's so sorry."

She runs her hand along my back and says nothing for a long time while I burrow myself against her shoulder. Everything feels like too much. I want to forget this mess. Let the men with the dynamite win.

"Was it a good dream?" Her words bring me back. Remind me that I can't be done yet. They'll never be good dreams again if I do nothing.

"It felt like I lost him all over again."

"Oh." Her voice catches, pausing in her throat. She makes a few of those familiar quiet grunts that tell me she's moments away from tears. "I'm sorry. I know it hurts. But you know what? It's good that you saw him. Means he knows how to come and see you now. I'll bet you'll see a lot more of him. That's what our loved ones do once they find their way around the Spirit World."

"What if something happens over there? Something that makes it impossible to move between doorways?"

She leans back and looks at me curiously, her ageless face lightly folded into intrigued confusion. "Can something like that even happen?"

"Maybe? I don't know."

"Hmm," she says, thinking it over seriously. "No. I don't think much would change. Our ancestors always find a way back to us."

I sigh, stepping away from her hug. "Not if their world is torn apart."

"What stories you been reading? Did that dad of yours put some crazy tales in your head while you were sleeping?" She looks at me indignantly.

I want to tell her the truth. Hope that she'll understand and not have me committed someplace. She deserves to know what's happening in her backyard and just beyond. This affects her too, in more ways than she can ever know. But I can't. How can I expect her to understand? Do I tell her that all the Spirit magic is real? That there are seven would-be angels watching over us, counting on me to do something about the man threatening the place they call home? No. Mom has always been supportive of my creative and overactive imagination, but this would be going too far.

"Yeah, I guess that's where I got it. It was a pretty intense dream," I say as casually as possible.

"I can't say I'm surprised, kid. You have the craziest dreams," she says. "But if you saw your dad, then I think you know how he feels about the mine."

"I do."

"Then that's that."

"What do you think we should do?"

"About the mine?" She shrugs and makes a noise with her lips. "Doesn't seem like there's much we *can* do. Ask your brother? He knows all about land claims."

"Gus is pretty set on ignoring the quarry."

"Tsk, of course he is. Stubborn arse." She places one hand on the edge of the counter. "Maybe you should get out of the house? A change of scenery might do you some good. Just make sure you dress for the weather."

I'm happy that she isn't prying. That's the good thing about Mom. She never asks more unless it's necessary. If I'm not offering her more information, then that's where the conversation will end. Took me a long time and many an angsty teenage brood to figure that out.

"Yeah, I guess I could go for a run. Might be the thing I need."

"Kinda greasy out there, though? Just walk."

"I'll be fine."

"Oh, go on, then," she says. "I'll make something to eat for when you get home. Think of it as a reward. Now, git outside, you."

Talking with her like this has lifted my spirit, made me feel better, lighter. I leave her to her backwards logic and get changed into warmer running gear, tucking my braided hair into a toque. Lacing up my shoes, I call out to Mom that I'll be back in an hour or so, and then head out the door. The cold hits me instantly, sending chills across my body, making the hair on my arms and neck stand on end. My breath billows out around my face like smoke. Everything is covered in a fine blanket of snow and frost. Maple and aspen leaves still dressed in the red and gold colours of autumn twinkle in the morning sunlight. The world looks frozen in place, as if the snowfall stopped time. Already the snow is starting to melt in the heat of the sun, but the cold touch of winter has left its mark.

It's so quiet that my footsteps sound like thunder as I hurry down the stairs. I walk to the end of the drive, pausing where the gravel meets the asphalt of the highway and then start running toward town. The rhythm of my feet as they pound the ground drums evenly and loudly through my body until I'm outside of myself. My mind runs as fast as I do, trying to find a solution to the problem.

How could we miss something like that? For years and years, that land has been in my family's name. It seems odd and perfectly convenient that now, once my dad is dead and without a voice, this new information surfaces. Every letter I've found that has to do with the quarry and the land it resides on has explicitly shown it as unsurrendered. Isn't that what old Côté said? The Indians of Spirit Bear Point made themselves very clear. No surrender. No mine.

The houses here are like clones of each other. Almost all of them were built by one of those companies that specialize in prefabrications. They're like the H&M of the real estate world. Nice, affordable pieces, but almost everyone's got them. I weave in and out of the streets of Ste-Marie des Oblats, doing what I can to up my kilometre count without having to run to the next town over. But I get turned around and wind up on some street with no exit off the main road. Cursing, I turn to double back but stop when I see the building I'm standing in front of.

"Gagnon et Fils. Of course."

—Call it fate.

Nanabush is sitting on top of the G, his talons curved around the metal. He looks down at me, his head twitching from side to side a few times before he flaps his wings and settles. He digs his claws into the sign, leaving a set of distinct marks.

"Coincidence is probably more likely. Seems to be a lot of that going around these days, huh?" I pace up and down in front of the building while I catch my breath, kicking my legs up behind me a few times to keep the blood flowing.

—Yes, I've been thinking about that. It's bothering me. Did you hear what year he said the land was surrendered?

"In 1912."

—Same year our old friend Philippe Gagnon became Indian agent.

My eyes go wide in a way that must make me look like a cartoon. "No way."

He nods.

—I knew there was a reason it stood out in my mind. It was in one of the letters that you found. One penned by Gagnon himself.

I stop pacing and look up at him, put a hand to my lips. "I know the one you're talking about. Where he bragged to Côté about taking his job and all but admitted he was going to find a way to get the mine approved."

Nanabush nods.

—That's the one.

"Then we have to go back there," I say. "We need to see what happened. Can you do that? Show me something in his memories?"

He clacks his beak a few times before answering.

—I think I can. The same way we went through your father's memories to find the handshake.

"Then let's do that. Come here."

—You think it's safe to go when we're out in the open like this?

I shrug. "It's Sunday. Sunday morning at that. Plus, it's cold and there's snow everywhere. Who's going to be out and about right now?"

Nanabush readjusts his wings, then flutters down to land on my shoulder. He's careful not to grip too tightly, even though my wounds have healed. This close, I can hear him breathing. His feathers brush smooth and cool against my skin.

—Close your eyes. I've found him.

I do as I'm told.

When I open my eyes, we're standing in front of the very same office but on a changed street. Here, in the past, it is night-time. Above our heads, a street lamp is alight with the soft glow of an oil flame. The street around us is smaller and the houses are made of tarpaper. The way that the road curves is different from the street I know now.

The office of Gagnon et Fils is small, modest. The large street-facing window is intricately detailed with gold filigree around its edges. The door is made of a deep-coloured wood, mahogany perhaps. Everything about the place reeks of small-town money. Inside, there is light despite the late hour.

"That must be him," I say, pressing my hands on the glass and leaning in as close as I can without whacking my head. "He looks different than I pictured him."

—Did you expect him to look like his great-great-grandson?

"Kinda, yeah. This version is so much pointier. Look at that nose. It's practically a beak."

—And what's wrong with beaks?

"Fine on birds, not so great on people with small features."

Philippe Gagnon is short, balding, with round wire-rim glasses perched on the end of his long nose. He's dressed in a brown suit with tattered elbows that looks slightly loose on him. The building might be impressive, but he looks like he's scraping by. He's hunched over something on his desk.

"Can we get inside?"

Nanabush nods.

—*Yes. You don't have to physically push anything open, but make sure you use doorways.*

"Wow," I say, turning my head slightly to look at him. "It isn't just our doorways that have power, huh?"

—*A door will always be a way in no matter how hard it tries to keep things out.*

"That's comforting." I move away from the window and toward the mahogany door. I feel a slight twinge of anxiety as I stand in front of it. Wary of what it might feel like to push my way into someplace, unannounced and uninvited. I hold my breath, bring my shoulders up to my ears, and step inside. There's no sound to announce my arrival. The little bell above my head is still and silent. I don't know what I expected. Silly. But not unwarranted. The last time I moved through time and memory with Nanabush, I fell down a big hole and almost died. So my hesitation is to be expected. Nanabush gently taps my shoulder with his foot.

—*Get closer. Don't worry, nothing can happen to you this time.*

"He can't hear us, can he?" I whisper.

Nanabush shakes his head.

—*No. We're not physically here. Besides, this place is different. The quarry has more energy and being so close to the Western doorway means it can exist in both worlds. All of this is just memory.*

"Huh," I say. "You know, you should have warned me about that last time."

—*I didn't know last time. The Seven taught me all of that when they called me to their camp a while ago. You know, before you showed up and yelled at me.*

"Okay, that's fair."

I move into the room, stepping lightly even though Gagnon can't hear me. When I reach his desk, I stop. Nanabush and I are directly across from him. He's got a mess of papers strewn across the tabletop. They're all in dark, thick ink with pencil scratchings here and there.

Gagnon rests his fists on the desk and leans forward to shift his weight as he looks down intently at the topmost paper. His eyebrows come together until they look like two caterpillars rearing up in confrontation.

"*Merde,*" he mutters under his breath.

I turn to Nanabush. "He looks upset."

—*Because he's looking at a map.* He bows his head slightly to point with his beak. *Hazel, that's Spirit Bear Point.*

"It is. Wow. It's odd to see something so old look so new."

A kettle whistles loudly from the next room. The sound makes us all jump. Gagnon glances in the direction of the sound but returns to the map. The kettle's screams seem to grow louder the longer it's left untouched.

"Oh my god, I'm going to go and get it if he doesn't."

He marches out of the room, cursing under his breath once more.

—*Quick! Hurry around his desk so we can see what's causing him trouble.*

Moving to the other side, I recognize the map. "This is from right before the road was completed. Oh, but look, there's the line of the road drawn in with pencil."

Nanabush hops down from my shoulder and lands on the desk. He walks across the map, his feet scraping the thick paper.

—*He has your lot circled. Right here. Lot 34. It looks like the road runs right through it. Wow, it was much larger before this construction.*

"Yeah, I remember Gus telling me about it. He said Quebec used to make these long plots of land that came from the river. When they made the road in 1910, it was cut in half. The lot reaches the river on both sides, so it's a bit confusing. This part here"—I point down at the map—"across the street from our house ended up belonging to the Band."

—*After each new construction, they'd need to bring in new surveyors, right?*

I nod. "Yeah, especially if they cut through plots like this."

Nanabush walks to the edge of the map and tugs on it with his beak. He pulls the map aside to reveal a new one beneath. This map looks freshly drawn with the road added. The date on the bottom is 1912. On this one, our lot is listed as 34a, with 34b being across the road. In pencil next to 34b is the word "Surrendered." Next to 34a it clearly reads, "Unsurrendered."

"Hang on," I say. "Look at that. Lot 34a is unsurrendered as of the 1912 survey. How the hell can it be unsurrendered *and* surrendered?"

Nanabush lets out a little caw to get my attention. He's holding another paper in his beak. I reach out and take it from him, squinting to read the handwriting.

DESCRIPTION FOR SURRENDER

Part of Lot 34 river front Spirit Bear Point Indian Reserve, described as follows;— commencing at a point in the far limit of said plot as it touches the river with allowance from said river; E-W vertical limits being three thousand two hundred eighty-four feet (3284); then N-S horizontal limits being one thousand

and seventy-four feet (1074); more or less to the place of begin-
ning, together with a road allowance of eighty feet from the
above described lands to the highway. Lot 34 being spilt into two
separate lots by road. Surrender is for parcel East of highway.

Signed,
R.H. Goode, Surveyor
Ste-Marie des Oblats, 1912

"What the hell? This parcel description says it's for the lot
east of the highway. That's the trailer park. The one across the
street from where we are—the one without the quarry." I look
at Nanabush.

—I hear him coming back. Put the paper down and hurry over here.

Nanabush flies back up onto my shoulder while I try to
rearrange the papers to the way they were. I step away from the
desk as Gagnon returns, placing a steaming mug of tea down
next to the maps. He pauses, reaches into his desk, pulls out a
flask, and dumps brown liquid into the cup. He brings it up to his
lips, sips, and sighs.

Nanabush and I watch closely as he returns to gazing at
the mess of papers in front of him. He scratches his head and
reaches for the parcel description. He slides into the chair, the
legs making an awful scraping sound as he scoots closer to the
desk. For a long while, nothing happens. He sits, stares, scratches
his head, sips his makeshift hot toddy. Then his expression changes. Frantically, he digs in the drawers until he finds what he's
searching for. Ink and quill.

He places the parcel description down onto the desk and
leans in close. Then, dipping his quill into the ink, with shaking
hands he strikes through the word "East" and writes "West" as

clearly and neatly as possible. There is sweat beading on his fore-head when he slumps back in his chair.

"There's no way that's going to work," I say, astounded.

The ink dries and Gagnon smiles.

—*It's going to work. That's why he never had to pay leasing fees. He couldn't be written up for trespassing because he was the one in charge. Who are the Indians going to complain to?*

"And I'll bet no one will even think twice about the fact that there's different handwriting on the document. It's already signed by the surveyor, so who are they to question it?" I curse. "Look at his smug look. He knows he's getting away with every illegal thing he does. I can't be in here anymore. Let's go."

Not waiting for agreement from Nanabush, I walk out the door and onto the street. I blink and we're back in the cold, bright morning. I look up at the sign. The colours have faded, but otherwise it's the same. I wish I had something I could throw at it, but I'm empty-handed save for my phone and there's no way I'm throwing that.

"What are we supposed to do now?" I say.

—*We know that he's trespassing, breaking the law. Working on unsur-rendered land. We have the ammunition.*

"But no real proof. We can't do anything without the original map. It's not like you can take me back and I can record him changing the description. It'll just look like some cheap attempt at a *Heritage Minutes* or something." I start to pace again, feel the weight of my muscles crying out to run.

—*What?*

"Oh, I guess you haven't watched TV, huh? Never mind, then." I'm trying to think of something we could do to prove what we know, but nothing is coming to me. If I knew more about criminal mischief, maybe I'd be able to disarm all their blasting equipment, but I'm almost certain that move's only reserved for movies and television.

—*If only there was some way that we could have gotten a copy of that map. Then maybe we'd be able to prove something.*

"Wait. That's it." I stuff my hand into the convenient pocket on the side of my running tights and pull out my phone. Swiftly, I tap the screen until I find Gus's number, then put the phone up to my ear. I shrug my shoulders to get Nanabush to move.

He croaks his offence at me, but I can tell he's too interested to be properly upset. He flies to a nearby cedar tree and sits in it, keeping his grey eyes on me.

The phone rings and rings.

A groggy voice says, "Hello?"

"Gus!"

"Did you expect someone else?"

I laugh slightly, nerves bubbling up into my throat. Already I can feel adrenalin starting to pump through my body, making me jittery. "No, I'm just impressed that you answered on the first try."

"It's nine in the morning on a Sunday. I thought maybe it was an emergency."

"You could say that, yeah."

"What?" He's suddenly alert, his voice even and low with seriousness. "What's wrong? Are you okay? Is Mom okay?"

"Oh, um, yeah, we're both fine."

"What the fuck, Hazel? Don't joke about that."

"Geez, you're the one who took it seriously right away."

"It's nine in the *morning*. On a *Sunday*. I'm off my game." He's back to his usual sarcastic tone. "If you don't want anything, I'm hanging up. Sleep needs me more than you do."

"I have a question about land stuff. What happens when a new survey is conducted? Like, what happens to the maps?"

"The Indian agent gets them. Along with any other documents regarding new surrenders and shit."

My shoulders droop and I feel my hope starting to sink into the ground at my feet. "That's it? There aren't any other copies made?"

"Oh yeah," he says casually. "The surveyors leave one copy with the Indian agent and they keep another for themselves. Well, not really for themselves. It goes to the surveyor-general or MNR or the Geological Survey of Canada."

I look over at Nanabush, who is watching me unblinkingly. I start to grin at him. "And that's in Ottawa?"

"You planning a field trip?"

"I need a favour. I need you to find a map."

"A map? Are you serious?" He's acting cool, but I can hear the genuine curiosity in the way his voice lifts. "What the hell do you need a map for? Joni have you on some mission to see which one of her sisters has the biggest lot? Or is this a history project?"

"No, this one's for us. It has to do with the quarry."

"Oh, for fuck's sake." I can practically hear him roll his eyes. "Not this again."

"Yes, this again. Listen," I snap, "there's something important I've found out and I just need the evidence to prove I'm right."

"Oh? And what's that? That the useless thing should be left alone?"

"Can you stop being an ass for a second?"

He groans. "Fine. I'll hear you out. But I already know that the mine is moving forward and they've been blasting."

"Did Mom tell you? Jesus, that's unfair. She told you and left me to find out the hard way."

"Yeah, sorry about that."

"Whatever, it doesn't matter now. Okay, look. I know for a fact that Gagnon and his company are trespassing. They've been doing so for over a hundred years. The land they're on is unsurrendered. It's never been theirs to work with!"

He clicks his tongue. "Uh-huh, right."

"No, I'm serious. I saw it happen."

"What?"

I cough, clear my throat. "I *swear* it happened," I correct myself. "There's a parcel description of Lot 34 from 1912 that says it's surrendered. I have reason to believe that that same document was altered so that it listed our lot, 34a, as surrendered when *really* it was for 34b. Someone just scratched out 'East' and wrote 'West.'"

His bed creaks as he readjusts. "You want me to find the parcel description?"

"Yes. And the map done in 1912."

"Those documents are on the Rez already. They should be in the pile of shit you're stuck rearranging."

"No, the altered ones are here. I'm talking about the originals."

"And you want me to go to MNR to find them?"

"Yes."

He groans again and hits the microphone with his hands as he rubs his face. "If I do this, will you finally shut up about the quarry?"

"Yes, promise."

He's quiet for a while. I start to chew on my lip nervously. Nanabush nearly loses his balance when he moves too far over on the branch in an attempt to get closer to me.

"You are so damn lucky I'm already set to go downtown tomorrow."

"Ah! Yes, thank you!"

"Yeah, yeah. I'm the best brother. I know, I know. Now you be the best sister and let me go back to sleep."

"Call me tomorrow when you find the documents."

"Sure."

He hangs up.

—*Sounds like you have a plan.*

I nod vigorously. "Oh yes. I know Gus is going to find the map and the parcel description. First thing tomorrow, we come right back here and tell Thomas Gagnon that he's wrong. We get him to stop everything. And he'll have to listen."

—*Then it all ends tomorrow.*

"Mm-hmm. Tomorrow's going to be the worst Monday Gagnon's ever had." I grin broadly.

Nanabush throws his head back. His cawing sounds like laughter.

—*Run home and be happy, Kotàganez-i Minisinòkwe.*

"*Meegwetch, Àndeg-niseyens.*"

I sprint home with the strength and wind of the ancestors at my back.

17

SASÀGIWICHÍGEWIN

The snow from the weekend is gone, but the frost and winter chill still hang in the air. I sit on the edge of my bed, fully dressed, staring out the window at the heavy fog. It's impossible to see across the street. Beyond the highway and the line of trees, the trailer park on Lot 34b sits with the undeserved claim of unsurrendered. I don't worry about what will happen to it once this wrong has been righted. That is something I do not have time for. Priority has been decided for me.

I don't know what's waiting for me today. I should be happy, thrilled, that I finally have proof that I've been right all along. *Will* have proof. I don't have it yet. Even if I know I'm right. I only hope it won't come too late. I have to count on Gus. This last stage is going to be out of my hands. For now, I have to hope Thomas will see reason. That he will accept my word as truth. It doesn't seem like a hard thing to do, but the last words we exchanged weren't kind. I can only hope that I haven't completely destroyed that relationship. He's a businessman, after all. He should be professional.

I bury my head in my hands, run my fingers through my hair, grip tightly. Frustrated. Nervous. Hopeful. I am too many things right now. If only one of them was brave. *Sôginijiwin*, I could use a bit of your thunder today.

I straighten and push myself up from the bed. Already I can feel sweat starting to dampen my palms, making them clammy and cold. I wipe them on the front of my pants and walk out of my room.

Mom is already gone for the day. She's made plans with my aunt. They're gone shopping in the nearest big city, which is at least two hours away. I've called in to work, left a message with the secretary that I won't be coming in this morning. I'm finally taking one of my hard-earned sick days. Well, half a day. I told her I'd call back if I needed the entire day off. Here's to hoping that I don't. I also thought about leaving a note for Joni that says I'm disappointed in her, but I figured that could wait. Might be best to say it in person and with some kindness.

I stand in the entranceway, zipping up my jacket until it reaches my chin. The zipper sounds impossibly loud in the quiet. I feel the pressure of the metal and fabric against my throat as I swallow. I hold my breath. Isn't there supposed to be some magic breathing pattern that works to calm nerves and anxiety? Breathe in for four counts, hold for seven, out for eight. I have trouble exhaling for that long without gasping. Don't know what that says about me. Guess I have trouble letting things go.

Today, that's a good thing.

I tug the door open and shut it behind me, sliding my key into the lock. The fog is hanging low in the air, feels so thick I can almost touch it. Hopefully, this weather delays the blasting at the quarry. Even if it stays just for the morning. Hell, even a few hours would be perfect. All I need is the time to convince one man that his ancestor was a cheating, conniving bastard. Shouldn't be too hard.

I get in my car and start it. The fog makes buildings appear as if from nowhere and the drive into town seems shorter. Time feels clipped because I want it to stretch out. If I've learnt anything the past few months, it's that time is the one thing beyond me, people, and even the likes of the Seven. Time rules itself. Which, of course, makes no sense beyond sounding cool. A famous theoretical physicist once said that time is an illusion. It's frightening that that makes sense to me.

I turn down the dead-end street where Gagnon et Fils stands overlooking the rest of the buildings like a stone statue of some colonizer overseeing the river that brings canoes full of pelted gold. Cold, unmoving, and with a religious stare. Parking across the street, I turn off the engine and look over at the building. In the cold morning light, it seems even more foreboding. The shroud of mist isn't helping either.

I drum my hands on the steering wheel, trying to release some of my nervous energy. I keep telling myself that on the count of three, I'll get out of my car, but so far I haven't moved. Closing my eyes, I breathe in for four seconds and quickly open the door.

I hold for seven as I step out into the street.

I look both ways and then walk across. Stuffing my hands into the pockets of my pants, I keep my eyes focused on the old mahogany door. I glance up and see Nanabush staring down at me from the marquee. He nods.

I nod in return and exhale.

My hand's on the doorknob. One more breath before I push my way in. The clear scent of citrus hits me as I stand in the entryway, letting the door shut behind me.

The office has changed in the past hundred years. What before was an open space with two separate desks is now walled off, creating two separate rooms. It's modestly decorated with white walls, clean dark bookshelves, a few brilliantly green plants. Minimalistic and chic. A testament to Thomas's big-city origins. I wonder if he finds this town dreadfully dull in comparison. Maybe that's why he decided to come after the quarry. Gives him something exciting to do. I spot an oil diffuser on the corner of the secretary's desk. Must be the source of the orange smell.

"*Bonjour,*" says the secretary in polite, joyful French. She's pretty, young. Her hair is pulled back in a slick bun and she wears pearls around her neck. Who wears pearls nowadays?

"I'm here to see Thomas."

"Monsieur Gagnon is a bit busy at the moment," she says in nearly perfect English. "Do you have an appointment?"

"No, I don't. But tell him Hazel Ellis is here," I say, fiddling with the ring on my middle finger. "Tell him I have some interesting information regarding the stolen land he's trying to blow up. Trust me, he'll want to see me."

Her demeanour changes. She's looking at me like I'm tramping around the place in muddy shoes. I give her a smile that I know will make her feel uncomfortable.

"*Un moment, s'il vous plait.*"

"*Merci,*" I reply.

She picks up the phone and dials. She angles her office chair away from me as she softly speaks French into the receiver. Her brow comes together, then she puts the phone down and gives me a forced smile.

"He will be right with you."

The door at the back of the room opens and Thomas fills the frame. He's dressed impeccably in a deep-grey suit with a thin black tie. He looks calm and self-assured when he smiles at me. He must not be taking my threat seriously.

"Hazel," he says, "please come in."

He steps aside as I move past him and into the office. The desk at the head of the room is the exact same one used by Philippe. It's in great condition. Thomas must've had it restored.

It shines in the grey light from the window behind it. The floor is hardwood, stained a deep brown to match the wood of the antique desk. The walls are lined with books that I don't recognize, most of them having something to do with engineering or natural resources. Thomas shuts the door and walks back over to his desk. He motions toward the chair directly across from his, but I stay standing.

"This won't take long," I say. Mostly, I want the distance between us to be as large as possible. That and I want a clear path to the door.

He raises an eyebrow. "So, you haven't come down here to shout at me again? I have to say, that's a relief."

"Not shout, no."

"But you're here to try to get me to leave the quarry alone?"

"Yes. I promise this will be the last time."

"Good."

"Because I'm going to win."

"Are you?"

I nod and walk toward the desk, my hands balled into fists at my sides. I can feel my heartbeat in the tips of my fingers. "Yes. I am."

He sighs, pinches the bridge of his nose. "Why is it so hard for you to understand that I'm not doing this because it seemed like a fun way to spend years of my time and money? I'm not here to steal from you. Don't you see that I'm trying to change that legacy?"

"That might've been what you thought when you started, but that's far from where you are now."

"How? Tell me, since you seem to be the authority on this." He's already starting to lose his patience with me.

"You're taking from earth that's already been bled dry."

"Oh, please. You're being dramatic."

"So what if I am?" I say, my voice rising. "That doesn't change the fact that it's true. There is nothing else you can take from that mine. Your plan to drain the water back to the river isn't going to work. You have no idea the damage it's going to cause."

Thomas shakes his head. "What kind of damage? You keep saying things like that, but you don't ever have proof. I'm starting to think this is all personal, spiritual nonsense that you're projecting onto me. You're upset because your father wanted this to happen and you don't. Can't try to convince a dead man to change his mind, now can you?"

Months ago, that would have hurt me more than anything else he could say. Now, I know the truth. "Say that all you want, but that's not the case anymore."

"What, then? What's the big reveal you seem to be building up to? Or are you going to make me wait all morning? Pretty silly plan to stop the mine—keeping me here won't do any good."

He looks at me and I hold his gaze unflinchingly. In the corner of my vision, I see the shape of a black bird as it lands on the pine tree outside. It stares at the two of us. Nanabush caws, lends me his support. I feel stronger, light with that clever sense of humour of his.

Calmly, I say, "You're a trespasser on unsurrendered land."

He's unfazed. "I'm not. We've been through this already. The land was surrendered in 1912."

I shake my head. "No, that's wrong. Look at the parcel description. Tell me what it says."

Thomas glances over at one of the meticulously organized bookshelves, but he doesn't move.

"Go on," I say, casually motioning to the bookshelf.

He exhales harshly and moves to grab a large black binder

from the shelf. Thomas takes it in one hand and carries it back to his desk. The binder thumps and falls open when he tosses it down. I watch as he riffles through it.

"You know," he says as he continues to search, "what I have are copies of the originals in *your* office. If you wanted to see them, you should have asked Ms. Kitchisabek. Here it is."

Thomas pulls the photocopy of the description out from its protective cover and scans it. "It mentions right here that it's for Lot 34—you know what that is, I presume. The section *west* of the highway. That means the exact lot your home shares with the quarry. Do you want to see it?" He holds out the paper to me.

"It's been edited," I tell him. "Someone crossed out 'East' and wrote in 'West' so that the description could match Lot 34a. Pretty easy considering how vaguely it's been written."

"It happens quite often," he says. "Surveyors sometimes wrote too quickly or got turned around."

"And if they did, they'd fix the mistake and send the right one off to the office of the surveyor-general," I say. "The maps there would match the maps here."

"You're telling me that you think this map has been altered by someone who wasn't the surveyor?" he asks. There's a difference in the way he looks at me. A hint of uncertainty in his eyes. This is something he hadn't considered. He moved on the quarry without thinking to double-check the validity of his claim.

"Mm-hmm," I say, nodding once. "Altered by someone who benefited the most from switching the lots. The person who dug the quarry in the first place."

His expression shifts, sours until he's glaring at me. "You mean Philippe Gagnon. I know he doesn't have the greatest reputation and I know that he wasn't a good Indian agent. But I'm not him, Hazel. I'm *not* him." There's sadness in his voice, but I can't tell if it's shame, guilt, or regret. He looks down at the map spread open across the pages of the binder.

Have I done him wrong? Seeing him as bare and vulnerable as he is now, I think that I have. He's the same as I am, trying to fix the mistakes of a man who came before. And I've gone and compared him to the colonizer that he's trying to forget. He wants to be better, to do better.

"Look," I say, gently this time as I walk closer to the desk, "I know you aren't him, but if you keep up with this plan to destroy that place, you'll only be furthering his legacy."

He lifts his head to look at me. "Are you trying to use my desire to change things against me?"

"What?" I recoil. "No."

He moves around the desk quickly, coming into my space. "This is because of that sweat, isn't it? You think you know me after one ceremony."

"No. I don't."

"You think a few nice words will change my mind? You beat me over the head with what my ancestors did to yours and then try to tell me I'm different." He's hurting. The fear he has of following in the footsteps of his forefathers is eating away at him. Like Dad said, he's just a boy in a fancy suit.

I can't think like this. I have to leave him be. I'll feel sorry later. Right now, I need to convince him to stop the destruction. Breathe in and speak firmly. "I think my damn evidence should be enough to change your mind."

"If it even exists."

"Excuse me?"

Thomas straightens up, crosses his arms. "Let's see this original map, then."

I step back, my face and ears going hot and red with embarrassment. "I don't have it."

He smirks and scoffs as he fiddles with the button at his wrist. "Ridiculous," he mutters. "You almost had me."

"It's *real*. I'm right!"

"Sure," he says, moving back around his desk. "But if you can't provide me with this 'evidence' of yours, how am I to believe you? You could easily be making all of this up."

My mouth falls open and I stare at him. Thomas is casual, nonchalant as he slides the copy of the parcel description back into the binder. He shuts it with a flourish that makes me jump.

"Until the time comes that you can show me proof that this wild claim of yours is correct, the mine goes forward. In fact," he says, glancing over his shoulder at the lightening sky, "I expect we'll continue with the blasting today."

"You can't do that. Please, pause it. Wait a day. I'll get you the map. I just need more time!"

He lightly shakes his head. "No, I don't think I will. Waiting a day will cost me too much money. Besides, I've wasted enough time trying to tiptoe around you. But go on and find this convenient little map of yours, bring it to me, and I'll order the construction to stop. Seems fair, wouldn't you say?"

Speechless. Nothing to say. They're going to blast and I can't do anything about it. The room starts to spin. I'm muttering, "No." Thomas has finished the conversation. He motions toward the door, tells me to leave, but I hardly hear him. I stop in the doorway and look over at him. I wish I had something to say, something clever or hurtful. But I still have nothing.

All I can do is leave.

I walk out, not bothering to say a word to the secretary despite feeling her eyes on my back. When I step outside, the light blinds me and I stumble. Thomas was right. Now that the fog has lifted, the weather is ideal for a day of work. The sun is brilliant in the blue sky above my head. Any hint of the gloomy winter weather is long gone. It's going to be a perfect autumn day. Only everything around me is dead. Frozen from the night before. Winter leaves a mark no matter how brief its stay.

Digging into my pocket, I fish out my keys and unlock my car. I'm about to pull the door open when Nanabush comes swooping down from the trees. He's cawing loudly as he circles overhead twice before finally landing on the car roof.

—*What happened? Did it work?*

I shake my head. My voice is tight when I speak. "No. He didn't believe me. He wouldn't even listen to what I was saying."

—*Have you spoken to Gus? It's possible that he's found it already. You could go back in and show Gagnon the proof.*

"No," I say. "It's hardly even half past nine on a Monday. I'd be surprised if he's even made it to the right office yet."

—*Try. Call your brother.*

Frustrated, I want to shout at him. Tell him to leave me alone. Instead, I take out my phone, find Gus, tap his number. I fidget impatiently while it rings, nerves and panic trying to win out over hope.

"Hey, you've reached Gus Ellis. Actually, you've just missed Gus Ellis. But leave me a message and I'll reach you."

Beep.

I hang up. Growl with frustration and try not to throw my phone across the street.

"He's going to find it. I know he is. All he needs is a bit more time."

—*How much time do we have? One hour?*

"Probably less than that." I start to chew my bottom lip anxiously. "And who knows how long it could take at the surveyor-general's? Government offices aren't known for their timeliness."

—*What you're saying is we need to do something that will delay the blasting for as long as possible?*

I nod. "You got any of that magic left?"

He shakes his head.

—*No, nothing that will have the power to do what we need done.*

"Maybe if you had let me fall into the quarry the first time, none of this would have happened."

—*Is now the time to bring that up again? You said we were done talking about it.*

He keeps talking, but I don't hear him. My mind is spinning, moving too quickly. That's it. I know what I have to do. It isn't the safest plan and I can guarantee I won't be the same when I'm done, but I can't afford to do anything else. This is bigger than me now. More is at stake. I redial Gus and wait for his voicemail to pick up.

Beep.

"Gus, you need to find that map and the parcel description. I don't know how to stress how important this is, but just trust me. Do it as quick as you can and then fax it to Gagnon et Fils. I'll text you the info. I'm going to buy you more time. Hopefully, it'll be enough." I pause, feeling emotion in my throat and my heart sinking past my stomach. "I love you."

I hang up and immediately text the contact information to Gus. My fingers are shaking as I type and I make a couple of mistakes that slow me down, but I get it sent. When I finish, Nanabush is looking at me curiously.

—*What are you planning?*

"You heard me. Buying more time, winning our fight," I say, pulling the car door open. "And I think I've figured out the cost."

The engine turns and I drive toward home.

¤ ¤ ¤

Standing at the heart of the Western doorway, I listen. The sound of the breeze as it moves in and out of the clearing, knocking the tops of the trees together and rushing along the yellowed grass, is music. Closing my eyes, my heart is the drumbeat. The sky is dark, peppered with stars and glimmering in the light of a deep blue aurora. There are whispers all around me—voices of thunder, water, oak, and fire. They're speaking too softly for me to hear, but my spirit knows what they say. It is time I live up to my name.

I open my eyes and let the light of day back in. The sun warms my skin, pushing away the lingering chill. I don't know what waits for me on the other side of the trees or what will happen at the bottom of the quarry. Uncertainty used to make me anxious. I would fear the unknown because there were too many factors out of my control. But right now, in this moment, I welcome uncertainty. I want murky, unclear, unsure. Messy is good. Plunge into the unknown.

Time to go.

I hold out my hands as I walk through the clearing, letting the yellowed stalks of the tall grass touch my open palms. Wiggle my fingers to feel the tickle and scratch of each blade. The clearing feels smaller, like walking across it takes less time. Must be the anticipation. The tree line towers above me. Now that the leaves have all fallen, the bare trees reach up into the blue sky like hands. I push branches aside as I step into the underbrush. Birdsong echoes around me, gets eaten up by the bush and then thrown out again in a different place. One voice speaks loudest.

—*What are you going to do?*

Nanabush is on the branch of a birch tree. He is sitting low on the trunk so that he's at the same height as me. We look into each other's eyes.

"I told you already," I say.

—*You were grossly vague with your answer. You're sounding more like one of the Seven each day.*

"I feel like that's supposed to be an insult."

—*A little, yes.*

I give him a smile, then sigh as I look away. I start to wring my hands together. "You aren't going to like what I'm planning to do."

He tilts his head to one side and then twitches it to the other. He acts more bird-like when he's nervous. Are these nerves for himself or for me this time?

—*I don't like that you aren't telling me.*

I move farther through the bush, twisting my body here and there to move as noiselessly as possible. The trees are so close here that the sun's heat hasn't made it through yet to melt the snow. Twigs and crisp leaves crunch beneath my feet. I hear the calls and shouts of the workers at the quarry nearby. The ground trembles lightly when the drilling starts. I walk to the edge of the forest and watch the work from behind the tree trunks. Nanabush follows me, darting through the thin spaces between the trees until he's near me again. We're both facing the quarry.

"They're setting up to blast," I say, quietly pushing a branch out of my way. "This one will be what destroys everything."

—*I know.*

We go quiet, listening to the forest sounds as they collide with the mechanical, industrial noise. They don't mix well.

"Nanabush?"

—*Yes?*

"Thank you."

—*For what?*

"Everything. For trusting me and teaching me. For showing me that I'm stronger than I think I am. For bringing me to all those memories. Letting me see my dad again. You're the kindest trickster god I've ever met."

Nanabush looks at me curiously, his head twitching back and forth. He blinks and laughs, cawing softly.

—*Guess you need to meet more tricksters, then.*

"Nah," I reply. "I think one is good enough for me."

His expression changes, the smooth features of his brow coming together in a downward point and his eyes darkening.

—*Why are you talking like you're saying goodbye?*

"You know, my dad used to avoid saying goodbye. He didn't like the finality of it," I say, moving forward and pushing my way through the trees until I'm out in the open and gravel crunches under my feet. "He'd always say, 'See you in the near future.' I think I like that better."

There's shouting from the men in orange and yellow vests when they see me. They call out to me in French, probably telling me to get lost, what am I doing here, this is a closed site, get back. But all I can understand is the swearing. Ignoring them, I keep walking. The shouting gets louder, more frenzied the closer I get to the edge.

—*Hazel! What are you doing?*

I kick a rock off the side of the quarry and watch as it falls. It hangs in the air before finally breaking the surface of the water down below. "They'll have to stop everything if I do this. No matter what happens to me, this will stop the mine, stop time."

More shouting from the others as they close in.

"*Es-tu folle? Ôte-toi d'là!*"

"*Fichez le camp!*"

Nanabush is in the sky above me, circling low so I can hear him when he speaks. His feathers graze my shoulders, wings beat a breeze that blows through my hair.

—*And you think* this *is the answer? You won't make it. This is suicide!*

I shake my head, tear my eyes away from the sunlight glittering along the water. Nanabush hovers in the air in front of me and I smile at him. "That's for you to decide."

There's the sound of boots behind me as the workers move in. They're still talking to me in French, their tone changed from frustration and anger to worry and panic. I turn to face them, look at the way they watch me nervously. Their concern is real and I start to feel guilty for putting them through something like this. After all, they're doing the job that was given to them. One of the men inches closer, making to pull me back from the edge. Nanabush dives at him, caws and croaks viciously, beating his wings until the man has no choice but to step back. Nanabush swarms the rest of them, forcing them away from me. He swoops back to me, his grey eyes wide.

Despite the well of emotions overflowing inside of me, I smile. "Catch me on purpose this time, okay?"

I spread my arms wide and kick off the edge. I feel like I'm hanging in the air a moment before falling, weight increasing and growing. I get heavier, start to fall faster. My eyes squeeze shut. I refuse to be blinded as I fall, so I force them back open. Above me, everything is brilliant blue sky. Air rushing underneath me, the cold closeness of water. Then a flurry of dark wings, shouting, cawing, screaming. Something grabs me. Slows me down. Hands pulling on my body until I feel weightless. There's a sound like rock on water.

Then nothing.

18

TEACHINGS

Whispers. Talking gently to me and softly about me. Voices that sound far away and close all at once. They're overhead and next to my ears, behind me and in front of me. They're telling me to wake up. Open my eyes. *Please, wake up.*

"You know, what you did back there was foolish."

"Dad?"

He laughs. "*Enhenh, nidànis.* It's me."

"Did it work? Are you okay?"

"Mmm," he says. "Hi-yah, my girl, you did good."

"I did?"

"Oh yes. Everyone is so proud."

I can't see him. I can't see anything. Everything is washed in darkness and sound. Slowly, I breathe in, smell sweetgrass and cold earth.

Dad speaks again and his voice is like warm cedar: "Do you want to stay here, Hazel? You can if you wish. There is a wigwam for you. You only need to decide to light the fire."

I let myself sink into the comfort of this place, accept the dark, and imagine what it could be like to stay. But something isn't right. "I want to, *Kaye We'osimidj,* but I don't think I can."

He chuckles. "Round pegs fit in square holes, but that does not mean they are meant for such places. I understand, *nidànis.* We will see each other again." He takes my hand in his, then leans over and kisses my forehead. "*K'zaagin.*"

When I open my eyes, Gus is asleep in the chair beside my bed. His hand is holding mine.

✖ ✖ ✖

It takes a few minutes for the room to come into focus. Using my free hand, I rub my eyes. There's a collection of crust in the corners like I've been sleeping for weeks. The room I'm in is unfamiliar. Everything is painted white save the floor, which is a creamy shade of yellow. There's a stuffed bear and a collection of flowers on the table at the foot of the bed. Three small bouquets and one aggressively large one.

There's an IV drip next to me, with tubes leading along my forearm and into my hand. The thought of having something stuck in me like that freaks me out, but I don't do anything about it. It's for the best, after all. Probably kept me alive for however long I've been out.

"Look who finally decided to grace us with her conscious presence."

I turn my head to look at Gus. He's smiling at me, trying to be his usual cocky self, but there's relief in his eyes. "Nice to see you too." At least, that's what I try to say. My words come out raspy and strained. I cough a few times to try to remind my voice how to speak.

He chuckles softly. "Don't worry. I'm used to people being speechless in my presence."

I glare at him. "Ass."

"How are you feeling? Do you want me to get the doctor?"

"No," I say. "I'm okay right now. I don't feel too awful."

"Being knocked out for four days gave you a lot of time to get better."

"I've been out for *four* days?"

"Yeah, which is a big deal on its own. Fall from that height should've done much worse." He looks at me hard, sighing. There's something on his mind that he's not sure he can say. I can see him weighing the pros and cons.

"Say it."

"Why'd you do it? Witnesses are saying it looked like you jumped on purpose." He keeps his grey eyes locked on mine. "Did you really want to hurt yourself?"

I take my time answering. "It looks that way, doesn't it?"

He nods. "Yeah, not too many people choose to swan dive off the edge of a cliff. How very 1995 *Pocahontas* of you."

"You know, Mia *has* been making a bunch of jokes about that lately. Maybe that was my inspiration."

"Okay, be serious now."

"I never wanted that to be the last thing I did, if that's what you're asking. I knew you'd need more time to find the stuff I asked you to, and I knew if an accident were to happen at the construction site, they'd have to shut it down for *at least* a day." I shrug. "You know, I put two and two together."

"And jumping into a pit was what you came up with? Jesus, Haze, you could have died. Why didn't you just wait the two days?"

"They were going to keep blowing shit up. I had to do *something*."

Gus flops back into his chair, runs his hands along the back of his neck. "You're dramatic. You know that?"

"So I've been told. Hey!" I sit up suddenly, too quickly. There's an uncomfortable rush of blood to my head and I get dizzy. I groan and lie back down. "Ow, okay. That was a bad idea."

"In the scheme of things, you've had worse."

I ignore him. "What happened after all? You found the map and the parcel description?"

Gus looks at me with a self-satisfied grin as he leans back in his chair, hands linked behind his head. "You're damn right I did."

Relief moves through my body. I close my eyes and sigh, sinking back against the pillow and the bed. Then I start to laugh. Joyful and light. I feel Gus gently kick the bed as he starts to laugh too.

"You were right, *àgawàdiz-ikwe*," he says. "The second I faxed those originals to Gagnon et Fils along with a signed letter from a government official verifying their authenticity, I got a phone call saying that the mine would not move forward. That guy, Thomas? He sounded pretty put out by it. Said he should have believed you before it got this far. Think he feels like he's the reason you jumped. Hence, the garden he had sent over here." Gus points at the biggest bouquet of flowers.

I carefully and slowly push myself into a sitting position. Gus puts a few extra pillows behind me to prop me up comfortably. "He's not wrong about that."

"Yeah, I didn't disagree with him." Gus grabs the envelope sticking out of the bouquet and hands it to me. "He visited yesterday. Insisted that I give you this when you woke up. Here."

I rip it open to find a handwritten letter. His penmanship is a bit messy, but his ancestor's was worse.

Dear Hazel,

I need to start by saying I'm sorry. I should have listened to you, taken you seriously. It was foolhardy and stubborn of me to forget to properly consult with the people on whose land I was working. For that, I'm deeply sorry.

Please take this letter as my solemn vow to work to heal the scars that I helped to reopen and the new ones that we created with this unfortunate venture. If there is anything that I can do for you as things move forward, do not hesitate to contact me. I am in your debt.

Rest up. Get better. I hope to talk to you soon.

Kindest regards,
Thomas

Must've been hard for him to write this. Even if we were on two sides of a blurred line, I do feel bad for him. That night in the sweat, he was open and honest about wanting to make things right between our communities. I can only hope he'll follow through with his promises.

I look over at Gus. "Wanna read it?"

He nods. "You have to ask?"

I'm quiet as I let him look it over.

"Huh," Gus says when he finishes. "What are your thoughts on this?"

"Depends," I say. "What did he look like when he came in to visit?"

Gus snorts. "Terrible. Sort of like he hadn't slept a good night in a while. Probably from the stress and guilt of all his *wabi-jishkish* bullshit eating away at him."

"Good. Then he's taking this seriously. We better make sure we keep this letter. Might have to call him up in the future to cash in that vow of his."

"Can do. I'm great at filing."

"What happens with the land now?"

Gus shrugs. "I've been looking into it since you bugged me about it last month, and it turns out that it never belonged to

Dad. Not the back part with the quarry and that freaky clearing, anyway."

"Okay, what does that mean?"

"It means that the lot we're on is unsurrendered, which, in turn, means that it still belongs to the Band. It's Rez land and no one can move on the quarry without proper authorization and leasing, plain and simple."

"So, what to do with it is up to the Chief and Council? Shit, they're just going to give it back to Gagnon and charge him extra for its use."

But Gus is shaking his head. "Nope. You see, in my digging—because I'm so good at my job—I found some old letters between the surveyor and an elder that state that everything back there is sacred ground. I have already taken the liberty of sending those documents to chief and Council as well as the rest of the Rez—you gotta love small-town post offices, just tell them you want this going to every Indian and they go ahead and send it off."

"Wow, you've been busy."

"I told you, I'm great at my job," he says, sitting back in his chair. "I got a call last night from old Chief Brian Howard himself saying that they've elected to leave the final call up to us. Since it's close to our house and any decision will likely have a pretty big impact on our family."

I click my tongue. "You get knocked out for four days and you wake up to a different world."

"Yeah, not the best time to take a leave of absence."

I relax into the pillows, fold my hands on my lap. "What do you wanna do with it?"

"Robby and I were talking about it and he suggested—"

"Robby was here?"

"Hm? Yeah. Those lilies are from him."

"Gee, that's nice."

"Are you blushing?"

"What? No. It's hot in here. Open the window, will you?"

Gus eyes me, but he gets up and walks to the window anyway. "Now, what I was *going* to say was that Robby suggested that we go with a cultural centre. Or a camp. I've thought about it a lot already. We could use that big open space as the main campsite, maybe put up a few rough buildings. Then reopen the road that leads down to the water in the quarry, so people could use that for canoeing and maybe even swimming eventually."

"Did you have any time to worry about me at all?"

He shrugs. "I hate not being busy. And, yeah, trust me, I was worried. Which is why I needed something to fill all the time I spent here. Hospitals are depressing as shit. If I was thinking about the quarry, then I wasn't thinking about how my little sister's brain was swelling."

Instinctively, I reach up to touch my head.

"You're okay now," he says. "Recovered pretty quickly. Which is why you're not wearing a breathing thingy. They said you were strong enough to go at it on your own."

"And I slept through all of that?"

"You were sedated."

"Oh, okay. That makes sense."

Gus stretches and then looks at his watch. "Shit, I told Mom I'd go and get her the second you woke up. She's going to be so pissed when she realizes you've been awake without her here."

"Aha," I say. "You're gonna be in trouble."

"Pfft, that's nothing compared with how much trouble you're in."

"Oh shit."

"Yeah."

"Maybe take your time going to get her?"

He laughs and comes over to the edge of the bed. "Sure, I'll try to buy you a few extra minutes." Gus leans in and carefully wraps his arms around me, squeezes. His voice is quiet and serious in my ear. "Don't scare me like that again."

I hug him back. "I won't. I promise."

He pulls away and smiles, making his way to the door. Before leaving he turns to me once more: "It's good to see you again, nishîmej."

"K'zaagin, niseyens."

Gus nods and shuts the door behind him.

I take time to stare at the flowers. There are cards that I can't reach because of my IV, but I'm content to look at the blossoms for now. There's a weight in my bones, aching from the stress and the trauma of my fall. Gus said I'm fine. I gingerly touch my head anyway. It's ridiculous, but I keep thinking that it should feel big and swollen. Out of the corner of my eye I see a dark shape as it moves by the window. Nanabush pushes himself through the small open space and then flutters over to my bed. He folds his wings along his back and walks toward me. I smile.

"You're still a crow."

—And you're still alive. You're welcome for that.

I chuckle. "It's very much appreciated."

He hops a bit closer and inspects me, his head twitching left and then right. The light from the window catches in the silver streaking his feathers.

—It was worth it. I'd do it again in a heartbeat. Turns out you're worth saving, Kotàganez-i Minisinòkwe.

"So are you, Nanabush Trickster. You have been the best teacher. All of this, I couldn't have done it without you."

He looks down to hide his face. I can feel him smiling.

—*I think, perhaps, you've taught me more than I have you. Because of you, I know what it means to be human.* He lifts his head, his grey eyes alight.

—*Thank you, Hazel.*

"You're leaving, aren't you?"

He nods.

—*A trickster's work is never done.*

"But what about your deal with the Seven?"

He shrugs.

—*That is for them to decide.*

"You earned it. You deserve the life that you asked for."

—*Time will tell.*

"That's a cliché. Time doesn't tell us anything."

—*Perhaps that is because we aren't patient enough?*

"Ah, you sound like one of Them."

—*I'll take that as a compliment.*

We share a laugh and then one last silence. I reach out for him and he moves closer to me. Gently, I let my hand glide along his smooth feathers. They're cool to the touch. I look down at him and smile despite my sadness.

—*Màdjàshin, nishîmej.*

The door opens and Mom explodes into the room and pulls me into her arms. I'm so startled that I hardly have time to bring my arms up to hug her back. I hope she hasn't squished Nanabush.

"Oh my god, you crazy kid! Thank the Creator you are alive! What the hell is the matter with you?"

"Ow, Mom. You're tugging on my IV."

"Oh, shit. Sorry!" She leans back quickly, readjusting to sit on the bed beside me. "Hey, you spend all that time knocked out and now you won't even look at me?"

I don't see Nanabush. I look around the room, checking the shadows for movement or some sign that he's simply slipped away, but there's nothing. It's a normal room in the ICU. He's gone.

"Hey," says Mom, reaching out to put her hand under my chin. She lifts my gaze to hers. There are tears in her eyes and she looks older. "I was only kidding with all that crazy talk. I'm just glad you're okay. You *are* okay, right?"

"Huh? Oh, yeah." I give her a smile. "I'm okay."

"Good." She lets me go and leans back to look me over. "What's that you got there?"

I look down. There's something dark between my fingers. Slowly, I open my hand. A single inky black feather is sitting on my palm. Mom starts to laugh as I pick it up, twirling the feather between my thumb and forefinger.

"Looks like I'll be putting some tobacco down for a trickster. That old Nanabush took good care of you, didn't he?"

A real smile parts my lips. I nod. "He did."

I bring the feather up to my eyes and watch the way the silver shimmers like lightning in the night.

Epilogue
==

AN OLD CROW

Smoke rises from the earth of Spirit Bear Point First Nation. It billows into the sky like thin, dark clouds from flames that are carefully watched over by keepers of less-than-sacred fires in nearly every backyard of the community. The annual burning of the grass has become a ritual for the people of the reserve. Something that they do every year to mark the change of the seasons. The snow may have melted, but the Algonquins know that the winter isn't truly gone until the first fires have been lit.

Spring has arrived.

The sun beats down from a clear sky, making the shadows of the budding trees dance along blackened grass. For what feels like the first time in months, the air is warm and smells of fresh earth and running water. Black-capped chickadees sing gleefully from the treetops.

Hazel Ellis steps out of the Band Office and into the sunlight. She smiles and waves goodbye to her co-workers as they head home for the day. She doesn't hear them whisper about her as they step into their vehicles. As with most things on the reserve, feelings toward her actions have been divided. Some view her as a hero who did what was necessary of a modern-day protector of Mother Earth. Others think she's batshit crazy.

More importantly, Hazel is happy. Leaving the dusty boxes and old letters behind is her favourite part of the day. She buttons up her denim jacket, stuffs her hands into her pockets, and begins her walk home. The co-workers who drive to work from their homes down the street think it's a bit of a trek, but Hazel doesn't mind. She likes the time to herself. And now that the spring grass fires have officially begun, she enjoys being outside.

The past few weeks of work have been the best Hazel has ever had. She splits her time between filing the archives of the Lands and Memberships department and consulting with the new project manager in charge of building the cultural centre. Joni Kitchisabek continues to repair the accidental rift she created between herself and Hazel by working closely with the young Anishnaabekwe on all new projects. Hazel has long since forgiven her missteps, knowing full well that Joni acted innocently and with good intentions, even if those actions almost caused a spiritual cataclysm. Fielding daily apologies is nothing new for Hazel, as she now works alongside her one-time adversary Thomas Gagnon. He has since become an integral part of the construction of the new cultural centre. As a means of reparation, his company offered to do all they could to ensure a safe and sustainable build. Gagnon et Fils lost a fair bit of money to their failed development of the land, but to the young CEO, investing in the proper future of the community provided more than enough reason to continue. Thomas apologizes to Hazel at every chance he gets since he still feels responsible for the way things unfolded at the quarry. She's accepted his apology countless times but is considering taking it all back should he continue to annoy her with his constant *I'm-so-sorrys*.

With the late-afternoon sunlight on her skin, Hazel takes in a slow, controlled deep breath, letting the air fill her lungs with the scent of rainstorm and fiery grass. She has plans to head into town with her mother this evening, rekindling their shared love of new books and old memories. Nora has found a peace in her solitude that she had been missing since losing her husband. Having her daughter home has helped. The Ellis women are not fully whole, but they are healing. Together.

Hazel heads home along her favourite route, through the trailer park. Last season's dead yellow grass is already peppered with tiny green shoots. The dust of the gravel from the dirt roads curving around each of the long homes is weighed down with water from the spring rains. A little white dog on a porch barks at Hazel as she walks by. The old woman sitting on a rocking chair next to the dog gives the girl a wave. Hazel waves back.

A small cloud glides past the sun, shining light on the trailer at the far end. Until recently, it sat empty, left to gather dust year in and year out. It's true, there was a housing shortage on the reserve, but no matter how desperate the people might get, no one wanted to live in the trailer park. The roofs leak and the windows let too much cold inside in the winter months. But to someone who has been without a home for so very long, it is perfect.

An older man is sitting on the front porch of the last trailer on the lot. He has long, black hair streaked with silver, high cheekbones, and a prominent nose that sits on a face with rich copper skin. There are lines on his face, but not enough to tell his age. When he smiles, crow's feet walk next to his eyes, which are both wise and youthful. Tobacco smoke rises from the ornately decorated pipe between his teeth. Above him, perched on the eaves of his trailer, two crows keep watch. The black birds stretch their talons. The larger crow adjusts on the eave and preens the feathers of his sister bird. They open their beaks and caw, sending their strong voices echoing into the spring air.

Hazel meets the man's gaze and she stops. He needs no introduction.

She smiles and nods.

He nods back.

The crows take flight, soaring higher and higher into the sky until they are little more than two black pinpricks against a sheet of blue.

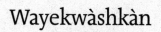

Wayekwàshkàn

Author's Note on Language

───

The language spoken by the people of Spirit Bear Point First Nation is Anishnaabemowin and, where possible, follows the dialect of my home reserve, Timiskaming First Nation. We don't speak the Language like we used to at home, but through the dedicated work of elders and teachers at Kiwetin Kikinamading, we are helping cultivate that knowledge in future generations. Hazel's Anishnaabemowin might not be perfect, but it is present and eager to be heard. The translations are taken from the *Anishinabe Kegonan Masinazowin Mazinahigan* (Algonquin Picture Dictionary) compiled by the Algonquin-Anishinabeg Nation, the *Algonquin Lexicon* compiled by Ernest McGregor, accessed from the collections of the Algonquin Nation Secretariat, and with great help from elder Bertha Chief. *Chi'Meegwetch!*

àgawàdiz-ikwe: crazy woman (roughly)
Anangininî: Star-man (roughly)
àndeg: crow
anganeshà: Englishman

animizie: bothersome (literal translation); playful, scamp (chiding
    term of endearment)

Anishnaabe(g): the People (plural)

Anishnaabekwe: woman

Anishnaabemowin: the Language

binòdjish: kid or child

dodem: clan

enhenh: yes

G'tchi Manitou: The Great Spirit

gashkenindam: sorry

gôkom: grandma

kakagi: raven

Kakone gîzis: September

Kaye Mâmâ: Mom

Kaye We'osimidj: Dad

kòpàdiz-i: stupid

Kotàganez-i Minisinòkwe: Fierce Warrior-Woman (roughly)

k'zaagin: I love you

màdjàshin: goodbye

madòdison: sweat lodge

madònewàbik: heated stone used in a sweat lodge

màg: loon

makwa: bear

manidò: spirit

meegwetch: thank you

migizî: eagle

minwa pijawok: welcome

nibi: water

nidànis: my daughter

nidijinikaz: My name is (introduction)

niseyens: older brother

Nish: shorthand slang for Anishnaabe
nishîmej: little sister
noshis: granddaughter
ogâs: pickerel
ogima: chief
onadotân: listens
sasàgiwichígewin: sacrifice
semà: tobacco
tagwagin: Fall
tcinedagan: relatives, family
wabi-jishkish: White asshole (slang)
Wabi-Mahigan: White Wolf (roughly)
Wàwàsamòg Kekinàmàgedji: Lightning Teacher
Wâwâshkeshîkwe: Deer Woman (roughly)
wayekwàshkàn: to reach the end
wemitigòji: Frenchman
wîgwas: birchbark

THE SEVEN GRANDFATHER TEACHINGS

Gweyâkwâdiziwin: Honesty
Kaye Nibwâkawin: Wisdom
Manadji'idiwin: Respect
Sagi'idiwin: Love
Sôginijiwin: Bravery
Tabasenimidiwin: Humility
Tebwewin: Truth

Acknowledgements

Crow Winter has been a labour of love, sadness, grief, and triumph. It is a story that showcases the ways in which strong women lift each other up and heal each other's hurts. I could ask for no greater inspiration for this than the intelligent, beautiful, supportive women in my family. To my mom, Audrey, thank you for showing me how a woman treats her friends, her loved ones, and her peers by proving that kindness is the truest form of strength. Thank you for teaching me how to continue on even when things seem their hardest. To my sisters, Kate and Alison, thank you for your never-ending support and laughter and for always proudly crying with me when we go out to dinner. Thank you to my aunties for the hugs, the flowers, the emails. *Meegwetch* to all the Anishnaabe women who have touched my life with their brilliance, their smiles, and their resilience.

My mentor, Susan Swan, deserves a big *meegwetch* for guiding me, teaching me, and helping me piece together the story that was to become *Crow Winter*. She gave me the permission to be confident in my work and to experiment with the stories of my ancestors in a way that brings them into the present. Thank you for your strength, your wisdom, and for being the much-more-put-together Nanabush to my Hazel.

Thank you to my amazing agent, Stephanie Sinclair, who has loved and supported *Crow Winter* from day one. She has been instrumental in bringing Hazel's story to those who need to hear it.

To Heather Sangster, thank you for taking what was a muddled thesis and turning it into a beautiful manuscript worthy of publication.

Thank you to the marvellous Iris Tupholme for believing in me as much as she believed in *Crow Winter*. With her gentle guidance and leadership, the manuscript became a beautiful story of loss and transformation. To Janice Zawerbny for her care, clever suggestions, and for wanting to know more about the Ellis family: thank you for letting Abraham sing. The entire team at HarperCollins Canada have been a dream to work with, and I'm so very thankful for their efforts.

Meg Desmond, my fellow MACRW, has been my first reader, editor, and confidante from the beginning, and I am so grateful to call her one of my friends. Thank you to my part-time roommate, Rachel Trombley, who let me crash on her couch when I came into the city and only ever asked me to read new sections to her in return while she made us delicious food. To Dr. Arlene Laliberté, who taught me how to welcome, cherish, and express my own grief so that I could better help Hazel with hers.

To the people of Timiskaming First Nation, thank you for your support, your belief, and your spirit.

Finally, to my father, Kenny, thank you for the years you gave to all of us. I only wish we could have had more. *K'zaagin.*

G'tchi Meegwetch.